THE LOST SUMMERS

JESSICA ANN

SOMEDAY LADY
PUBLISHING LLC

THE LOST SUMMERS

Published by Someday Lady Publishing LLC

Copyright © 2025 by Jessica McQuaid

All rights reserved.

ISBN-13: 979-8-9992879-4-6

This story is dedicated to the indomitable Harriet Kelley.
For the sleeping bags, the wrestling, and the Mountain Dew.
And I'm still so sorry about the alfalfa.
Love, Heidi

Note to Reader

Note to reader:

This story mentions rape culture and hazing throughout. It does not depict details. Both concepts are merely mentioned as part of the story.

However, the story does depict an on-page suicide in Chapter 29.

And as always - nothing happens to the dog.

ONE

I always knew I'd die because of a dog.

I just thought the culprit would be *my* dog.

The incessant chatter of sparrows wakes me as it usually does in the summer, and I blink to awareness, my body coming alive piece by piece. At first, the cacophony of the birds—the chatter of the sparrows replied to by the sharp chirp of the cardinal, which in turn is bemoaned by the mourning dove—and the wash of early morning sunlight that sneaks its way past the window curtains fills me with a sense of anticipation for a new day.

One that is quickly doused when the cloying sensation of humidity rushes back to me, and its sticky fingers crawl along every inch of exposed skin. I sit up, heedless of where my Labrador retriever, Henry, may be sprawled in oblivious slumber on the bed with us, my arms held high to catch any breeze that might stir the suffocating air.

A noise comes from the other side of the bed, something incomprehensible, but the sentiment still understandable.

"The humidity didn't break," I manage through my cracked lips.

I must have slept with my mouth open again. Humidity makes me congested, and I touch my lips gingerly, wincing when I find new cracks in the delicate skin.

Eventually my husband hauls himself to a seated position beside me. His black hair stands straight up at the back of his head from the sweat I know drenches his pillowcase without having to look.

I'll be washing the sheets again today.

"I thought it was supposed to break." I interpret this more than hear my husband say it as the words mostly come up garbled.

"Lake," I say at the same time Logan mutters, "Shower."

Our cottage sits on the east end of Bear Lake in the village of Bellegrave, which boasts a comfortable elevation of approximately fourteen hundred feet in the Adirondacks. I can count on one hand the number of times the temperature has climbed above ninety degrees in July since the year I was born. We don't even own an air conditioner.

The heat wave that has gripped Bellegrave for the past four days has brought the town to a standstill and turned the lake into Miami at spring break as everyone, locals and tourists alike, seek comfort in her cool waters. People with no experience and no business operating motorized watercraft zip back and forth across the surface, heedless of boating regulations. The beaches are packed with out-of-towners who think the open-container laws don't apply to them, and the daily exercise of picking up litter that washes up on our lakefront has become a nuisance.

It's almost made me retreat to the aquatic center for my morning swim.

Almost.

As mountain lakes go, Bear Lake is frigid most of the year, and I habitually perform my doctor-ordered morning swims at the indoor pool at the village's aquatic center. But lake swimming is always my preference, and you'll find me there starting June first, wetsuit on and cold-water swimming floatie in hand.

Except now, with temps and tempers so high, everyone wants what only the lake can offer.

Relief.

The meteorologist on Channel 13 has been promising a break in the weather any day now, and yet, I have once again awoken in a puddle of my own sweat. I tumble from the bed, my hand already reaching for the swimsuit I've discarded on the chair in the corner.

"Henry." I tug at the bedspread where the dog lies sprawled. "Henry. Lake," I manage, peeling off my sweaty pajamas. I eye my swimsuit, already feeling the tug of spandex ripping against my skin and wince.

Henry opens one eye, glaring at me as though I've just asked him to give up peanut butter.

"I get it, buddy," I say, adjusting my swimsuit straps as the water in the shower of the connected bathroom comes on.

I give Henry a scratch between his ears before slipping out of the room. I pause on the landing, my eyes resting on the closed door opposite. It's a room I haven't gone into in thirteen years. I know Logan does once or twice a year to check the storm windows, but I don't.

I continue down the stairs.

I brace myself for the cold water to hit my sticky, overwarm skin as I take a shallow dive off our dock. The water hits me like a freight train, and I plunge through it, letting its icy grip chill me instantly. I'm several yards from the dock when I finally come up for air. I shake the water from my face and start my swim. I swim laps from the end of our dock out into the deep water of the lake in a northeast trajectory that keeps me a safe distance from the small island that runs east west in the middle.

The island used to be an all-girls camp, but its operations shuttered the year after I was born. Its remnants litter the island like an eerie abandoned amusement park you'd see in a horror movie. I only know this from secondhand accounts. I haven't stepped foot on the island, not in the forty some years of my existence.

I cut through the water, keeping my eyes moving left and right, alert for the unusual traffic the lake has been seeing lately. I'm one small swimmer in a vast expanse of dark water and could be easily missed.

I usually swim for about forty-five minutes. I don't keep track of how many laps I complete or the distance I swim. For me, exercise is only about keeping my body moving after my left femur was broken in a car accident that also killed my daughter in the seventh month of my pregnancy. I often think about Audrey while I swim, marking the passage of time. I picture her first steps, her first day of school, her first lost tooth, how her grandfather would have interrogated her prom date, and every milestone in between. That's what I think about with every meditative stroke. My daughter who didn't get to live because of a distracted tourist, and the moments she never got to achieve.

I'm so preoccupied by my thoughts it takes me several seconds to realize there's movement in my peripheral vision. I jerk upright, treading water to look around, sure a speedboat is coming straight toward me. But that's not what has caught my attention.

It's movement on the island.

At first, I think to ignore it and pivot to go back to my swim, but the movement comes again. It's just odd enough to have me turning back, my eyes scanning what little of the shore I can see from this angle.

Over the years many developers have tried to strike a deal to purchase the land and the camp remnants, but every deal has fallen through for some reason or other. The island has remained empty and desolate for forty years, and now it's wild with overgrowth, the once manicured pathways and clearings long consumed by nature. There's only the stony beach along the shore that provides any opening to see what the island hides, and I study it, sure that what I thought I saw are just water droplets stuck to my eyelashes.

But this time when the movement comes, I can't miss it. Because my eyes are locked on the very spot when it appears.

A dog.

My heart lurches, panic and fear warring at the thought a dog has swum out to the island and become trapped with all its ghostly inhabitants.

That's the thing about the island. If this were a B horror movie, this is the part where I would say not all of the campers have left.

In reflex, I start swimming toward the island, intent on rescuing the dog, before reason kicks in. I can't swim back holding a dog. I need a boat.

"Wait there," I yell above the slap of water around me. "I'm coming to get you."

The dog tilts its head as if it's understood me. It's a black dog of middling size, stocky and with a box head that would suggest some kind of pit bull mix. I don't know if pit bulls are swimmers, but I don't take the time to contemplate it.

I turn and head for the dock where my aluminum fishing boat sits. I've only gone a handful of strokes when the noise reaches my ears.

The hum of a motor.

I jerk upright again, my head swinging wildly around me, hoping to spot the motorboat and alert them to my presence long before they're a danger.

But as soon as my eyes lock on the boat I know it's too late. I was distracted by the dog, and my distraction has wasted time. I scream anyway, lifting my arms out of the water as far as I can. The boat is planing, its bow high above the water as it gains speed, and I know the captain cannot see me. I stop screaming and start swimming, my arms cutting through the water, my legs thrashing wildly behind me.

My heart pounds so hard I'm afraid of having a stroke. At least then, the speedboat won't be such a worry. My arms ache, from the cold and the exertion and the adrenaline, but I push through. The hum of the motor is a roar now, and the water rises up beneath me. I think it will push me forward, out of danger, but instead it swamps me, pulling me under. I catch a glimpse of the end of our dock before I get sucked under. The dock is so close but when I flail for it, my hand only strikes water.

I emerge in a rush of limbs and gasping lips, pulling in air, knowing if the boat hasn't hit me, it's going to swamp me. It's too close, going too fast.

It's over in a second. The roar of the motor zooms past me as its wake takes me under again. I don't have enough oxygen in my lungs for how far the surge of water pushes me under, and a burning takes up in my chest. The need to breathe almost forces open my mouth, but I resist, pumping my legs in the direction of what I think is the surface. I'm turned upside down, the water pushing at all angles, and I don't know where I am.

I know I'm going to take a breath just as hands grab me from above. I break through the water, precious oxygen rushing into me, filling my head until I think I'm going to pass out. The rough boards of the dock scrape the backs of my thighs as I'm hauled bodily out of the lake. Water sluices off of me, soaking the boards that are now under me. I blink, trying to orient myself when the hands that pulled me out of the lake move and wrap around me, pulling me against a warm body that cradles me there on the dock.

"I'm calling Chief Tom," Logan says from somewhere above my head. "These tourists are going to get someone killed."

I blink again and realize I'm staring at the mat of hair on my husband's chest. I touch it, just to assure myself he's real, and he made it in time to pull me from the water before I drowned.

"The dog," I say, but the words don't really come out. My throat aches from the water I likely inhaled but can't remember inhaling.

Logan eases me back. He's only wearing a pair of old jeans, and his hair drips with water. I stare at him.

"You heard me from in the shower?"

"You screamed really loudly." He nods in the direction in which the speedboat disappeared. "I don't know how he didn't hear you."

I touch my husband's face. I'm not sure why, but I do. Things are messy between us after we finally had a conversation thirteen years too late, and touching him feels like a novelty, something I'm doing for the first time after being deprived of it for so long even though I wasn't.

"I'm sorry," I say. "But I need to go out to the island."

His expression pinches in concern. "You've never stepped foot on that island."

"There's a dog out there. I can't leave him. We need to rescue him."

Logan looks over my head, and I know he's studying the island before he looks back at me. "I don't see anything."

I turn to look and see the empty, stony beach. "He was right there," I say, pointing. "We need to go get him, Logan. You know what's out there. He can't be left with them."

Logan studies me long enough that I think he'll try to stop me, but instead he only says, "You'll need to put some pants on."

Two

I run into the cottage only long enough to pull on a pair of jeans and a long-sleeve t-shirt and stuff my feet into some sneakers. Despite the heat, the island is overgrown, and I want to protect as much of my skin as possible while we search for the dog. Passing back through the kitchen, I grab some of Henry's biscuits and stuff them in my pocket.

By the time I get back to the dock, Logan is untying the boat, the engine already humming. I let him take the helm as I perch in the bow, my eyes sweeping the rocky beach of the island as we motor across the lake. I see no signs of the dog, but then, it might have been spooked when I screamed earlier and taken off into the brush.

It takes less than a minute to cross the small expanse of lake between our dock and the island, and the bottom of the boat scrapes along the stones as Logan beaches it. I hop from the front, taking the mooring line with me. I find a tree farther up the bank to secure it, and only then do I let my senses open.

The flood of energy is overwhelming, and I grind my back teeth, forcing out the voices trying to worm their way into my mind. I only want to get their measure. I don't want to hear what they have to say.

I don't know how many spirits linger here, but it's a lot. The camp was open for several decades, and I wonder how many girls camped here over the years and how many have now departed, leaving behind an echo of their energy that lingers on the island. This is why I've spent forty years avoiding this place and so many like it.

It's a congregation of souls, and I'm the only one who can hear them.

When Logan touches my elbow, I jump, and only his hand on my arm keeps me from falling back into the water.

"Is it bad?" he asks.

I can only nod.

"Then we should hurry." He helps me up the shore until our feet find the relative stability of dirt rather than beach stone.

Tangles of brush and vine capture my legs as I try to move forward, and for every three steps, I slip and catch myself against a branch or sapling. The island rises up on all sides to a plateau that sits above the water. It's this rise that makes the island so valuable as it keeps any structures above safe from spring flooding.

It takes precious time for us to reach the crest of the ridge, and the palms of my hands are scraped raw by the time the brush and saplings are replaced by tamarack and elm, the forest that grows unchecked across the island.

I stop, planting my feet as I let my heart rate slow.

"There's no way a dog could be up here," Logan says beside me, his head turning back and forth as he takes in the thick woods before us.

"I know what I saw," I say.

Movement to my left has me turning before I remember to check myself. I find two girls leaning out from behind a tree, their expressions mischievous, their eyes nothing more than black holes. Youthful energy likes to play games on the living. They are spirits trapped in a place from their memories, and they yearn for the chance to have a bit of fun.

I reach out to touch Logan beside me. "We need to be careful," I whisper.

The girls disappear, only that familiar eerie laugh, the one I've heard for years from the lake shore, echoing through the trees.

We press forward. Logan lets me lead as I can see what he cannot, and my only hope is to keep us both safe from the spirits that haunt the island until we can find the dog and get out of here. I reach into my pocket and take out one of Henry's biscuits, breaking it in my hand.

"Here, boy," I call. "Treat."

I hold up my hand, but there's no response. We keep going.

Soon the monotonous curtain of trees is interrupted by soft shapes that are likely remains of the cabins of the old camp. We're not quite close enough to see them clearly, and their soft silhouettes make me pause.

"Can you see that?" I ask.

Logan comes up behind me. Although the forest is cooler, I can feel my husband's heat as the humidity presses in around us.

"The cabins? Yeah." He points to the side. "I think that's the old mess hall over there."

There's a larger structure through the trees to our right, but it must be the rear of the building as there's only a single door and no windows that I can make out.

I nod, assuring myself they're real. I take a step, but my foot snags on a root, pitching me forward. Logan is close enough to catch me easily, but when I straighten the dog is there, directly in front of me in a clearing in the brush.

He wasn't there a moment ago, and I didn't hear any noise of an animal trotting through grass.

I freeze, the small hairs on my arms standing up. "Logan." I keep my voice as low as possible. "The dog is directly in front of me. Can you see him?"

Logan shifts, and his hot breath trails along my ear as he says, "No. There's nothing in front of us."

I swallow and tuck the treat back into my jeans' pocket. I lick my lips. "Logan, the dog is a ghost."

He takes both of my upper arms in his hands, and the sweat on his palms dampens my shirt. "Good ghost dog or bad ghost dog?"

"I'm not sure yet," I say. "I think good ghost dog."

The dog watches me as though he can understand what I'm saying. Standing before him now, I see he's stockier than I first noticed from the water, perhaps a mix of Labrador and pit bull. His ears fold forward on either side of his boxy face, and he's wearing a red collar, the brightness gone rusty with age and use. He studies me, a small line between his eyes as he tilts his head in question.

"Show me," I say.

I'm not sure why, but I get the sense the dog needs to show me something. That he appeared on the beach to get my attention, to bring me to the island, to show me...something.

I reach behind me and take Logan's hand, squeeze it once. "I think he needs to show me something. You don't need to follow me. I'm not sure..." I can't finish the sentence because standing there on the island, the disembodied voices springing from one tree to the next, my senses strained, I can't tell my husband whether or not it will be safe to keep going.

"I'm right behind you," he says.

The dog must have heard him because he turns and trots away, his paws soundless as he cuts through the fallen logs that lie between him and the shadowy outlines of the cabins beyond.

I follow, going slowly and watching my feet as much as the dog. The last thing I want to do is break my leg again on this possessed island.

When we step out of the forest, I'm surprised by how untouched the camp cabins and buildings remain at the heart of the island. Beyond the voices whispering through my mind, I hear the lap of the water at either shore and know it can't be more than one hundred yards on either side, the island being longer than its width.

The dog stops at one of the cabins to look back as if making sure we're following him. I nod, and he turns, trotting around the side of the cabin.

I don't look directly at the cabins and their empty windows, splinters of glass hanging like rotten teeth in their wooden frames. The sickening laughter is louder here. I squeeze Logan's hand, and he squeezes back. The laughter grows, and while the dog remains unfazed by it, I cannot let it go.

I stop so abruptly Logan walks into me. I turn, my eyes sweeping from cabin to cabin, broken window to broken window.

"I'm not here for you, and I don't give you permission to enter my mind or touch my person or the person of this man beside me. Go away." I speak as loudly and firmly as I can with my heart thumping in my chest, my stomach roiling.

The laughter ceases at once. I know I have only bought us minutes. The dead do not abide by any rules, only courtesies that they grant and revoke when it suits them.

The dog has disappeared around the corner of the building that must be the old mess hall we'd seen from the forest, its front adorned with a sagging screened porch, the three wooden steps leading up to its front door broken nearly in half by a fallen tree.

When I round the corner of the building, I step nearly straight into the dog, and I lurch back, once more colliding with Logan.

"The dog stopped. I almost ran into him."

"Geez," Logan mutters. He shifts to look around me. "Where is he?"

Three blue fuel drums, their paint speckled with rust and dirt, sit alongside a large piece of equipment with a cylinder of some kind on one end. It probably was once painted orange, but it's faded to a peach color, the insulated wires coming off of it and hanging loose, the insulation worn and in some places chewed.

"It's an old generator," Logan says. "Did the dog want to show you this old generator?"

As if he heard my husband, the dog nudges the fuel drum next to the generator.

My heart rate slows to an impossible beat. "I think he wants us to look in that drum."

I feel Logan's breath stop, his body stilling, the rush of warm air against my ear ceasing. "Why?"

I give him a disappointed look.

He shrugs. "I thought maybe he could tell you. Telepathically."

I look back at the dog. He only nudges the drum again.

"We need to open that drum," I say, even as my stomach tightens at the thought of what we might find in there.

Logan turns. "I'll need to go back to the house and get—"

There's a sickening scrape of metal against metal, the further rumble of rust and dirt grinding. The dog's stare is intent on the barrel, and I wonder if he's somehow directing his energy toward it.

"Okay, okay," I say, but the dog doesn't stop.

I lurch forward, careful to sidestep the ghost dog as I take in the barrel from a closer angle.

"I think the top is rusted off. That's why the dog is able to move it like that." I scoot in between the generator and the barrel, cringing as I picture the colony of spiders that make this godforsaken island its home. "Help me." I gesture to the other side of the lid.

Logan steps forward nearly into the dog, and I hold up both hands. "Stop." I gesture to the side. "Over there." I point to the side of the barrel. "Don't step on the dog."

He looks around as if he's dropped something but sidesteps as I direct him.

We each take a grip on the rusted edge of the barrel lid. I meet my husband's gaze, but I can't speak, the tension in my stomach traveling higher to squeeze my throat. We tug off the lid.

I'm not sure what I had been expecting, but what I see when I look down is only the gummy film of old diesel fuel. The barrel is nearly full, the aged fuel congealing into sludge at the sides. We push the lid farther until it tips over the side, crashing into the long grass between the mess hall and the generator. The entire surface of the barrel is exposed, and still there's nothing but the shiny gloss of dark fuel.

I glance up at Logan, but he's staring at the barrel.

"That's it?" he finally asks.

I look for the dog to find him standing on the other side of the barrel, looking up, expectant.

Logan touches my arm, and I look down.

Air bubbles litter the surface of the diesel. They pop one by one like a pancake frying on a sizzling griddle. I watch each one evaporate as more take their place.

Pop. Pop. Pop.

The first part of the body we see is a hand. It floats to the surface like a dead fish, pale and lifeless, breaking the surface in a quiet plop. The skin is grossly preserved, decay suspended by the likely lack of microbes and fungi in the fuel, sealed into the quasi-sterile barrel upon death.

The hand bends, flopping through the oil as the wrist comes into view. Sickeningly, there's a bracelet on it. A charm bracelet with a single charm that looks as though it's been carved from wood. A bumble bee.

I look up, not wishing to see more, and the dog's eyes catch mine just as he bursts into a halo of warm, glowing light.

The dog vanishes at the same moment my husband vomits into the grass at my feet.

THREE

I sit on the grassy hill that rises up from the dock to our little cottage. I have one arm wrapped around my husband who sits in the grass beside me, his head between his knees, and I rub his back in slow, soothing circles.

"The dog crossed over," I say, watching my fishing boat cut through the water, Bellegrave Police Chief Tom Reznick and my best friend, Detective Carmen Neil, the only occupants as it makes its way from the island back to our dock. "I think he waited here to make sure someone found her."

Logan lifts his head long enough to look at me, a watery smile turning up the corners of his lips. "We don't deserve dogs. Not even in death." His voice is raw from vomiting, and he lets his head drop again.

Once we determined there was indeed a body in the barrel, we got off the island as quickly as possible and called Carmen. We waited there on the grass until she arrived with the police chief. I explained as succinctly as possible what had happened that morning, and they wasted no time in going out to the island themselves to see what we had uncovered.

My abilities in speaking with the dead are well known in

our small Adirondack lakeside town, so when the chief of police heard my story, he didn't balk.

Especially as I'd only recently uncovered, with the help of the ghost of a Bellegrave school teacher, an embezzlement scheme and a murder made to look like an accident.

The boat knocks softly against the dock, and Carmen steps lightly from the craft, her cell phone already coming out of her pocket. She holds up a single finger in my direction before bringing the phone to her ear. Chief Tom ties up the boat and makes his way up the slight rise to where we're sitting.

"Well, Dr. James, you've done it again," Tom says, taking a handkerchief from his pocket to wipe the sweat from his brow.

Chief Tom is wearing a short-sleeve, pale brown uniform shirt with jeans and boots, and it's strange seeing him so formal. It's probably the influx of tourists that has him donning the uniform shirt instead of just his badge, which he usually hangs from the pocket of the flannel shirts he tends to favor.

"I thought you'd at least give me a little break after the Reynolds affair," he adds, tucking the handkerchief back into his pocket.

"Sorry, Chief," I say, looking up at him.

I'm forced to squint against the sun that's just peeking through the canopy of trees above us, and Chief Tom shifts into shadow.

"How you holding up, Logan?" The chief kneels then to get a better look at Logan, who still has his head between his knees. "Need me to call in the boys from the firehouse?" he asks, referring to the EMT team that is part of the fire department in Bellegrave.

Logan waves him off with a hand but doesn't pick up his

head. "No need, Tom. Just need a little more time off that island."

Chief Tom looks up and over his shoulder at this, his eyes falling on the island. I follow his gaze, unable to stop myself, as I remember the soulless eyes of the youthful spirits so gleeful at the chance to torment unknowing visitors. I swallow and look away.

There's a noise behind me, and I look back to see Henry at the glass patio doors of the cottage. He sits, one paw on the glass, an expression of extreme sadness on his features because there are visitors who haven't pet him, and he resolutely believes he's been forgotten in the house.

"You okay for a minute?" I ask Logan, who waves me off much as he did Tom.

I stand and take the few steps to the patio door to release Henry, who goes straight for Tom. Tom catches him and gives him a full-body hug.

"Hey, old friend," Tom says. "You taking good care of your mom and dad?"

I adopted Henry from a police deputy who found out too late she was allergic to dogs, but it meant Henry spent some of his youth in the Bellegrave police station. As it goes with most dopey, lovable dogs, Henry was instantly adored, and I still let Carmen take him for visits.

I don't go into the Bellegrave Police Department. Or at least, I try not to. But that's a different story.

I nod in Carmen's direction as she paces along the hillside, phone pressed to her ear. "What's happening?"

Tom gives Henry one last scratch before pushing to his feet with a noise only men over sixty make. "Detective Neil is calling in the state police. We don't have the forensic resources for a crime like this. We'll need the state lab to process the evidence we recover on the island if we hope to find out anything about the victim."

Victim.

"You're thinking foul play?" I ask.

Tom glances in the direction of the island again. "We can't assume anything at this point, but reason would suggest our victim didn't climb into the barrel herself after she died." Tom looks back at me. "You said a dog led you to her?"

I nod and explain again about the dog I'd seen on the beach that morning.

Logan interrupts, finally picking up his head. "And a tourist in one of those rented speedboats nearly ran her over when she was swimming back to the dock. What are you doing about those tourists, Tom? They're worse than ever this summer."

"I'm afraid it's the heat," Tom answers, pushing the matted hair from his sweaty brow. "It's got everyone going crazy. I've hired as many temporary deputies as my budget will allow, and I've asked the DEC to step up patrols on the lake at least for the weekend."

"Then where are they? It's nearly noon," Logan says.

Tom shrugs. "The hell if I know. Probably dealing with their own problems."

Carmen joins us then, tucking her phone back in her pocket. "State police are sending a team. I've asked the DEC to have their patrols cordon off the island until the state police can get their forensics team out there."

Logan looks pointedly at Tom who looks away.

Carmen notices the exchange but ignores it. "You said you saw a dog? How did a dog get on the island?"

I shrug. "If I were to make assumptions, I would say that dog belonged to the girl in the barrel in life. She must have brought him on the island at some point for him to have left a strong enough imprint to bring me to her."

"What do you mean?" Tom asks.

"Ghosts are echoes," Carmen answers, probably because

I've explained this to her so much. "Ghosts can form in places where they've left an energy imprint. So the dog Della saw had to have been on the island at some point in its life."

Tom's expression is more twisted up than a pretzel, but he waves a hand in dismissal. "I do not want to get into this hocus pocus stuff."

"It's a question that needs to be asked. The dog didn't just get there on its own, and figuring out how it got there, might help us identify the victim," Carmen goes on.

Tom doesn't look away from the island, so I ask, "Did you see more of her? I made Logan leave after we were sure it was a body."

I don't mention how I ran for the first time since being forced to run laps in the high school gym in ninth grade, nor how much my leg is hurting me now. As soon as the dog crossed over, the air had solidified, the humidity coming together with an almost audible snap, and I knew the dog had been holding them back. But he wasn't there to protect us any longer.

As soon as Logan could rein it in, we ran.

Carmen only nods, and that's enough for me. While I went to grad school for history with a concentration in archive management, Carmen came home from college and joined the Bellegrave Police. She's been a detective for almost eight years now, and even though I speak to the dead, she knows when to stop talking about their remains. A flash of that eerie hand rising out of the murky diesel fuel resurfaces in my memory, and I trust my friend not to elaborate.

"Tom, we've got a bigger problem than your fear of the hocus pocus," Carmen says.

Tom turns back to us. "What's that?"

"State police are going to send in a team to take over this investigation, and there will be a detective on that team that will probably want to know how Della knew to look in that barrel."

Tom doesn't move, nor does he answer.

My ability to speak to the dead may be well known in Bellegrave, and I've even been a state witness a few times, giving testimony in Monticello. But when I've been called to be a witness, it's usually in the capacity of my day job as the executive director of the Bellegrave Historical Society. I'm either called up to give testimony regarding historical facts about a location, especially on cold cases, but sometimes it's because I've stumbled into an investigation on my own.

As in the case of Bellegrave school teacher Victoria Gustafson.

When doing a search of the local newspapers archive for Carmen, I'd stumbled upon a photograph that led me to Victoria's ghost and her revelation that her death had been no accident. Victoria's murderer, Martha Pruitt, was now awaiting trial, and I was sure I would be called to testify. I did shoot the woman after all. But my involvement in the case was easily explained without relying on my supernatural abilities.

This situation was entirely different.

"I'm not going to lie to the state police." I make a face. "I still can't lie to my own mom."

Carmen waves a finger at me. "That's true." She turns to Tom. "In summer between ninth and tenth grade, we made friends with those girls who came in on that church camp exchange. Remember the ones? With the roller blades?"

Tom rolls his eyes. "You weren't a part of that crowd, were you? I've never gotten so many complaints. Those girls kept racing up and down Main Street on those blasted things."

Carmen purses her lips and nods. "We were going to go into Plattsburgh and get our own blades, but Mrs. Hopewell wouldn't let us. So we talked those girls into giving us a ride in the church van when they went into Plattsburgh for a supply run." Carmen's expression sours further, and I avoid her gaze. "Little Miss Perfect here couldn't hold it in and blabbed to her mom the night before. We were so grounded."

I cringe. "We were. That was my fault."

Logan lifts his head. "You were grounded without doing the thing?"

Carmen's expression turns fierce now. "Hell hath no fury like Maxine and Vanessa when they combine forces."

Tom shudders. "I can only imagine." He looks to me. "So you're going to tell this state police detective you see dead people?"

I shrug. "That's the truth, so that's what I'm going to say."

"What if that makes her a suspect?" Logan asks. This is the longest he's held his head up since vomiting on the island, and it's reassuring to see his face has a little more color now.

Carmen looks away uncomfortably. "That shouldn't be a problem." She hesitates, and I know she's trying to decide how best to say what she needs to say. "Evidence on the body would suggest she was placed there either before Della was born or shortly thereafter. You couldn't possibly have murdered her and put her there." She directs this last part to me.

"You saw her clothing," I say.

Carmen doesn't say anything.

"I didn't know a body could be so well preserved in a barrel of fuel," I go on.

"A drum like that tends to act like a preservation chamber. Especially if it was sealed tightly enough for long enough to keep out the oxygen," Carmen explains.

"And petroleum hydrocarbons prohibit the growth of microbes that speed decomposition," Tom adds.

"Petroleum hydrocarbons? Not diesel?" Logan asks.

Tom shakes his head. "Looks like those drums were heating oil for a furnace somewhere on the property. There used to be a caretaker that stayed on the island year-round. His residence likely had a furnace that required oil."

"A caretaker?" I shudder, thinking about what that kind of life that must have been.

Tom nods. "The Carmichaels, the owners of the island and the camp, didn't like it being left unguarded in the winter."

I glance at Carmen to find her lips pursed before she says, "Bored teenagers doing dumb stuff in small towns."

"Well, I certainly wouldn't have wanted the job," I say. I look to Tom. "Do you know of any reported deaths on the island?"

I think of those soulless eyes, so many of them, and wonder at their number. Based on the feelings emanating from the island and the noises I'd heard drifting across the water from it, I'd assumed the ghosts that inhabited it had died elsewhere and had simply returned to the island to recapture a moment in their life that was happy. After being on the island, so close to those souls I had before only heard and felt, I wasn't so sure. I had felt many projected feelings while on the island, but happy wasn't one of them.

"As far as I know, Bellegrave Police have never had a single issue with the island until now. Nothing serious anyway." He nods in the general direction of the village that sits nestled in a bay at the west end of the lake. "I heard Barry Wise came home for the summer to show his new wife Bellegrave, pack up his house, and sell it. You might ask him if he ever heard of anything."

I tuck that piece of information into the very recesses of my mind, trying to convince myself I won't go looking for trouble. But there's something about those empty eyes that still haunt me even from the safety of my own backyard.

Henry has come to sit on Carmen's feet, and she reaches under his chin. He tilts his head back and nearly purrs as she gets that good spot along his neck with her blue and yellow polka-dotted nails. "You might want to take this time to get cleaned up. State police will be here soon, and then I can't guarantee what will happen to the rest of your day."

I nod and stand, pulling Logan up with me. "Can I get you guys some water or lemonade or something?"

They are both visibly sweating, and the sun is only rising higher in the sky as it's not quite noon.

Carmen opens her mouth to answer, but a familiar hum from the lake has her stopping and turning. A midsized watercraft with the emblem for the New York Department of Environmental Conservation approaches from the west, followed by two smaller aluminum boats. The DEC is New York's version of fish and game officers, and this team is probably the patrol Carmen asked to come secure the island until the state police could arrive.

She turns to me with a smile. "I'll have to pass on that. Looks like my day has already begun."

———

I take an icy shower, the effects of which last for about three seconds after I step out.

The humidity ruins any chance I have of feeling clean, and I stare at my bra as if it's betrayed me before tossing it aside for a cotton bralette that although won't provide as much support will not require me to become a wrestling champ just to get it on.

I find a dress in the back of my closet. It smells musty from going unworn, but it's made of cotton with thin straps, and it's about all I can tolerate. I slip on my cork-bottom sandals, tousle my short curls until they look like something intentional, and go downstairs in search of coffee. I find both coffee and my husband at the table in the dining alcove in our kitchen.

Our cottage once belonged to Logan's great-aunt Marge, and while she kept up on the maintenance, she wasn't keen on spending money on new kitchen cabinets when the old ones worked just fine, even if all the doors had fallen off of them. The kitchen had been our first renovation project when we moved in and remains the only updated room in the whole cottage.

Shortly after that was the car accident, and in an effort to save my life from a uterine rupture I had suffered in the accident, Logan gave consent for the surgeon to perform a hysterectomy. It was a decision that had sent me into a foggy limbo of being neither alive nor dead that I had wallowed in for the past thirteen years until I discovered my husband having an almost-affair.

The one thing social media got right was having a relationship status that simply said it's complicated.

"I called your dad," Logan says when I take the seat across from him. "He's on his way over." He pushes my University at Albany mug toward me, already filled with coffee. "Despite what Carmen says, I think it would be best if we had a lawyer present for both of us when the state police get here."

I take a sip of the coffee, strong and bitter like I like it, and close my eyes for one blissful second, pretending a ghost dog didn't just lead me to a dead body in an oil drum on the old girls camp island.

When I open them, Logan is smiling softly at me. I stick my tongue out at him.

"You must be tired," he says in response.

"Thank you for calling my dad," I say and set down my coffee mug. "And yes. Very. I'll probably try to take a nap this afternoon in the freezer."

Keeping the spirits on the island at bay had taken more

energy than I could have ever guessed, and I'm feeling far more drained than my swim alone usually makes me. I want to crawl on the couch and hog our one fan for myself, but I know the state police will be here soon.

Logan pushes a plate of toast toward me next, and I pick up the jar of peanut butter he's put on the table next to the butter dish and a pot of my secretary, Frances Blum's, home-made strawberry jelly.

I've hardly turned the lid on the peanut butter jar a quarter of a turn when Henry appears at my elbow. He executes a perfect sit, his eyebrows neutral in an expression of serene dogginess.

I pick up a spoon from the table and scoop some of the peanut butter out for Henry. I sit, letting him lick the spoon while Logan takes the toast back to spread peanut butter on it for me.

"Did you eat something?" I ask, and he cringes.

"Not yet," he says.

"It might help settle your stomach." I offer him my own toast after he pushes it back to me with a healthy swipe of peanut butter on each piece.

He takes an overzealous bite of it from my hand, and I laugh before the moment can hit me and erase my smile. It's funny having to rebuild intimacy with someone you're comfortable peeing in front of, and these awkward moments poke at my heart a little more than usual.

Logan had not been having an affair with a client as I'd suspected, but it had been enough to unlock something inside of me, and I'd finally said how I felt about his decision after the accident. We'd said a lot of things the night I'd shot Marty Pruitt, and it was as though a river had been undammed. Only now we were standing on opposite shores, trying to figure out how to make our way back to each other.

I've nearly finished my toast when the first state police

watercraft appears around the western curve of the shoreline that makes up the cove in which our cottage is nestled. A second appears shortly behind it, headed in the same direction.

Carmen turns from where she's been waiting on our dock to look back at the cottage. I wave a hand so she can see me through the windows of the dining alcove. She holds up a single finger indicating I should wait and then turns back to drop into my fishing boat with Tom. They make it to the island just behind the state police boats, and I watch Carmen approach a man in a black polo on the rocky beach. Even from where we sit, I can tell he is someone of authority, and I wonder if he is the officer in charge.

"It feels like we're on our own episode of one of those live cop shows," Logan says.

I nod, unable to say more as I watch two teams climb the hill into the woods on the island. My stomach tightens remembering those eerie eyes that had followed us through the woods, the haunting sound of disembodied laughter.

How is it that a joyful sound can evoke such terror?

I take another sip of my coffee, holding the warm mug between my hands as I've suddenly grown cold. Alarm shoots through me, and I nearly drop my coffee mug as I stand, my gaze swinging about the kitchen behind me, but there's nothing there.

Logan stands too, his hands reaching for me.

"Whoa," he says. "What just happened?"

"I got a..." but I don't finish the sentence. I shake my head. "I thought I felt something, but there's nothing." I shake my head again and slowly sink to my seat, even though my eyes still search the room around us. "It's nothing," I assure Logan and pat the table where he'd been sitting. "It's really okay. I'm just a little jumpy, I think."

This doesn't stop me from looking around the kitchen

one more time. I was sure I had felt a ghost, but it wasn't like the usual feeling I got. It was almost as though—

I can't bring myself to finish the thought.

But when the back door bangs open seconds later, I still start.

My dad appears in the kitchen from the mudroom. Concerningly, he's dressed in chinos and a polo shirt and even more concerningly, he's carrying the leather satchel he took into his office every day before he retired.

"You came in lawyer mode," I say.

He sets the satchel at the empty spot at the table, his eyes transfixed by the sight through the windows.

"Dear God," he whispers before dropping his gaze to me. "Did you talk to the victim?"

I shake my head. "I didn't stick around long enough to see if she could gather energy to appear." I glance back at the island. "It's not the most welcoming of places for me." I nod in the direction of the door. "Mom didn't come with you?"

He pulls out the chair and unlatches his satchel, withdrawing a yellow legal notepad before setting the satchel on the ground so he can sit. "She's at yoga in the square with Mel. She'll hear about it soon enough. DEC has the boat launch roped off, and their launches are patrolling the lake, sending people back to their docks and the marina."

"They're shutting down the whole lake?" Logan asks.

"It's just a dead body," I say carelessly before realizing.

Logan and my dad stare at me.

Dad says, "Not everyone sees dead people as frequently as you do, Del."

"Point taken." I tap his notepad. "Do you think this is necessary?"

"It's better to be prepared than to be caught unawares," Dad says. "Now walk me through it from the beginning."

"I'm going to take a quick shower," Logan says and heads up the stairs two at a time.

I turn back to my father and start with the black dog and go through the story one more time. When I've finished, Dad pushes up his glasses to rub the bridge of his nose, something I've only ever seen him do when helping my little brother, Ryan, study for the SAT.

"A ghost dog led you to the body?"

"Yes, sir," I say and stand to get my dad a cup of coffee.

He hooks an arm over the back of his chair so he can watch me walk around the kitchen. "What do you plan to tell the state police?"

"The truth," I answer, pulling a mug from the cupboard and filling it from the carafe on the counter. "I'm the one who must live with the decisions I make, and I choose to tell the truth. It's up to the state police to decide whether or not they believe in ghosts."

I set the coffee down in front of my father and take my seat before I register the odd expression on his face.

"Are you sure you're okay?" he asks.

"Of course, I am." I take up my own coffee mug, but the coffee's gone cold.

"You look...strange," Dad finishes.

"I just found a body in an oil barrel after a ghost dog showed me where to find it."

Dad shakes his head. "It's not that. It's almost as if—" He stops himself and shakes his head again.

"What is it?" I set aside my coffee mug.

My father has never hesitated in speaking his mind to me, and that he should do so now is alarming.

He shrugs. "You just—" But he shakes his head and swallows hard.

Concern has me sitting up. "I just what?" I press.

He looks straight at me. "You look like you did when you were pregnant. Almost like you're glowing."

Something hard hits me in the chest, but I shove it aside. "Glowing? Are you kidding?"

He shrugs again. "It's probably the adrenaline."

I'm stopped from further questioning my father when Logan comes back down the stairs into the kitchen. His hair is damp again, and he's put on another pair of jeans and an old t-shirt from a triathlon he did once when he was in law school.

He sits at the table to put on his sneakers but freezes, his attention caught by something out the window.

Dad's the first to register his look and turns to the window before I can. Carmen has returned to the beach along with the man I'd seen her speaking to earlier. She hops back into my boat, and the man follows behind her.

A sudden unease strikes me, and I wrap my hands around my coffee mug out of habit.

"It looks like it's time to test that theory about telling the truth," my dad says as Carmen pulls the engine to a start and shoves off, my little fishing boat headed back to its dock.

Four

We go out to the patio off the kitchen to await the arrival of Carmen and the state police detective she's bringing with her. Henry remains in the kitchen, seated behind the glass sliding door as though he were an art exhibit depicting pity.

The heat is nearly unbearable, and I reach over to open the umbrella in our patio table even though the sun is not the worst of it.

"Hi, Mr. Hopewell," Carmen says, and I can hear the smile in her voice before I turn to see them at the edge of the patio. "Logan call you?"

My dad nods. "Of course, he did."

Carmen shakes her head with a small laugh. "Lawyers." She gestures to the man standing beside her. "Mr. Hopewell, this is Detective Daniel Hanratty. His team will be taking over the investigation."

I'm not sure when it happened, but Logan and my father have come to stand in front of me like I'm a middle school nerd in need of saving from the class bully. I elbow my way between them and extend my hand to Detective Hanratty.

"Hi," I say. "I'm Dr. Della James. I see dead people."

Detective Hanratty is somewhere in his mid-to-late thirties with dark blond hair cut short and a face that would be called handsome if it carried a little more weight. His teeth are brilliantly white though when he smiles in response to my statement, and his smile speaks of kindness and understanding. I wonder if this will go better than I imagined.

"Dr. James." He takes my hand. "Detective Neil has been telling me about you. Do you mind if I ask you and your husband some questions?"

His smile is friendly, his eyes exuding warmth, but my other sense picks up on something that's not quite right, and I hesitate a moment too long.

Dad steps back in front of me as soon as Detective Hanratty lets go of my hand. "I represent Dr. James and Mr. James, and I will be present for any questioning."

Detective Hanratty has a slow smile that kicks up the side of his mouth now. "Mr.—"

"Hopewell," my dad supplies.

"Mr. Hopewell, Dr. James is not a suspect, nor can she be one unless she chose a life of crime in her toddler years."

My dad doesn't back down. "Still, I will be present for the interview."

"That's fine," Detective Hanratty says with that same smile.

His straight teeth suggest a history of braces, and parents who loved him enough to pay for orthodontics. But beneath that charm, something darker lingers. I just can't quite put my finger on it.

His voice genuflects on the word fine, and I tilt my head.

"You're not from around here, are you?" I ask, my other sense pushing me to ask the question.

Detective Hanratty's eyes come back to me, and I realize they're a deep green, an unusual and intense color. "No, I'm not. I grew up outside of Manhattan." He pauses before adding, "Kansas." His grin is entirely lopsided now.

"Your accent's gone soft," I say, and I'm not sure why I'm having this conversation with this man, but I can't shake the uneasy feeling he projects. Maybe I'm subconsciously trying to find a logical reason for my unease.

I can feel Logan watching me, but the events of the morning have me unsettled, and I don't back down.

"So it has," he says. "I haven't been back to Kansas in a while." He gives a grin then that's not like his usual smile, this one is tense and forced, and I realize the topic is an uncomfortable one for him.

He shouldn't be the uncomfortable one here. I'm about to explain how I almost drowned because of a ghost dog that then led me to a dead body in a barrel. I indicate the patio table behind us.

"Please sit," I say. "Can I get you some water or something?"

He shakes his head. "No, that's all right. I'll just get to my questions and be on my way."

He takes a chair, and I take one beside him while Dad, Logan, and Carmen linger around us like sharks, as though if they stop moving they'll die.

"Let's start with why you and your husband were on the island, Dr. James."

I explain once again about the black dog and how I almost drowned from the motorboat and lost sight of the dog and how I went to search for him on the island.

Detective Hanratty holds up a hand. "I'm sorry, Dr. James."

"Della," I say.

"Della." He gives that slow smile. "I'm not familiar with dogs myself. Are they able to swim that far out?"

I point to the glass door behind me. "Henry's done it a

time or two. He's always swum back though, so I haven't been forced to go get him from the island."

Detective Hanratty glances behind me to where I'm sure Henry still sits pathetically behind the glass door. Hanratty's smile is swift now.

"Oh, there's a good boy," he says before turning back to me. "You said his name is Henry?"

I nod. "Professor Henry Jones."

He nods in appreciation. "Because it was the dog's name."

I shrug. "It's kinda on the nose for the director of a historical society, so I thought Henry was a good compromise."

The detective's tone is jovial, the conversation benign, and yet that lingering sense of unease has me wary.

I continue. "I assumed the dog had swum out there and gotten trapped. The island is haunted by spirits that like to torment the living, and I couldn't leave him out there."

"When did you realize the dog was a ghost?" He asks the question so seriously it takes me a moment to realize he's not questioning my ability, and this heightens my unease.

"When we reached the summit of the island." I gesture to the girls camp. "You might have noticed the island goes up to a plateau. The lake was formed by glacial movements that carved out what would become the lake around that spot of land, leaving it elevated and flat at the top. It makes the land valuable."

"And yet it hasn't been redeveloped since the camp closed."

I shake my head. "That's not land that should be lived on."

"What do you see on the island, Della?"

Again the question catches me off guard, and I recognize it for the mark of a good detective.

"Spirits of youths. Anywhere from probably thirteen to

eighteen. Their eyes are empty though, and I can feel their evil intent."

"Their evil intent?" Detective Hanratty raises his eyebrows at this.

"Ghosts are just accumulated energy. You know how you can feel the air crackle before a thunderstorm? It's mostly the same thing, only I can feel energy on a different level."

Detective Hanratty sits back in his chair. "How long have you had this ability, Della?"

"Almost my whole life," I say, glancing back at my dad over my shoulder, and he nods in confirmation.

Detective Hanratty glances between us. "Does this ability run in your family?"

"Yes," I say, surprised by the turn the questioning has taken. "It comes from the paternal side of the family. My great-grandmother had it, then one of her daughters, and then it seemed to skip a generation before falling on me."

"These ghosts that you see. When they tell you something, how accurate do they tend to be?"

"Very," Carmen says from behind me before I can answer. She leans forward, putting both hands on the back of my chair. "I'm afraid to tell you, Detective Hanratty, but Dr. James likes to create a lot of paperwork for me."

Detective Hanratty takes this in, his eyes narrowed in thought. "So the ghost dog lures you to the island and then takes you to the victim in the oil barrel. That's it?"

I nod. "We ran from the camp after that. Got back into our boat and came back here to call Carmen and Chief Tom."

The detective looks to Logan. "I'm going to assume you have a similar story, Mr. James?"

Logan nods. "Except my wife has kindly left out the part where I vomited after seeing the victim."

Detective Hanratty smiles. "You're just showing your humanity, Mr. James." Detective Hanratty looks back at me.

"Is there anything else I should know about that island? Any other insights you're picking up on? It might help if you've sensed any leads we should follow up on in our investigation."

"You're taking me seriously," I say.

He laughs, a little self-deprecatingly. "Of course, I am, Della."

"Do you believe I see ghosts?"

He leans forward, his face suddenly serious. "I believe that you believe you see ghosts, and for me, that's the only thing that matters."

It's not as though he's admitted to believing me, but rather something adjacent to it.

I shake my head. "There wasn't anything else. It's hard to filter through the background noise on the island to concentrate, and I think having the body sealed like that in an oil drum prevented her from gathering energy to form." I swallow, remembering the press of energy after the dog crossed over. "I didn't stick around to see if she would appear so I could talk to her."

The detective blinks. "How's that?"

"Ghosts need energy to form. That's why a room will grow cold, or batteries drain before a ghost appears. I think the victim was deprived energy, so she didn't form. I, therefore, couldn't speak to her directly."

Hanratty looks back at the island. "Do you think there's a chance she will manifest?"

I open my mouth to answer but pause at his use of the term *manifest*, an unusual term for someone who likely didn't wake up this morning thinking he was going to interview someone who can see the dead.

"There's always a chance. But I hope for her sake she crossed over when she died," I finally say.

"How likely is that?"

I look back out at the island, but in my mind I'm seeing

Victoria Gustafson as she first appeared to me that day by the river where her body had been dumped. "For a murder victim?" I frown and look back at the detective. "Not very likely."

The detective stands, and I realize our conversation is already over. He digs into his pocket for a moment.

"Thank you for your time, Della." He pauses long enough to nod in the direction of the island and then hands me his card. "If our victim does appear, you'll let me know, right?"

"Of course," I say, taking in the details of the card. "Detective, there's one other thing that's bothering me." I study the island as I talk. "There are a lot of spirits out there. It doesn't mean they've died there. It just means they're drawn back to that place for some reason."

"Perhaps it's happy childhood memories," Hanratty offers.

I shake my head. "No, those spirits aren't happy." I glance at the island, the feelings that had been just out of reach since fleeing the camp finally righting themselves. "It's like they're waiting," I say.

Logan's hand finds the small of my back suddenly, and I lean into his strength.

"They're waiting for something, but I can't figure out what," I finish.

When I rouse myself from my thoughts, I find a curious expression on Hanratty's face. I don't get to ask him about it as he exchanges pleasantries with Dad and Logan before heading back down to the dock with Carmen. I watch them retreat.

Logan touches my elbow now.

"You've got that I've just seen a ghost look on your face," he says when I turn.

I shake my head, looking back to the dock, my fingers absently tracing the raised print of the card. I study the retreating figure of Detective Hanratty, my other sense pulsing even as he moves away.

"There's something off about that detective."

"Off?" Dad asks.

Carmen pulls the engine on the outboard to life once more and navigates the boat in a perfect U-turn back in the direction of the island. I watch the boat grow smaller and smaller while I gather my words.

Finally I say, "It's like he's haunted."

———

I don't have time to consider this development or what it might mean if I'm forced to work further with Hanratty because just then my mother comes tearing around the side of the cottage.

"Delia Ann, what have you done?" She's striding at a clip an Olympic walker would admire while also trying to keep her purple flip-flops on.

She's absolutely, without question, wearing the lavender leotard with the leggings that resemble a splatter painting that she first wore during her jazzercise era in 1994. She's put on an oversized, teal t-shirt over this that reads *Namasté Here* with the outline of a martini glass complete with olive underneath it.

"I haven't done anything," I immediately reply, but I feel the stares of my father and husband. "I haven't done much," I amend.

My mother tosses her tote on a patio table chair, her yoga mat nearly toppling out, as barking erupts from the other side of the sliding glass door behind us. Logan goes to release Henry who has spotted Grammy and will not settle until he's frisked her for treats while I wait for my mother's barrage.

"Elmer McQuiggan is down at Shelly's telling everyone

you found a mass grave on the island." She flings a hand in the direction of the village and diner on Main Street.

"Elmer McQuiggan has run a business based on gossip for the past seventy years. I'm lucky it's only a mass grave," I say.

My mother straightens and crosses her arms, and I know I've tripped a booby trap wire.

"Age is not a disease, Della," she says crisply.

I hold up both hands. "It is not. You're right. But I did not find a mass grave. You know how Elmer likes to spread gossip. It's why he took over the launch in the first place. It's the best place to do it."

My mother's frown could cut bricks. "That is not true. He voted for Obama."

Anyone who voted for Obama is a god in my mother's eyes.

"I didn't find a mass grave."

She takes a step toward me. "Don't lie to me, Delia Ann." Her voice drops. "Elmer said it was some kind of sex thing."

For the first time, I want to stay in this conversation just to see where it leads. I put a hand on the back of the chair next to me and lean in. "What kind of sex thing exactly?"

She looks left and right, but the only people who could hear her are standing right next to her, so I'm not sure what she's looking for.

"You know. One of those sex cults. Elmer says they all died at an orgy."

Logan covers his laugh by reaching for a jumping Henry and turning them all back toward the cottage before Henry can knock over his grandmother. My father has had nearly fifty years to practice the art of turning his head as though he's suddenly spotted something interesting. He does it now, but I still hear the inhale of an aborted laugh.

"Mom, I want to say this with the absolute most clarity. I am not familiar *at all* with sex cults."

She considers this and takes a step back, a single eyebrow going up. "But did you find a dead body?"

I hold up a single finger now. "Just one."

"Della!" She drops her arms in frustration.

"It's not my fault. The ghost dog made me do it."

My father coughs and heads in the direction of the cottage where Logan has disappeared.

"Are you serious right now?" my mother says. "A *ghost* dog made you do it?"

"Yes." I let out the word with a sigh. I'm so tired of saying *ghost dog*, but I guess it's better than having to explain a sex cult.

"A ghost dog made you find a dead body? You couldn't just toss him a bone and tell him to take a hike?"

"That's not how this works."

She shakes her head, her eyes pinching, and she looks as though she's going to cry.

I straighten. "Mom, are you okay?"

Something tells me this is not about the dead body or the ghost dog or sex cults. Sweat has pooled along my mother's upper lip, and the neck of her t-shirt is damp.

"I knew something like this was going to happen," she mumbles through the tears she's trying to hold back.

"You knew I was going to be led to a dead body by a ghost dog?" I soften my voice, unsure what's happening here.

My mom shakes her head, but it seems to only dislodge the tears that start to fall down her checks. "I knew something bad was going to happen when I retired," she finally cries, doubling over the back of a chair.

"Mom, you need to get inside out of the sun. I think something's happening with you."

I'd moved forward to help her into the house, and she straightens so abruptly she nearly smacks the back of her head into my teeth.

"Of course, something is happening, Della. I'm retiring!" she says like she's contracted an STD from a public toilet.

"Yes," I say. "And we're going to have a wonderful party to celebrate. Joan and Joyce are coming from San Diego, Maeve and Poppy are—" I don't get to finish the list of college and high school friends that are coming to Bellegrave for the extravagant retirement party my mom has planned because she suddenly seizes my shoulders and gives me a not-delicate shake.

"Della, do you know what happens to people when they retire?" She doesn't give me a chance to answer and instead blurts out, "They die! That's what happens, and it will be so much worse for me."

"I don't think there are degrees of death. It's like pregnancy. You either are or you aren't."

She lets go of me to stab her chest with a finger. "For me, there is." Now she stabs me with the finger. "Because you'll still be able to talk to me, and I'll never escape the sex cult!"

She dissolves into tears again, but now she lets me take her by the shoulders and steer her in the direction of the cottage. I find Logan and Dad in the kitchen. Logan is trying to convince Henry to drink his water without playing with the ice cubes while my dad stands at the kitchen island pouring glasses of lemonade. When he sees my mom, his expression doesn't change.

I close the sliding door behind us, blocking out a good deal of the heat. "She's been doing this a lot, hasn't she?"

"Yep," he says, going back to pouring glasses of lemonade. "Change is tough. She's worked for Kirkland and Martinelli since it was just Jeff senior. Now it's Jeff senior, junior, and the third. That's a lot."

Mom lets me take her into the living room where I plop her on the couch in front of our only fan. Dad brings her a glass of lemonade. She tries to drink it, but she's crying too hard, and it mostly spills down her t-shirt.

She swipes at her mouth with the back of her hand. "Bad things always happen when people retire," she says and meets my gaze. "I don't want bad things to happen to us."

I can't stop my eyes from going to Logan, who stands in the doorway, holding back a vibrating Henry. Once something hard and unyielding would have been caught in that stare, but now it's only soft, tender, and waiting. I look back at my mother.

"Nothing bad is going to happen." I signal to Logan to release Henry.

He lopes over to Grammy and plows into her legs, dropping his head on her knee. She laughs and scratches the spot between his eyes. He lets his head roll back in bliss.

"You can't know that," my mother whispers to Henry.

"No, I can't, but you know what I can know?" I look to Logan more assuredly now. "I know we'll get through it." I wrap my arm around her, and she's so startled by the contact she stops crying. "We'll get through it together."

She blinks, tears falling from her lashes. "When did you get so demonstrative?"

"I prefer it when we make passive aggressive comments about one another that are vaguely cloaked in love," Dad mutters before taking a sip of his lemonade.

I ignore them both. "Mom, Dad's right. Change is hard. That's what's happening here. It's okay to have these feelings of uncertainty, but I don't think you need to worry about having to talk about sex cults with me in the afterlife. How about we make a deal?"

My mother holds up the hand she's been scratching Henry with, and he lets out an annoyed huff.

"I don't want to know about what you found on that island."

I shake my head. "I won't tell you, but you might want to avoid the paper in the morning." I pause, consider. "And maybe the counter at Shelly's."

She gives a solemn nod. "Fine. What is it?"

"I promise not to get involved with what's happening out there." I gesture to the window, the island framed perfectly within it, showcasing the law enforcement boats now swarming the rocky beach. "So far as I can without obstructing an investigation or refusing to cooperate with the police."

She tilts her head back and forth as though weighing every word. Finally, she nods again. "Okay. What's my part of the deal?"

"You concentrate on your party."

She twitches her nose. "How can I—"

"Uh uh," I interrupt. "We're making a deal. No focusing on the tumultuous feelings stirring inside of you. We're looking for healthy ways to cope with those feelings and turn them to the positive."

"Did you finally go see Carmen's therapist?" Dad asks.

"No, Daryl sometimes tells me what he overhears the tree hugger groups saying in the rec hall during their meetings." I smile at my mother who does not return the expression. "Doesn't that sound nice? Focusing on something positive while you make your way through this transition?"

She toys with Henry's ear before answering. "I was looking forward to a nice party. We haven't done anything with the whole family since your wedding." When she looks up again, her eyelashes are free of tears. "And it's not like I can depend on Ryan to give us a wedding any time soon."

I pat her hand. "He's only thirty-eight. Give him time."

Mom snorts. "I'm more likely to join a sex cult than Ryan is to marry."

The idea of my mother in a sex cult has me wishing for a martini like the one on her shirt.

"Do we have a deal?" I ask.

She looks at my father. I'm not sure what passes between them, but like Logan and me, they have a silent language of their own. If Ryan and I had ever been able to interpret it, we would have held more power over them, but alas, we never did.

"Fine." She exhales the word.

"Good," I say and hand her the glass of lemonade again. "Now drink this. The news said I should check on the elderly, and I always do my part."

My mother takes the glass of lemonade and glares.

FIVE

The blare of my alarm clock nearly sends me toppling from the bed the next morning. I catch myself on the edge, my hand flailing blindly until I can turn the damn thing off. It's a second before I remember what day it is and why my alarm is going off this early.

It's my Sunday on duty at Lady Josephine Lodge, and I need to have the front gates open before seven for the sunrise yoga session that takes place on the lawn every Sunday in summer, weather permitting. I glance to the window, and it has the gall to be filled with buttery, warm summer sunshine. I'd groan, but it would wake Henry and Logan, so instead I stumble into the shower.

There's regular staff at the Lodge, but during the busy summer months, the staff of the Bellegrave Historical Society rotate weekend shifts so someone from management is on the grounds at all times. Logan had tried to talk me out of going into work today, but after spending the previous afternoon after Mom and Dad left on the couch hogging our one fan—an effort ruined when Henry climbed on top of me and draped his body over mine—I'm feeling marginally human.

Still, I skip my morning swim. For many reasons.

I dress in an equally as musty smelling cotton dress, and sandals in hand so I don't wake Henry, I sneak from the room. I pause on the threshold, my eyes going to the door across the hall and back to my husband asleep in the bed. For a second, I have the urge to kiss him goodbye, but it feels too weird, so I go down the stairs instead.

I don't have time for breakfast, so once I'm in the car, I call in my order to Shelly's and pick it up as I go through the village on my way to the lodge. I make it just in time to have the gate open before Hilary Vandecamp pulls up in her station wagon. She waves a hand out the window as she passes, and I secure the iron gate against the brick pillars to keep the drive open for the day.

The camp is quiet when I let myself in, and I stand in the foyer for a moment, enjoying the smell of old polished wood and the tick of the hand-carved grandfather clock in the conference space.

And the incredibly modern and soothing HVAC installed years ago to preserve the lodge, which currently has it at a comfortable seventy-two degrees and humidity levels I can live with.

My peace is interrupted by a string of curse words floating down the hall. I turn my head in the direction of the sound. I'm sharing today's shift with my Director of Programs Allie Kim, but that distinct string of curses can only originate from none other than my Director of Operations Steve Fitzpatrick, which absolutely cannot be good.

I make my way down the hall that leads to the management offices and find Steve in his, cursing at his computer screen.

"Hey," I say from the door.

He doesn't look up. "Some kid slipped his head through the safety fence blocking off the creamery and got stuck yesterday. I had to call the fire department, they had to cut him out, and now I'm trying to find someone who can come this morning and fix the safety fence before we open the exhibits." He slams his mouse onto his desk like he's striking a hammer against a nail.

"Ah, summer," I say because I don't have anything helpful to add.

Steve finally looks up, a grin on his face. It's such an about-face I know with a great deal of certainty what's next.

"I heard you were the reason they shut down the lake yesterday. You won't be able to go into Super Duper for a week without hearing about it."

My smile is tight. "It's not my fault," I say. "These things just happen."

Steve snorts. "Yeah, to you maybe." He gestures with his chin. "I heard it was some kind of mass grave. It's gonna take weeks to catalog all the bodies."

Nothing sprouts rumors faster than a small town, and I just hope he doesn't say the words *sex cult*. I may never be able to look at him in a budget meeting again.

"Nope, not a mass grave," I say. "But I don't think I'm supposed to talk about it."

Steve holds up a hand. "No need to. I got all my info from Elmer down at the dock. He said he saw the whole thing. Said the state police filled an entire cadaver van."

I'm saved from responding when Steve's phone rings, and I slip away while he answers it. I retreat to my office, drop my backpack on the floor, and dive into my bag from Shelly's. The egg and gouda on a ciabatta roll is still warm, and I dig into it while I go through my email.

As executive director of the historical society, it's my job to oversee the running of the living history museum at Lady Josephine Lodge, and as I scroll through my emails I feel the pinch of overwhelm that's familiar this time of year. There are summer camps for school children from kindergarten all the way through twelfth grade. These are overseen by Allie as part of programs with a summer staff composed of area school-teachers.

There are corporate retreats for businesses from Syracuse, Albany, and even New York. Diana Milton, our director of development, takes these on in the hopes of securing corporate sponsors for future projects.

Then there are classes ranging from plein air painting to mycology and foraging, live re-enactments, and at the end of the season, a pig roast open to the public. The grounds are filled with visitors from open to close, and it's a delicate operation to keep everything running smoothly.

Now is not the time for me to investigate another murder, and I know I shouldn't have any trouble keeping my promise to my mother. Not this time.

I continue through my email, putting out several fires while my egg and gouda goes cold next to my laptop. I'm not sure how much time has passed before a voice comes from the door.

"I thought you might need reinforcements."

I look up to see Lisa Reynolds holding a familiar mauve box from Cake & Cookie. My tastebuds stand at attention.

I reach up and give a *gimme gimme* gesture with both hands. "Yes, please."

Allie Kim comes in behind Lisa, carrying a tray of paper coffee cups. "Lisa and I had a funny suspicion the little scene we witnessed on the lake yesterday had something to do with you," she says, setting the tray down on my desk.

I pluck a still warm croissant from the box Lisa has offered me. "I don't know why you would think that," I say innocently.

Both of Allie's black eyebrows go straight up. "What did you do this time?"

"I hope it's something juicy," Lisa adds, selecting a cranberry and orange muffin from the box before passing it to Allie. "After the week I had with those kindergarteners from the Kid Center, I could use something grown-up."

After witnessing her mother murder a beloved teacher, Lisa Reynolds had faked her own kidnapping and murder to escape Bellegrave. She had only been eighteen at the time. After I uncovered her mother's actions and discovered Lisa's whereabouts, Lisa was able to return home where she's now caring for her ailing father and serving as the Lodge's volunteer music teacher for the summer, teaching visitors about the importance of music at the time the camp was founded and how it was used to pass on history and local tradition. We're lucky to have her before she starts as the choir director at the Bellegrave Middle and High School in the fall.

What I hadn't expected when I solved the murder of Victoria Gustafson was how easily Lisa would slip back into the small-town life in Bellegrave. Not only did it seem like she'd never left, but she'd also formed a fast friendship with Allie. Allie, a transplant from Massachusetts, had struggled to fit into the small town of Bellegrave. As was the case in most small towns, Bellegrave was a tight-knit community that protected itself from outsiders like Allie, and I was happy to see this particular friendship blossom.

Especially when I benefited from it in the form of caffeine and sugar.

This thought has me stopping, and I eye the two of them.

"You guys did something crazy this morning, didn't you?"

Allie shrugs. "We just ran up Sutton Hill. It's only like five miles round trip."

"We made it back for Hilary's session this morning, so we could cool down with some vinyasa. It was a beautiful way to start the day," Lisa adds.

I wrinkle my nose. "Were you being chased?"

Allie sets down the box after extracting a cheese danish. "It's an easy run. You should come with us sometime."

"I'll stick to swimming. Thanks." I grimace to let them know my true feelings, but they only laugh.

I take a sip of my latte and close my eyes in glee. I was sore in places I couldn't imagine, and my leg felt stiff after my unplanned sprint through the woods the previous day. The caffeine and sugar were medicinal at this point.

"So what happened?" Allie prompts, taking one of the chairs in front of my desk.

"It was not a mass grave," I start and lean back in my chair to relay the events of the previous day to Allie and Lisa. I give them the version that has hopefully been printed in the *Bellegrave Bulletin*. I don't divulge any details to them because I know this could derail an investigation, and I hope to do everything I can to ensure justice for the girl in the barrel.

By the time I've finished, Allie is on to a blueberry scone, and Lisa is nervously picking at the remains of her muffin.

"She was in the barrel?" Lisa asks. "Did you"—she licks her lips—"see any of her?"

I shake my head. "I didn't stick around. That island is... not right," I decide to say, remembering my father's and Logan's reactions yesterday.

Sometimes I can be too comfortable with death.

"Is that the first time you've seen a dog?" Allie asks.

I pull the pastry box toward to me to see what's left. "The first one I've seen. I might call my aunt Janine to find out if she's seen a dog. I suppose they have enough of a conscience to remain as ghosts."

"This is all so weird," Allie mutters.

"Do the police have any idea who she is?" Lisa asks next.

I shrug. "I have no idea. I only gave the state police detective what I knew, and he didn't offer anything in return. Just that Logan and I weren't suspects based on certain factors at the crime scene." I glance out my office window at the lake below, and a shudder passes through me. "She doesn't belong on that island though. I only hope she's passed."

"She didn't come to you?" Allie looks up from where she's dissected her scone on a napkin.

"No. I think the barrel might have prevented her from manifesting."

The word stops me, remembering Detective Hanratty's use of it.

"The barrel stopped her? How?" Lisa asks.

"Iron," Allie says for me with perhaps a little too much enthusiasm. "Iron is believed to contain a life force that stops spirits. Ever seen a fence around a cemetery where the top portion curves in? Victorians especially believed in the power of iron and designed cemetery fences like that because it was believed the iron in the fences and the curved top would keep spirits in the cemeteries."

Lisa looks between Allie and me. "You history nerds are weird in the best way."

"I know," Allie says with a grin before popping a bite of scone into her mouth.

"I can't say I'm surprised they found something on the island," Lisa says, bringing my attention back to her. "Not after what happened that last summer the camp was open."

She has my full attention now, and Allie stops chewing.

"What do you mean?" I ask.

Lisa points at me with a bit of muffin. "I know I ruined your summer with my disappearing act, but remember I was five in 1984, and Sadie Beaumont ruined my summer that year." She looks up nostalgically. "The year my dad took my training wheels off my bike. It was going to be the biggest summer of my life." She drops her eyes, her expression sorrowful. "And then Sadie Beaumont drowned at the camp."

"Who is Sadie Beaumont?" Allie asks.

Lisa shakes her head. "I didn't know her because she was much older than me. Seventeen or eighteen, I think. She was the daughter of the camp's caretaker. It was horrible."

Something inside of me clenches as I remember Chief Tom mentioning a caretaker. I can't stomach the thought of someone living permanently on that island.

Lisa takes a sip of her matcha before continuing. "It was only the middle of the summer too. I remember that. Camp had been open for maybe a month, and I saw my whole summer rolled out in front of me, training wheels free." She shakes her head. "Then one morning I woke up, and my bike was locked in the shed. Off limits. My dad totally freaked out."

"What happened?" I hold my latte cup absently in one hand now, that creeping sense of falling into a new investigation enveloping me even though I had only minutes before convinced myself it would be easy to stay out of it.

Chief Tom had said they'd never had any trouble out at the camp, but I wonder if the incident of which Lisa spoke happened before he was on the force. I only vaguely recalled Tom coming to Bellegrave later in his policing career, even though it felt like he had always been here.

"I don't know exactly," Lisa says. "You know how it is as a child. You only understand events through the lens your parents give you. My dad used this as a way to tell me I was never going to date. I was five."

"Never going to date?" Allie asks as she draws her legs up to sit crisscross style in the chair.

Lisa nods. "Sadie had always been a do-gooder before that summer. Good grades, volunteered with the youth group at church, helped out at the animal shelter, all sorts of things. Then she started dating some boy she met from the other camp." Here she swishes a finger back and forth. "Remember Camp Tomahawk over the hill? They would come over to the girls camp for dances and stuff. Very old-school. I remember because the boys would wait at the boat ramp for Elmer's launch to take them over, and they were always dressed up." She stares at a spot behind me for a second. "I was always bummed I didn't get to see the girls. I bet they had pretty dresses." She shakes her head as if bringing herself back to the present. "Anyway Sadie started seeing one of those boys, got into some kind of trouble. I don't know how bad because as a kid everything seems huge, and I was a do-gooder too. I was too scared to play tic-tac-toe on the back of the church bulletin even when Pastor Philips was doing the sermon."

"Pastor Philips?" Allie asks.

"He was the pastor of the Baptist Church back then," I say. "That man could put a Puritan to shame."

Lisa nods. "Had a tendency to spit when he got really excited, which was usually when he talked about the second coming."

Allie wrinkles her nose in disgust.

"So Sadie became a typical teenager?" I ask.

Lisa nods again. "Yeah, but of course, she was the only one anyone talked about. I don't think I ever even heard the boy's name. You know how it is. Boys will be boys, but girls must be saints."

"So how did she drown?" Allie asks.

Lisa shakes her head now. "Nobody knows. Her father reported her missing, and one of the camp's canoes was found capsized on the lake. One of Sadie's sneakers later washed up on shore, but they never recovered her body. They called in the dive team from Albany for that one. It was a big deal then. No one around here had ever heard of a dive team, and when they rolled into town, it caused a hubbub." Lisa sobers and shakes her head again. "They never found Sadie's body though."

"That's awful," Allie whispers.

"They found her sneaker on the shore of the island?" There's a click somewhere inside of me, and a sense of foreboding washes over me. The last time I had a preternatural click I nearly got myself killed.

"Yeah, just one sneaker though." She nods in the direction of the windows. "I saw Barry Wise at the Super Duper last week. He's in town getting his house ready to put on the market. You should swing by his place. I'm sure he'd be able to tell you more."

Chief Tom had mentioned the same thing. Barry Wise was the town's police chief before Tom took the job, and I bet he could tell me everything about Sadie Beaumont's drowning. It was odd that a girl had drowned at the same time the girl in the barrel was likely murdered. Were they connected? Had the girl who drowned known the murderer? Had she maybe witnessed it and needed to be silenced?

I can't let myself get ahead of the facts.

"I think I just might do that," I hear myself say, apparently completely forgetting my promise to my mother. "Thank you."

Lisa smiles. "Least I can do." She tosses her empty cup into the recycling bin. "I'm off to listen to five-year-olds try to sing the word macaroni for the next half hour." She rolls her eyes dramatically before slipping out the door.

"Thanks for the sugar and caffeine," I call after her, and she waves a hand in acknowledgment before disappearing down the hall.

I look at Allie. "Do you regret moving here?"

Allie shakes her head and downs the last of her coffee. "Not for a second. Where else would I find someone I can share macabre history with?" She wiggles her eyebrows and tosses her cup into the recycling bin with a flick of her wrist.

"I'm not sure that's a compliment," I call after her as she sails out my door, her laughter trailing behind her.

———

Barry Wise owns one of the few Victorians still standing off Clinton Street that runs behind the Super Duper at the west end of the village. That section of the village used to be all Victorians until the McMansion craze swept in, and some beautiful old houses were torn down to make way for modernity.

That part of the village is close enough to the main street that it tends to get congested with overflow parking, so I catch a ride into the village with Steve, who is bringing in the lodge's motorboat to fill up on fuel at the marina and pick up some supplies to restock the lodge's boathouse while he's waiting for Terry Parker to finish up the repair on the creamery's safety fence.

Barry Wise's Victorian is just a short walk up from the boat launch, and the exercise feels good. Not as strenuous, or potentially life-threatening, as my swim, but it still stretches the muscles enough to see what is working and what isn't. My leg even feels better by the time I reach Chief Wise's house.

I keep telling myself the whole way up the hill that I'm just going to talk to an old friend. It doesn't mean I'm investigating. Still, I hope no one I know sees me and calls my mom.

I knock on the front door at just after eleven, and I see a shadow shift in response behind the stained-glass panel insert in the door.

I wait, nearly calculating the rate at which the humidity condenses against my bare arms. The forecast is calling for storms this afternoon, but I've been promised storms before and had my heart broken. I won't be fooled again.

"Della Hopewell, is that you?"

Oddly, the voice comes from behind me. I glance over my shoulder to find Barry Wise standing at the bottom of the steps that lead up to the Victorian's wrap-around porch, his hands full of some kind of potted fern. A woman stands next to him, her smile nearly taking up the whole of her face.

I glance back at the door and the inset of stained glass but look away before the chill can crawl up my arms.

"Hi, Chief Wise," I say, stepping down off the porch. "I'm sorry to just show up like this."

He shifts the potted fern into the crook of his elbow so he can wave away my concern with his free hand. "Not a surprise at all. Carmen called me." He gestures to the back of the house. "We were just sprucing the place up a bit before David comes with the photographer. Come and have a bit of lemonade with us, and you can get to know Sheila."

The woman next to him makes a twittering sound of delight, and I think her smile grows bigger.

"That would be nice. Thank you." I follow them as they head to the back of the house. "David is taking the listing?" I ask, referring to Bellegrave's premiere real estate agent, David Knolls.

"Sure thing," Chief Wise replies. "Says he's already got an interested buyer from Watertown."

I glance at the house just as a shadow flicks past one of the large windows. I look away.

"That's awesome." I follow them to the back where a brick patio spills from the rear steps of the porch.

There's a small wrought iron table with four chairs positioned around it. A glass pitcher of lemonade sits in the middle surrounded by several glasses on a tin tray.

"I don't want to interrupt if you have a schedule to stick to," I say when I see the tray, realizing David and his photographer must not be far behind me if Sheila's already brought out so many glasses.

I know this is Sheila's work because she adjusts the tin tray the slightest bit as she picks up a glass.

"Nonsense," she says, her voice huskier than I would have guessed. "You have a seat, and we'll get to know one another."

Chief Wise sets the potted fern down by the table.

"I met Sheila on Duvall Street in Key West, Della. Just standing there in three-inch heels and a Buffalo Bills jersey." Chief Wise's eyes crinkle. "It was love at first sight."

Sheila's laugh is loud and full, and she lays her hand on Chief Wise's arm as she tosses her head back. "I was on my way to a football watch party. The jersey had been a gift from my nephew who was doing his residency in Buffalo." The hand she laid on Chief Wise's arm curls possessively now. "Who knew it was such good bait?" She laughs again, and Chief Wise stares adoringly.

I can't help but smile. The woman radiates nothing but warmth, and after the turbulent years Chief Wise faced just before his retirement, I can't help but feel genuine happiness for him. Belinda Wise, the chief's wife of forty-two years, had passed away after a ravaging battle with breast cancer shortly before the chief was due to retire. It was said that was why he had delayed his retirement. He couldn't stand being in their home without her. It was heartwarming to see he had found someone.

"I'll have to remember that," I say and take a seat facing the house. I scan the windows that dot the rear of it, but they all remain empty.

"Della's jerking your chain, Sheila. She's been happily married to her high school sweetheart for eons," Chief Wise says as he takes a seat opposite me.

Thankfully, I accept a glass of lemonade from Sheila and take a sip, so I'm not required to respond to that.

"Well, I guess we'd better get to it before David gets here. Carmen said you might have found yourself another investigation." Chief Wise's smile holds a touch too much glee.

"Chief Tom called you about my last little investigation, didn't he?"

Chief Wise's laugh is more of a guffaw. "He had paperwork for days after that." He sobers and shakes his head.

"Never would have thought that of Marty Pruitt. Bellegrave is lucky to have you, Del."

"That's kind of you to say, but I'm not always so sure."

"Are you some kind of amateur sleuth?" Sheila asks, handing a glass of lemonade to Chief Wise before taking her own seat.

"Something like that," I say, and I can feel Chief Wise's gaze on the side of my face.

"Della here sees ghosts," he announces like he's telling Sheila I'm a piano virtuoso.

She nearly chokes on her own lemonade. "You do? Oh that's wonderful. I could really use that skill every now and then." She points to the house. "There's something in there that makes an awful racket at night. I tell him to be quiet, but he doesn't listen to me."

Chief Wise chuckles. "I keep telling her it's just the pipes. It's an old house. It makes noise." He says this with a shrug.

I only smile. "Did Carmen tell you what Logan and I found on the old girls camp island?"

Chief Wise shakes his head as he leans forward, his face settling into lines deep with age and repetition. "No, it's an active investigation, but that doesn't stop you from telling me."

I take a sip of my lemonade before relaying the events that led to the discovery of the girl's body.

At the end of my story, Sheila lets out a long, slow breath. "Your energy must be very weak right now." She shakes her head and makes a sorrowful sound. "And the Buck Moon is less than two weeks away. I hope your energy is restored by then."

I'm not sure how to respond to this.

Chief Wise leans forward in his seat. "A bee charm? Carved from wood?" He turns his head to the side as if sorting through his thoughts. "Now that sounds an awful lot like Maurice."

"Maurice?" I prompt.

Chief Wise turns back to me. "Maurice Beaumont. He was caretaker at the girls camp since the Carmichaels bought the land in sixty-eight. He used to whittle." He taps at the edge of the table with one blunt finger. "People just don't do those sorts of things anymore."

The name Beaumont sets off an alarm in my head. "Maurice Beaumont? He wouldn't be Sadie Beaumont's father, would he?"

Chief Wise's eyes widen. "You know about Sadie?"

"Lisa Reynolds told me about her."

Chief Wise takes Sheila's hand in his before continuing. "Poor girl drowned. What a waste too. She was a good one."

"Drowned?" Sheila breathes.

Chief Wise meets her eyes with a nod. "That last summer the camp ran. That summer was a hot one. Kinda like what we're going through right now. Everyone was lulled into a sleepy slumber by the long, hot days." His face pinches with old grief. "Such a tragedy. Poor Maurice."

"How can you be so certain she drowned? Lisa said her body was never recovered," I say.

"Well," Chief Wise says, settling back into his chair although he never lets go of Sheila's hand. "That there is a long story, Del. As far as we could piece it together, Sadie got into an altercation with her father that afternoon." He hesitates, his free hand tracing the end of the arm of the chair. "Sadie was a good girl. A great one. Always doing for others. Did good in school. Ran a food drive every Christmas for the pantry. Heck, she was even the one to report Lionel to the EPA." He shakes his head vigorously. "The town council had been trying to shut him down for years, and it was Sadie that stopped pussyfooting around. Went right to the federal government." He snaps his fingers. "Got that place shut down within the week."

I lean forward. "I'm sorry. Lionel?"

Chief Wise laughs. "I forget how young you are sometimes, Del. You've got such an old soul." He points vaguely to the west and the outskirts of the village. "Lionel Melrose used to run a junkyard out behind where the Gale Center is now. He never took any precautions about engine oil going into the ground. Folks around here got concerned about their drinking water, the effects it would have on their kids." Now he points in the general direction of the town hall. "The town council hit him with every fine they could, but he just ignored them. Couldn't ignore the EPA when they showed up at his door though." He laughs again. "Old Lionel. Served him right."

I make a mental note to follow up on the name Lionel Melrose. Not as part of an investigation. Just to help Hanratty if I can.

"So Sadie was a good kid until something changed?"

I don't mention what Lisa told me about Sadie seeing a boy that summer. I don't want to sway the chief's memory of that summer in a certain direction.

Chief Wise sobers. "Yeah, it was one of those kids from over at Tomahawk. Can't remember his name. Sadie started stepping out with him." The chief shakes his head. "Quite frankly, with how Sadie's death shook up the whole village that summer, I don't think my brain took the time to remember the kid's name."

"You know Sadie took the canoe out?"

Chief Wise nods. "Yeah, after she and her father had words, she told him she was going over to the camp to spend the night with some friends. Some girls at the camp confirmed it."

"Was that unusual for her? Making friends with the girls at the camp? She was the caretaker's daughter after all."

"Not at all," the chief confirms. "Sadie grew up on that island. It was her home more than any of the Carmichaels or the girls who came to camp there. She was good friends with several of the regulars at the camp. That I remember because it was those girls who told us she'd taken the canoe out." He shrugs. "They said she was still hot after the fight with her father and wanted some time alone. Hard to find solitude on a packed island like that, so she went out in the canoe. Her friends warned her not to go. It was already dusk at that point, but she went anyway." He shakes his head. "That was just like Sadie. So stubborn."

"And this Carmichael family, were they present on the island when this happened?"

Chief Wise's eyebrows go up. "Oh no, no, not at that point. Well, I guess, Ashley might have been, but Miriam was long gone by then. Lung cancer. Their daughter Ashley still went to the camp every summer, but Don had passed on the running of it to a manager of some kind with Maurice handling the facilities and such."

"Any idea how I can trace the Carmichael family? It would be helpful to get their take on what happened that summer."

Chief Wise gives a soft laugh. "Oh, that won't be hard. The Carmichaels moved into their summer place up on the hill right after Don's accident. It was easier for Ashley to care for him there, I understand. Been there ten years or more now."

"Their place up on the hill?"

"That post and beam monstrosity that cuts up the trees there. About a mile up the road from the old Bellegrave Manor."

I glance instinctively at the house at the mention of Bellegrave Manor and swallow uncomfortably before continuing. "And Maurice Beaumont? What happened to him?"

"Last I heard he went down to Raquette Lake. Got

another caretaking job there. Hasn't been back to Bellegrave as far as I know."

"And Sadie's mother? Any other family?"

"No, no," Chief Wise replies. "Sadie's mother died when she was very young, and she was an only child. It was just her and Maurice out there on the island."

I think of the malevolent spirits that now haunt the old camp, and a chill of lonely desperation ripples through me.

"Any thoughts on who our victim might be?" I ask.

Chief Wise shakes his head slowly. "No, can't say I do. Now if you had said she'd drowned, then I'd say you finally found Sadie Beaumont." He does the same slow shake of his head. "But no, I'm afraid not. Can't tell you how many girls were in and out of that camp any given summer."

"She had a dog," I say.

Sheila had been watching Chief Wise, but at this, her attention slowly swivels to me. "A dog?" Her voice is bright with wonder.

I plunge ahead. "It was the dog that led me to the oil barrel. He crossed once we got the lid off and discovered the body. The dog couldn't have materialized on the island unless he'd been there in life. I don't think the victim was a summer girl."

"You saw a dog cross over?" Sheila's eyes cannot get any wider, and it's like I've just told her the truth about the Tooth Fairy.

I nod. "It happens sometimes."

She doesn't say anything else, but her lips remain parted.

"I'm sure the state police will follow up on this, but you might want to ask Chief Tom if there were any missing persons reports from that summer. Maybe even check surrounding towns. Your girl could be one of them."

I thank the chief for his time and Sheila for the lemonade just as David Knolls appears around the side of the Victorian.

He stops so swiftly his shoulder bag swings until he catches it with one hand. His blue button-down has an embroidered pair of otters holding hands over the left breast pocket.

"Do not tell me someone's died in this house, Della," he says when his eyes land on me. "I do not want to have to disclose that."

I stand and say my farewells to the chief and Sheila before going over to David.

I place a light hand on his shoulder as I pass him. "Okay," I say. "Then I won't tell you."

I walk away as he sputters my name behind me.

Six

I nearly run into Detective Hanratty on Water Street.

I mean literally as I'm preoccupied with all that I've just learned from Chief Wise, making mental lists of everything that will require follow up even as I try to convince myself I'm not investigating and thus not breaking my promise to my mother. Detective Hanratty steps out of Cuppa, the sandwich and coffee shop along the lake, a paper coffee cup in one hand, forcing me to stop abruptly before I walk into him.

I have only a second to brace myself, remembering the haunted feeling that had washed over me at our first meeting the previous day. But standing there in the heat and sun, the street clogged with people headed to the boat launch, it's just Detective Hanratty.

He turns, his face hard, guarded really, until I see in his eyes he has registered it's me. Then his face opens into its familiar grin.

"Dr. James," he says. "Funny running into you here."

"Is it?" I ask just as another man steps out from the coffee shop behind the detective.

The man is a few inches shorter than the detective. He's thicker with nearly shaved black hair. He's wearing loose-fitting chinos with a button-down shirt open at the collar. A badge hangs around his neck on a chain, and it bounces as he takes a generous bite of his bagel sandwich.

Hanratty gestures to the man. "This is Detective Perez. He's been assigned to the case with me. Perez, this is Dr. Della James."

Hanratty doesn't need to specify which case, and Detective Perez smiles around the mouthful of sandwich.

"Hey, you're the doctor who can see dead people, right?" He points with his sandwich hand, and I see his fingers are covered in hummus. "That keep you up at night? I heard ghosts are more active after dark."

I'm staring at his hummus-encrusted fingers, so it's a second before I realize he's serious. When I take in his expression, his eyes are intense with curiosity as he chews thoughtfully.

"They can be," I say. "Spirits pull energy from the atmosphere around them in order to manifest, and I think lights are an easier source. So when it's dark and people have lights turned on, it's an accessible energy source."

Perez has stopped chewing by the time I finish. "Are you for real?" he asks around the remainder of his bite.

I nod. "As real as I can be." I shrug. "To be honest, I don't know how any of this works. I've just formed theories based on my experiences over the years."

I can feel Detective Hanratty watching me, and I haven't forgotten about what he said, how he believes I believe I see dead people.

I face him directly. "Have you gotten the results from the autopsy yet?"

I ask the question knowing he won't answer it, but my directness has unsettled him as I intended it. There's something in me that wants to find out what this man's deal is, but he's so closed off I can't get close enough to find out.

Detective Hanratty blinks and shifts his weight from one foot to another as he thinks. "We should have the results from the autopsy by the end of the week."

His answer is vague enough to not jeopardize an active investigation, yet it still answers my question. He's good at playing detective, and I wonder how long he's been doing it.

"I suppose you're trying to find reports of any missing persons from that time period to see if the victim is a match," I say, remembering Chief Wise's advice to me.

Detective Hanratty stills, and I recall too late about his concern I might try to investigate on my own, having thought it was only my mother I was trying to convince I wouldn't.

"Our first priority will be to identify the victim, so we can then notify next of kin. Once that is done, we'll know where to take our investigation." He hasn't answered my question, but then I think he never intended to.

"Then I suppose you have your work cut out for you, Detective." I gesture to the launch behind him. "If you'll excuse me, I'm meeting a colleague for a ride back to work." I smile at Detective Perez who has finished his sandwich. "Detective, it was nice to meet you."

I check the street for traffic before I take a step to move off the curb and into the crosswalk leading down to the launch, but Detective Hanratty grabs my arm.

When he suddenly tugs me backward, the surprise stops my shock from coming out audibly. I had one foot on the street and one on the sidewalk, and his forceful tug sends me off my feet. He catches me easily against him, my body connecting fully with his in a way that makes it instantly awkward. I find my feet quickly and spin around, every question on my lips.

"Detective—"

He holds up a single finger in my face, and my annoyance sparks.

"Wait, just a second," he says, his eyes on the street behind me.

I open my mouth to demand an explanation when the sound of boyish laughter reaches my ears along with the squeal of bike tires on pavement. I turn in time to see a pack of tweenagers on bikes round the corner from Church Street heedless of any traffic laws. They zoom into the street as they head toward the public docks, cutting straight through the place where I would have been standing had Detective Hanratty not stopped me.

I close my mouth.

"Whoa, slow it down!" Detective Perez calls after the tweenagers who ignore him.

Detective Hanratty finally meets my eyes with that ubiquitous grin of his. "You okay, Doctor?"

"How did you do that?" I ask.

"Do what?"

I point in the direction of the boys. "How did you know they were coming around the corner?"

He shrugs. "Instinct, I guess," he says before taking a sip of coffee. He steps into the crosswalk I had just been trying to use and gives me a farewell salute with his coffee cup. "Nice seeing you again, Doctor."

Perez follows him, and I'm left alone on the sidewalk, a sudden chill dimpling the skin of my forearms in the midsummer afternoon heat.

———

It's after six when I finally poke my head into my kitchen.

Logan sits at the table in the dining alcove, his laptop open on the table, files scattered around him, and a yellow legal pad caught under his elbow. Henry is asleep on one of his feet beneath the table.

"Psst."

Logan doesn't change his focus from his work.

"Psst." I try again.

He doesn't look up but instead says, "Are you pssting at me?"

"Is my mother here?"

I didn't see her car out front when I pulled up, but I can't see the dock from the driveway. She and Dad sometimes come by boat from the marina, and I don't want to be caught unawares.

Logan finally looks away from his laptop. He spins to face me, barely catching the legal pad before it falls on Henry's head.

"You're investigating," Logan says, his smile smug. "Just when you promised your mother you wouldn't."

I make a face, an ugly one. "I'm not investigating." I shrug and toss my stuff on the stools at the kitchen island. "Some stuff just came up."

He slouches back in his chair and crosses his arms. "Is that what you're going to tell the judge?"

By this point, Henry has realized I'm there, and the sound of his tail thumping the tile floor reverberates through the kitchen. He doesn't, however, pick up his head or move to greet me.

It's my turn to cross my arms. "What did you give my dog?"

Logan refuses to look at me. "I didn't give him anything."

"Liar."

"Cheeseburger."

I stare. "You got cheeseburgers without me?" I move my gaze between my dog and my husband.

Logan shrugs. "I had to go over to the marina and get new

spark plugs for the outboard. It was too hot to cook lunch, so we stopped at Shelly's." He reaches under the table and scratches Henry's head. "He's a good copilot."

"The betrayal," I breathe.

Logan straightens. "I would have stopped by the lodge, but I know Sundays are tough."

I slump into my chair at the table and kick off my sandals. "Today was particularly tough."

Logan's brow creases. "Want to tell me about it over dinner?"

"It's too hot to cook," I repeat his words back to him.

"Takeout?"

We both turn to look at the sky through the alcove window. It's turned the color of hope, steel gray and cluttered with thunderclouds. Perhaps the promised storms are truly coming, and the heat will mercifully break.

"Maybe not," Logan says. He turns to me. "There's a half gallon of mint cookie ice cream in the freezer."

"I'll get spoons," I say.

We adjourn to the living room couch with ice cream and spoons. Henry joins us, slipping into his spot at our feet on the floor.

I stab the block of ice cream with my spoon. "I went to see Chief Wise today."

Logan stops with his spoon just above the creamy mint surface. "Wow, you're diving right in, huh?"

I scowl. "It just seemed convenient. Chief Wise could sell his house tomorrow and be gone, and he's likely the best source for information about the camp when it was still operational."

"You're forgetting the Carmichael family," Logan reminds me.

I point at him with my spoon. "Best source for the good

stuff including probably the facts I need to figure out who we found in that barrel."

"I thought the state police were going to find that out."

I can't scowl anymore, so instead I tell him what Chief Wise told me about Sadie Beaumont.

When I've finished, he shakes his head. "I don't remember anyone talking about her when we were kids, do you?"

I shake my head. "No, but the camp was shut down so quickly after we were born. I wonder if the memory of her just faded away like memories tend to do when there isn't a reminder there."

"And her father is now in Raquette Lake?"

"That's what the chief said."

"When do you want to go see him?" Logan asks.

I pluck a chunk of chocolate cookie from the ice cream with my spoon. "I'm not. I'm not investigating. Detective Hanratty seems perfectly capable of figuring this out."

"You just said you were going to figure this out."

"Stop twisting my words around."

He steals a chunk of chocolate cookie out from under my searching spoon.

"Hey," I scold.

He parries with my spoon like our utensils have turned into swords. "Stay on your side of the carton."

"We're married. Your side is my side."

"Not if my side has the better chunks," he mumbles. "So what are you going to do next?"

"Nothing," I say, even as I don't believe it.

"Liar," he says.

I stop, letting the last bite of ice cream melt on my tongue. "Something else happened today. Something really weird."

"Really weird?" Logan raises both eyebrows. "Weirder than finding a dead body in a barrel?"

"Mhmm," I say and tell him about my encounter with Detective Hanratty on Water Street.

"That's really weird," he says when I'm done.

"I told you it was." I steal another chunk of cookie from his side of the carton.

"How did he know those boys were coming around the corner?" Logan asks.

I shrug. "I haven't a clue. It's been bothering me all day. Even after the cow crapped on that Karen."

Logan lowers his spoon. "A cow crapped on a Karen?"

I nod. "A literal Karen. The woman's name was Karen. She wanted a selfie with the cow in the creamery, the one Helen brings from her farm for milking demonstrations. There's a big sign there saying stay away from that end of the cow. Stuff comes out of it." I shake my head. "She just had to get it for social media."

"How much of it got on her?"

"Enough that she started screaming she was going to sue." I shake my head again. "I had to call Carmen when she started making the kids from the Baptist Church VBS camp cry. She sent over a deputy who trespassed her and made her leave the premises."

"This heat needs to break. I think it's making everyone tense."

I glance out the window behind the couch. The sky is still promisingly gray, but there's no sign of rain yet. My gaze inevitably falls on the island. It's a dark, impenetrable mass in the shadows of the thunderclouds.

Logan touches my arm to get my attention.

"I know you made that deal with your mom, but you know it's all right if you keep looking into this."

I look back at the island, but it remains quiet.

"I know," I say. "It's just..." I shift in my seat, propping myself back up in the couch. "Something doesn't feel right about this whole thing."

"Tell me," Logan says.

I study his face for a moment. Henry has rolled onto his back at our feet and stuck his paws in the air. Logan reaches down with his free hand to rub his belly, and I see my husband in profile. The lines around his eyes have deepened, and new ones have appeared at the corner of his mouth. They're smile lines. I know because it's been the two of us for so long I've memorized the shape of his smile.

"There are too many spirits out there," I decide to say first. "There are just so many of them, and they have this intensity to their energy. It's like they're waiting for something to happen."

"Like a charged battery," Logan offers.

"Yes, that's exactly it," I reply, sitting up farther, the ice cream forgotten between us. "It's all pent up on that island, and I think at some point it's going to..."

"Blow," Logan says.

I don't say anything. I just watch him, sitting there, scratching our dog's belly.

"What happened on that island?" I say, my eyes once more going to the window.

The sky is darkening now as night approaches, and I wonder if the storms will pass as we sleep.

"I don't know, but if anyone can figure it out, it's you," Logan says.

"Why do you say that?"

Logan straightens and picks up the ice cream carton as he stands. "You're in a unique position to uncover the truth."

I consider his words as he walks back into the kitchen. I listen to him rummaging around while I stay on the couch and contemplate the island. Henry crawls up after several minutes and takes Logan's spot. I let him. I rub absently along his back, and he settles against me. Soon he's asleep.

Logan comes back and leans against the door jamb.

"Something's not right with Hanratty," I say. "And something's not right on that island. I can't make sense of it all."

Logan makes his way to the couch and sits on the arm across from me.

"You don't need to make sense of it all. You can just listen."

He's right. I shake myself from my troubled thoughts and attempt a smile.

"Do you remember how to turn on the TV without the remote?"

He frowns and glances at the TV. "Can you do that? I didn't think modern TVs even had buttons."

"Well, Henry's asleep on the remote, so if we want to watch anything, you're going to have to figure it out."

He does, in fact, figure it out, and we watch the end of *North by Northwest*, careful not to wake Henry. The first rumble of thunder vibrates through the air when I take Henry out for his bedtime business, and by the time we climb the stairs to bed, the storm has unfolded.

But it isn't until the dead of night that the screaming wakes me.

Seven

I sit up, but sleep still clings to me like a cobweb, and I struggle through it to make sense of the noise assaulting my ears. At first, I try to cover them to save them from the attack, but it takes no more than a moment to realize the sound isn't real.

It's supernatural.

My eyes fly to the windows, my hands dropping uselessly in the bed sheets bunched at my waist. Carefully I slip from bed, not to keep from disturbing Logan and Henry, but from a preternatural sense that I don't want to disturb her, the girl in the barrel. For somehow I know that's who is screaming.

A chill spreads up my arms, and I wipe senselessly at it, my confused mind not understanding that the heat and humidity should keep the chill at bay, the storm from earlier having given little of its promised relief. The floorboards are unyielding under my bare feet, but I take no notice, my eyes fixated on the open window, the curtain fluttering as though someone has just touched it. The air is thick with the storm that still lingers. Distantly, I hear its rumble, but it's gone from here now, leaving petrichor in its wake.

When I reach the window, I draw the curtain to the side. It's only when I finally see the island shrouded that I realize I've been bracing myself.

"Della?"

I don't startle when I hear Logan's voice behind me, hoarse with sleep.

"She's awake," I whisper, that feeling of not wishing to draw attention still strong even though sleep has receded.

"Who's awake?" Logan's voice is closer now. He must have risen from the bed.

My other sense has sharpened before the usual ones, and I give myself a mental shake to finish waking up.

I hold out a hand to stop my husband from approaching the window, but I don't look back to meet his gaze. I don't know why, but I reach out and crank the window shut.

"The girl in the oil drum. She's awake." Finally, I turn to face my husband. "I need Aunt Janine." I gesture to the island out the window. "I think the dog was protecting us last time. I can't go out there alone. I'm not strong enough."

Logan takes a step forward, his hands reaching for me, but he stops. "I can't tell you not to go out there," he says, dropping his hands.

I shake my head even though it wasn't a question. "She's wailing," I say. "The girl on the island. It's almost as though..." I turn back to the window.

The treetops of the island forest glow in the silver of the moonlight, and I picture her there alone, just now understanding she's dead, those haunted black eyes watching her.

Can they hurt her, the other spirits? Is this what they've been waiting for? For her to wake up?

Logan touches me then, just a soft hand to my shoulder, but it's enough to pull me from the mire of my thoughts.

Now I can look at him. "She's angry about something. Maybe she can tell me what happened to her."

We both know this isn't how it works, but Logan's blue gaze softens then, and his hand slips from my shoulder. He turns away.

There are too many things tugging at my emotions just then, both real and supernatural, so instead of thinking through them, I simply do the next thing that needs doing.

I find my cell phone on its charger on my nightstand.

"Who died?" Aunt Janine says on answering my call.

"That's what I'm trying to find out," I reply. I quickly explain about the island and the girl in the oil barrel as the supernatural wailing grows keener.

"Don't do anything until I get there," she says, her voice sharp. "I'm leaving as soon as I can find some underwear."

She hangs up before I can say anything else. I look at my husband, standing by the window now in jeans and a t-shirt, his gaze on the island even though he can't hear the screaming or see anything.

"I'm going to find some clothes," I say.

He turns from the window. "I'll make coffee. We're going to need it."

He slips out of the room as I go in search of a clean pair of jeans.

My great-aunt Janine taught me about our gift of speaking with the dead, something that was passed down to us by Great-Grandmother Theresa, Great-Aunt Janine's mother, and if I am going back on that island, I want someone of her strength with me. She's had seventy-six years to strengthen her abilities, and that is the kind of power we're going to need.

Henry hardly stirs as I put on my hiking boots. I want more than sneakers protecting my feet this time. I grab a sweatshirt before I stop at the bed and touch Henry's paw. He opens one eye.

"Want to come with me?" I ask.

He closes the eye in response, and I leave him be.

Logan is finishing up the coffee when I step down into the kitchen. I get a mug from the cupboard by the sink and pause, my attention arrested by the sight out of the window there. The island is in shadow at this angle, too low to see the moon's spotlight on it, but the wailing is just as strong, and I wonder at the girl's energy.

"She must have been young when she died," I say, my hand still on the cupboard door, unopened.

Logan steps toward me with the glass carafe of coffee and stops, his head turning to look out the window.

"How do you know?" He whispers the question.

I turn to see his face warmed by the under-cabinet lights in the kitchen. "Because she's still going." I glance at my watch. "It's been almost fifteen minutes." I look back out the window. "She must have the ability to draw a considerable amount of power if she can emit a force for that long."

"Do you think she's dangerous?" Logan asks as he reaches around me to open the cupboard I've failed to.

He unearths a mug and fills it for me, setting down the carafe on the counter so he can take my hand and put the mug directly in it.

The warmth of the coffee shocks me back to the present, and I look away from the window.

"I don't think so," I say. "Her screams seem more like..." I glance at the window but don't allow it to hold my attention this time. "It's like she's venting."

"Should you call Carmen?"

I shrug. "And tell her what? The ghost woke up? Need me to ask her anything?" I shake my head. "I can't be sure it's even really her until I get out there. We could have stirred up some other energy. I know the dog was protecting us, but maybe he was keeping something else at bay too."

"I don't like the sound of that." Logan moves his gaze back to the window.

"Me either," I mumble and take my first sip of coffee.

I'm not surprised when Aunt Janine arrives hardly an hour later. The drive from her condo in Lake Placid takes forty minutes at the minimum, and I know Aunt Janine never leaves home without packing for a thirty-day cruise. She also drives like a sixteen-year-old who's just gotten her license.

I meet her in the drive as she parks her faded red jeep behind my SUV. The sky is the surreal color when night meets the coming dawn, and I don't need the motion-activated floodlight above the garage door to see her spiky white head pop up through the roof of her jeep.

"Is she making that awful racket?" Aunt Janine wrinkles her nose. "I heard it all the way out on the county highway." She hops out of her vehicle and comes around to the front where I'm standing to take my upper arms into her hands. "Jesus, Moon Pie, what have you done?"

Aunt Janine is the youngest of seven children, and because of the range in ages, she was only ten when my father, her nephew, was born. I've always been grateful for that as I've had Aunt Janine with me through this whole paranormal journey.

She's taller than me with defined features she got from my great-grandfather, but somehow on her they look beautiful and feminine. Her eyes are a soft brown, and her mouth is just a little too small for her face.

"I think she's scared," I say. "We need to go talk to her."

Aunt Janine might be seventy-six, but she spent her spring break in Croatia on a biking tour, pedaling more than ten miles a day.

"You say she was murdered?" Aunt Janine asks as we make our way into the house.

We find Logan in the kitchen already pouring new mugs of coffee.

"Logan, dear," Aunt Janine says, going up to him for a one-arm hug. "I'm so sorry we're affecting your sleep like this."

Logan laughs. "Still think you're tougher than me, huh?"

Aunt Janine blinks. "No. I'm seventy-six. I've already slept my usual four hours. I was catching up on my BeepBeep feed when Moon Pie called. Lots going down after Josh Carter married his girlfriend in a surprise Vegas wedding yesterday," she says, referring to the popular social media app.

"Who?" I ask.

She looks at me, and with genuine earnestness says, "I don't know how you don't know what I'm talking about. He's an MVP quarterback, and she's that actress."

"I don't have a BeepBeep account," I tell her.

Her mouth opens for a full ten seconds before she speaks. "Is that even legal?"

"No," Logan replies, deadpan.

Aunt Janine gives him a resounding smooch on the cheek that leaves a crimson imprint and takes a mug of coffee from him just as a cacophony of pounding paws erupts from the stairs. Aunt Janine manages to set down the mug of coffee just as Henry catapults himself across the kitchen and into her arms. She kneels to wrap him in a hug he falls out of in his excitement, his wiggling body falling to the floor for a belly rub. Aunt Janine obliges before taking his face in her hands.

"Professor Henry, do you know who's a good boy?" she coos. "Who is the goodest good boy?" She pauses dramatically, and Henry goes entirely still, his body radiating forward even as he doesn't move. "Do you know who needs..." Aunt Janine's voice trails away as she slowly pulls a strip of cooked bacon from her jean jacket pocket. "Bacon!" she finishes as Henry goes into a down and accepts his treat as though he's done something to earn it.

"You brought him bacon?" I ask.

Aunt Janine shrugs as she gets to her feet. "I always carry bacon. You never know." She retrieves her coffee. "Now tell me about this girl."

"It's not the girl I'm so worried about," I say, taking a fresh mug of coffee from Logan. "It's the island I don't like."

Logan takes Henry out on a lead, which Henry despises and which I insist on. I don't care if a strip of water separates us from the island, I'm not letting my beloved Labrador wander around in the dark while the spirits out there are active. While they're gone, I catch Aunt Janine up on the island, the youthful, menacing energy, and how the ghost dog seemed to prevent them from harming us.

Aunt Janine sips her coffee as she considers my words. "Any idea why there are so many different imprints of energy out there?"

"I can only assume it's because there were so many different people on it over the years. I'm not sure how long it operated as a camp, but I think it was for more than a couple of decades. That's a lot of summer camps."

Aunt Janine makes a noise of agreement. "Are there any stories about terrible things that might have happened there?"

I tell her about Sadie Beaumont, but she's already shaking her head before I've finished.

"That's not enough. One hot-head teenager storms off and meets a tragic end? That wouldn't explain the noise we're hearing." Aunt Janine glances out the window in the dining alcove. "How long has she been going?"

I glance at my watch. "Almost two hours now."

Aunt Janine winces. "Jesus, poor thing." She turns a concerned expression on me. "Do the police think they can identify her? She might be able to cross over if her people know what happened to her."

I relay what little conversation I had with Detective Hanratty, but I pause before saying what really concerns me about the state police detective.

Aunt Janine doesn't miss my hesitation. "Out with it, Moon Pie."

"There's something off about Hanratty. He has an aura about him that makes me uneasy." I shake my head. "Not in a bad way. I don't think he's evil or anything. I think he's... haunted." I say the word reluctantly, much as I had done the day before when I watched Hanratty retreat back to the island.

Aunt Janine watches me. "Haunted? Did you see a presence with him?"

I shake my head again. "No, it wasn't anything like that. It was a heaviness that he carried. He seemed uncomfortable when I asked him about where he's from. I wonder if something happened back there. Something that left a mark."

Aunt Janine shakes her head now. "We're all entitled to our baggage. Maybe what he's carrying is heavier than most."

"Maybe," I reply, and we both turn back to the window.

Logan returns with Henry and gets him a fresh dish of water just as the first puddles of sunlight paint the horizon.

Aunt Janine sets down her mug. "Looks like it's time to go."

———

The puddles of orange have leaked from the horizon into the sky when we make our way down to the dock. We leave Henry in the house, and Logan comes with us. He'll motor the fishing boat over and stay in the boat offshore until we return. I don't trust the island's spirits not to tamper with it while we're gone if we leave it moored on the beach.

Just as before, Logan beaches the boat long enough for Aunt Janine and me to disembark before I shove it off. He gives one last wave as he turns the boat around toward open water.

I look at Aunt Janine. The wailing has grown uncomfortably louder.

"Ready?" I nearly shout to be heard over the keening.

Aunt Janine only nods and starts up the plateau cliff like she's taking a mall walk. I pull my jeans up over the pouch of my tummy and follow her.

The energy hits us as soon as we crest the hill, nearly stopping us in our tracks with its force.

Aunt Janine takes my hand. "This place is bad," she says, her eyes scanning the trees around us.

I follow her gaze. The eyes I'd seen the previous day aren't there, but I can feel them, lurking in the trees, waiting. It's darker here in the forest, and I let go of Aunt Janine long enough to hand her a headlamp and put one on myself. Aunt Janine takes my hand again, and we start the trek through the forest.

It takes us longer to get to the camp than it did Logan and me as the forest is impenetrable even with our headlamps, the sunrise unable to pierce the density. The going is slow and treacherous, and twice we trip, each catching the other. The energy hums in our ears, the wailing a mournful tone above it, growing in crescendo as we near the camp.

The eyes don't appear until we step in front of the first cabin on the outskirts of the settlement. They come in pairs as they had that day we'd followed the dog. Soulless voids but now their bodies aren't visible, only the outlines of cold skulls. Through the wailing, I hear the echo of laughter like the feeling of walking through a spiderweb.

"Jesus," Aunt Janine breathes when she sees them and squeezes my hand. "Hang on to me, Moon Pie."

I squeeze her hand back, but I can't speak. It's taking all my energy to keep the ghosts out of my head.

We follow the worn path between buildings to the generator where the oil barrels were, but we're stopped by a string of yellow police tape, eerily still in the predawn light. It flashes in the beam of our headlamps as we lift it to sneak under.

I glance around, but the state police haven't left anything

on the scene. No evidence collection kits, no white tents. If it weren't for the police tape, it would look like nothing had happened.

We round the corner of the mess hall to find only trampled overgrowth. I stop, causing Aunt Janine to tumble back toward me.

"She was right there," I say, pointing to the barrels that still remain. "The state police must have taken the barrel she was in," I explain, pointing to the bald spot in the grass by the generator.

"That hasn't stopped her energy," Aunt Janine says.

When the wailing stops so suddenly, we both instinctively clutch at our ears at the swift ringing there.

We let go of each other, stumbling backward to regain our composure, and in that lapse, the energy pulses around us.

The voices I've been trying to keep out start to form, their hissing whispers taking shape.

Go away.

You're not welcome here.

Come play with us.

I shake my head, trying to force the words out, trying to find Aunt Janine in the fog that has become my mind. I flail blindly at where she was just a moment ago, but she's not there.

"Della!"

Her voice is so far away. I can't reach her.

I blink, hard, forcing my own conscience through the spirits that try to command it, and that's when I see her.

The girl from the oil barrel stands in front of me. It's hard to make out details in the dim light, and I realize my headlamp has gone dead. I strain, trying to take in as much as I can while keeping the others out, but I know I'm going to drown.

"You're dead," I shout over the roar in my mind. "You died. Please. Tell me what happened. I can help you."

The girl tilts her head, and I can make out the shape of her long hair, wild and big. She's wearing a jumpsuit in a light color, maybe yellow, with a stream of pockets down each side, the pant legs tucked into tall white socks and white sneakers. The jumpsuit is open at the throat, and she's wearing a lighter shirt underneath it. Maybe it was once white, but it's soaked in blood that's probably come from the hole oozing in her chest.

I think she's not going to respond, but then she holds up her hand. The bumblebee charm dangles from her wrist.

Save them.

Her voice penetrates the discord like a pick driving through the ice that traps the lake in January.

She disappears before I can ask her anything more. The confusion of spirits rears up in my mind, but they're no longer soothed by the girl's wailing.

Shapes form before me, one, two, three, five, eight. They morph and shift and float toward me, drawing closer and closer. I reach again for Aunt Janine's hand, but I can't find her.

"Della! Where are you?"

Her voice is still so far away. Without our headlamps, it's impossible to see more than a few feet around me, and that space is taken up by the ghosts who press closer. The chill comes swiftly, frost forming on my clothes. They're too powerful. I can't...

What happens next will be explained to me several hours later.

All I remember is a warmth as powerful as fire and as soft as a mother's touch enveloping me, and the world glowing bright before darkness takes me completely.

EIGHT

The first thing I see when I open my eyes next is my mother's face.

"I'm dying," I manage through a groan.

"Delia Ann," my mother scolds. "Why would you say that?"

I try to raise my hand to my throbbing head, but my arm won't move. I give up.

"Because you wouldn't be out of bed before eight for anything less," I say.

The rest of the room comes into focus behind my mother's scowl. I'm back in our cottage, lying on our living room couch. I can't raise my arm because Henry has dropped himself between me and the back of the couch like a hot dog into a bun. His breath is warm against my neck, the faintest whimpers soft against my skin. I nuzzle him with my nose as I can't move anything else, but he doesn't take the solace and only whimpers more.

Behind my mother, I see Logan perched at the end of the sofa, looking worn and tired. The lines of his face are hard with worry, but it's his shirt that draws my attention. It's covered in mud and grass stains, and one sleeve is ripped.

My father stands next to him, and while his face is grave too, it's more in an annoyed way like when Ryan spent a summer racing golf carts at the country club where he had a job caddying and ended up crashing his cart. Not only did my dad have to pay for the damage, Ryan ended up in the hospital for a week because of an infection in the arm he broke.

Aunt Janine sits in the chair in the corner at the end of the couch, and on the arm of the chair sits a...

I blink, sure I've hit my head at some point while I was out, because sitting on the arm of the chair next to Aunt Janine is a priest.

And Aunt Janine is crying.

I close my eyes and groan again.

My mother's hand is cool on my cheek. "Delia Ann, what is it? You need to tell us where it hurts."

"Just tell me if I'm dying," I say.

"Why do you keep saying that?" my mom nearly squeaks.

"Because the only time I've seen Aunt Janine cry is when they brought back high-waisted jeans, so if it's anything less than death, she wouldn't be crying."

My mother's face goes flat as she glances in Aunt Janine's direction. Now real concern flares inside of me. I wiggle my way out from under Henry and sit up. The room spins, and I immediately collapse back against the couch as everyone surges toward me, arms outstretched with cries of *don't get up*. Henry lets out a yelp and drapes his body over mine. I clutch him to me as Logan shifts to the arm behind my head, displacing my mother as he moves. My mother emits a low moan and drifts back to my father who wraps an arm around her.

"Someone had better tell me what's going on," I say, trying to glare at my husband, but he only avoids my stare.

Aunt Janine finally stands to come perch on the sofa next

to me. The priest hovers behind her, and I wonder if he's going to start speaking my last rites.

"Della, Moon Pie, listen to me." Aunt Janine takes my hand in hers, and I feel like I'm eighteen again, and she's telling me the Spice Girls have broken up. "This is my friend Father Patrick. Pat is a special kind of priest. He deals mostly in..." her voice drifts away as her eyes skitter to the priest and back to me, "exorcisms," she finishes.

I blink again. "I'm not sure one man can handle what's on that island—"

"It's not for the island, Moon Pie," Aunt Janine says, squeezing my hand so much it hurts, but I let her, knowing it's more for her than for me. "He's here for you." She chokes out the last word.

I can only stare at her before switching my glare back to my husband again, but I find his eyes glassy with tears, and I can't take anymore. I sit up, the room tilting wildly as I clutch my giant dog to my chest.

"Aunt Janine, what the hell is going on? What happened out there?"

It's then I notice the grass stains on Aunt Janine's black capris. She's missing one gold hoop earring, and there's a twig stuck in her hair.

"Listen to me, Moon Pie," Aunt Janine repeats and leans in. "The spirits on the island are evil. You were right about that. They're strong. Much stronger than either you or I could manage, and they separated us." She shakes her head. "I know you were standing right there, but they played with my mind and made me think you were somewhere else. Somewhere far, far away." She licks her lips. "Moon Pie, I think they separated us so one of them could...could..." But she can't seem to get the next word out.

The priest comes up behind Aunt Janine, resting his hands on her shoulders. The living room was too dim when he was on the other side of the room for me to see him clearly, but I realize now he's hot. Not in a *Thorn Birds* forbidden kind of way but genuinely. He's younger than I thought, probably somewhere around thirty, with a thick flop of dark hair that falls across his brow, and solid, round features that give him a welcoming look. If he were my priest, I'd go back to attending Mass.

"Della is it?" he says, his voice soothing and a touch alluring. "I'm Father Patrick. I'm your aunt Janine's friend. I understand you have a similar talent to your aunt. That of seeing and communicating with the deceased?"

I nod, and pain tears through my neck. I wince, and my mother squeaks and buries her face into my father's chest.

I turn my attention back to Father Patrick. "Yes," I say. "I can see dead people."

Father Patrick nods slowly. "I understand you had an encounter with malevolent spirits this morning."

I've not heard the word *malevolent* used outside of a fairy tale discussion, and it takes me a moment to process it. I shake my head and regret it.

"I don't think they're malevolent. They're just...bad." I know I haven't proven any points.

My mother makes a deranged noise then, and my father holds her tighter.

"Logan," I say now. "If someone doesn't tell me what the hell is going on right now, I'm going back out to the island to ask the ghosts."

"They think you've been possessed by a ghost," my husband blurts.

Aunt Janine sucks in a breath that stops her soft mewling even as tears silently roll down her cheeks. Father Patrick presses his hands together in prayer and holds them against his chest. My mother might have entered a catatonic state. I'm not sure.

"Possessed?" I repeat and then laugh. "I'm not possessed." I pause. "Am I?"

Father Patrick presses his hands to his lips before lowering them. "A demonic possession often takes over control of their host's body while leaving the host's spirit isolated inside the body. Della, do you feel you're in control of your body?"

I attempt the motions of the Macarena over the prone body of my dog. I stretch my arms into the air before folding them to touch my shoulders and then my head. I try to find my hips but encounter mostly fluffy Labrador butt.

"Yeah, Macarena," I declare when I finish. "I think I'm okay."

I try to sit up again, but this time Aunt Janine pushes me back down, her eyes suddenly dry.

"Della, you *glowed*." She says the last word as though accusing me of eating crunchy peanut butter. "I saw you," she goes on. "You lit up like a—" She flails her hands around in front of her as if trying to find the words through touch. "Like you had a Christmas tree stuck up your butt."

I still, the seconds before I passed out coming back to me.

The girl from the barrel floating in front of me, the bracelet on her wrist, her words echoing through my head, the press of spirits around me.

The glow that made everything feel safe.

Glow.

My father had said something similar that day we'd found the girl. That I looked like I was glowing.

I make the mistake of shaking my head again. "You must have seen something else, Aunt Janine. I can't possibly glow."

Although I try not to, I remember sitting in the kitchen, waiting for the state police, the chill that had spread over me in the impossibly warm room, the feeling as though...

It was coming from inside of me.

I swallow. "It was probably a trick of the spirits on the

island. You felt them, Aunt Janine. They're mischievous. I'm sure they wanted you to see something that wasn't there."

"Then why were you unconscious for so long?" She gestures to Logan beside me on the arm of the sofa. "I had to scream for Logan to come help me drag you out of that forest. If I didn't know better I would say you were—" She stops herself, but my mother fills in the silence with another strangled cry.

That would explain the torn shirt, missing earring, and grass stains. For a second, I feel bad for having put them through that.

"Dead?" I supply.

Aunt Janine's expression doesn't change.

I've managed to wedge myself in the corner between the arm of the sofa and the back. Henry has melted into a puddle on my lap. I touch my temple where a headache pounds. It's not a typical headache. It's deeper and pervasive, the kind I often get after speaking with the dead for too long.

"I'm sorry you had to go through that," I say now. "I really thought we'd be strong enough together." I lay my hand on her arm. "I'm sorry you were forced to carry me out of there. That must not have been easy for you."

She purses her lips. "Well, I knew you weren't dead because I didn't see your ghost, so that was at least something." She shakes her head. "Della, whatever is out there is bad."

"I know," I reply. "But I saw our girl."

Aunt Janine straightens, and Father Patrick presses his hands back together in prayer.

"You saw the girl in the oil barrel?" the priest asks.

"Someone catch you up on what's going on here?" I answer with a question.

His smile is sheepish and only makes him look hotter.

"Your husband filled me in when I arrived. It must have been so unsettling to discover her in that barrel."

"It was," I agree. "She was shot or stabbed or something. Right here." I press a hand to my chest where I saw the depression of blood on her spirit. "She showed me the charm bracelet and told me to save them."

"You won't be doing that," my mother scolds just as the sound of the screen door at the back of the kitchen slamming filters through the room. "We have a deal, Della," my mother goes on.

Carmen appears seconds later. She has her natural curls wrapped in a hot pink scarf, her earrings don't match, and those are definitely her cat and mouse pajamas under her windbreaker.

"What in God's name happened?" she says before her eyes find Father Patrick, and I swear she turns nearly as pink as her head scarf. "Oh, hello," she says to the priest. "Sorry," she mumbles.

He raises a hand and gives a soft smile as if to say she's forgiven.

"What happened?" she starts again, coming over to the couch to peer down at me.

"I saw the girl in the barrel. She has a wound here on her chest." I indicate again the place where I saw the blood. "She's really mad. Like really mad. Remember when the basketball team lifted Principal Jordan's car onto that snowdrift, and he had to call a tow truck to get it out, so the school board canceled the Valentine's Day dance, and you were furious because your mom had taken you all the way into Plattsburgh because you got all As the semester before, and as a reward she took you to Montgomery Ward to get a dress, and then you couldn't even wear it?"

Carmen's lips thin so far I'm sure they're going to disappear, and her nostrils flare. I point at her face.

"That mad," I say. "But I don't think she's mad about being dead. She's mad that she was…" I search for the right word, and again, the image of the girl drifting in front of me enters my mind. I meet Carmen's eyes. "I think she was mad that she was stopped."

I try to stand, easing Henry from my lap, but everyone surges forward again with outstretched hands and worried exclamations of needing to rest.

I flop back down, Henry clawing for purchase back into his spot on my lap.

"I'm fine, really," I say through the pounding that is growing in my head. "I need to get up. That girl—"

"That girl is dead. The police are handling it," my mother says before pressing her fingers to her lips. "Oh, Greg, I told you something was going to happen."

"Maxine, nothing is happening. Della is fine. She always is, remember?"

Carmen puts her hands to her hips, and I try to give her a death stare before she can speak.

"Carmen—" Logan says somewhere over my head, but he's too late.

"What do you mean something was going to happen?" Carmen asks.

My mother makes a noise of anguish a telenovela star would envy and collapses against my father's chest. Dad pats her back ineffectually while making incoherent shushing noises.

Carmen looks at me.

"Mom is retiring in two weeks. She's afraid something bad is going to happen before she makes it."

"Eleven days." She whips her head up from my father's chest so quickly I'm afraid she's going to whack my dad's chin with her forehead.

He manages to dodge as she turns to face Carmen, her face

a map of red blotches, and oddly, mascara streaks. Did my mother take the time to put on mascara before coming to my possession? I look at Logan with a questioning glance, but he only returns the same look to me.

"Eleven days, Carmen Rebecca." My mother middle names Carmen, causing her to back up.

"I've worked my whole life, and in eleven days, that's over, and I knew something bad was going to happen." She throws out her arm. "My daughter is possessed."

Carmen holds up both hands as she pivots slightly in my direction, her eyes taking up more real estate on her face than I thought possible.

"I'm not possessed," I say.

My mother wails, and Aunt Janine starts crying again.

"I'm not possessed," I say over the racket. "There was a little incident on the island when the ghosts made Aunt Janine think I was glowing, but it was just them messing around. I'm fine."

Carmen takes in all the faces in the room before stopping at Father Patrick. "That why you're here?"

"Yes, ma'am," Father Patrick replies, and I swear the tips of his ears turn fuchsia.

"You going to perform some sort of exorcism?" Carmen goes on.

"No one is performing an exorcism," I say. I nudge Henry, sliding him carefully from my lap. "I'm going to get up and get my dog some cheese, so he knows I'm not dying," I say when the room leans in again with their overbearing concern. "That's all. I'm fine."

Carmen lets me stand but asks, "Okay, but if there's an exorcism happening here, you know I need to call Raymond. He'll be so mad at me if I let him miss it."

I try to glare at her, but she's right. Raymond, her husband, wouldn't want to miss an exorcism.

"Sorry to disappoint, but I don't need an exorcism." I lay my hand on my best friend's arm. "Maybe next spiritual crisis."

Carmen's face turns puzzled then. "Why do you think she was stopped?" she asks, referring back to my statement before my mother's small meltdown.

"Because she told me to save them," I reply. "I think she was trying to stop something bad from happening to some people, and the murderer killed her to stop her from doing it." I lick my suddenly dry lips. "I think whatever she was trying to stop is the same thing that's causing so many spirits to be out there."

"That would make for a convenient motive," Carmen says with a slight edge of warning.

She's done this before, cautioned me not to make pieces fit that don't go together.

I hold up both hands. "I'm just telling you what I felt. She wasn't scared. Most ghosts I encounter are frightened at the prospect of staying trapped between this world and the next. This girl wasn't. She was—" I glance at Father Patrick but finish anyway. "Pissed."

Carmen's face turns more confused, but I hold up a finger to stop her.

"I promised Detective Hanratty I would call him if I saw the girl. Why don't I tell both of you everything at the same time?"

She shrugs. "All right. I'm still disappointed there's not going to be an exorcism."

I pat her shoulder. "We all are," I say and head in the direction of the kitchen to find Henry some cheese.

Maybe I'll get some for myself too.

NINE

I use the half bath off the kitchen first. It's tucked under the stairs, and I maneuver carefully to sit on the toilet fully clothed and close my eyes. I press my hands to my chest and abdomen, releasing my senses. Aunt Janine saw the glow too. Even if I want to ignore it, I should still perform a little due diligence. What if I've brought a ghost home? But as my inner sense opens, I already know. There's nothing there.

The glow that had enveloped me on the island is gone without even a trace of echo left behind. I open my eyes, take in the cramped bathroom, but the chill I experienced that day doesn't come.

All of me is simply empty.

I touch my temples lightly. Maybe I imagined it. Maybe the stress of the situation made me hallucinate. Maybe the ghosts themselves made me see things that weren't there just as I'd told Aunt Janine.

But then what about the warmth? I had most definitely felt the warmth. Could that have been a hallucination too?

I stand up carefully, avoiding hitting my head on the slanting ceiling to look in the mirror above the sink, but I find it's only me in the reflection. I touch my face with the fingertips of my right hand, tracing the faint spray of freckles under my right eye. I sometimes wonder if my daughter would have had that same spray of freckles.

I catch my own gaze in the mirror, and for just a second, I don't feel alone. I let my hand drop, and the feeling vanishes.

I turn on the tap and splash my too warm skin with cold water before burying my face in the hand towel on the hook beside the sink. I draw a deep breath, replace the towel, find some ibuprofen in the medicine cabinet, and head back out into the fray.

The first words I hear upon emerging are *foreign tongues* and *contorted body movements*, so I divert to the coffee carafe on the kitchen counter.

"Hey."

I glance behind me to smile at my husband who has just come in from the living room.

"Coffee?" I ask.

"I'll make it," he says, moving to take the carafe from me.

"I got it," I say, cradling the carafe in both my arms.

His smile is knowing. "Need to feel normal again?"

"Please," I reply, filling the carafe with water from the tap. "What are they talking about in there?"

"Father Patrick is going through the signs of demonic possession with your mother."

I grimace. "He really shouldn't do that. She doesn't need any ideas."

He leans against the counter by the stove. "I know."

I start the flame under the tea kettle and move to find a filter and the coffee grounds when Logan taps me on the shoulder with a fist bump.

The level of affection between us since I'd walked in on his near-affair hovers around that of a teenage boy for his mom. It's awkward and reluctant at times, but I know it's Logan's way of giving me the space I asked for. I look back at him now and find his face is etched in real worry.

"Hey," he says softly.

The survival instinct inside of me wants to hold back, but I know what I've put him through in the past few hours was bad. I don't know exactly how long I'd been unconscious or what it must have been like to hear Aunt Janine screaming for him or what he had felt carrying my unmoving body through the forest.

So I say, "Hey," back to him and let myself sink against his chest as his arms wrap around me. "I'm really fine," I say then. "I truly don't think I'm possessed, and if I am, it's probably just the spirit of a deceased Bond girl, so that should be good for you."

He laughs softly, and I feel some of the tension leave his body.

I ease back so I can see his face. "There is something you should know."

I spent thirteen years not saying things that needed to be said between us, and witnessing the destruction of our marriage has made me painfully aware of when I stop saying them again.

I lower my voice, not wanting the exorcism cohort in the living room to overhear me. "I think something's going on with me." His eyes flash with concern, and I quickly go on. "Not something bad." I try to reassure him, but his eyes remain wary. "It's just..." I swallow. "Aunt Janine was right. I did glow on the island." I step back out of his arms to press my hands to my torso. "It came out of me." I shake my head. "Like something was inside of me trying to get out, but it wasn't bad. It was warm and caring." I shake my head again. "I can't describe it because I don't understand it. But—" I lick my lips now, feeling the edge of the precipice on which I stand. "Remember when I freaked out in here the other day? I felt a chill, the kind I get when a spirit is forming near me, but there wasn't anyone there. I was sure of it." I swallow and force out the last part. "The chill felt like it was coming from inside me."

Logan continues to lean against the counter, his arms still suspended where he held me.

"You're sure you're not possessed?" he asks softly.

"I don't think so," I say. "The chill I got happened two days ago, and I didn't glow until this morning."

"But you were on the island that day. Without Janine to help you."

He's right, and his words strike an ominous bell inside me. I'm saved from having to contemplate it further when my phone buzzes from where I left it on the kitchen island.

It's the weather app notifying me of imminent rain. Relief floods through me, and I glance out the window to make sure it's right. The orange hues we'd seen in the sky when we'd embarked on our ill-fated endeavor have been smudged out by rumbling gray clouds, and a sense of anticipation runs through me at the thought the humidity will finally break this time.

But the phone buzzing reminds me I need to call Detective Hanratty. I take the phone to the fridge where I've put his card under a Super Duper magnet. I type his number into the phone, but I chicken out and send a text instead.

Girl in the barrel is awake. I spoke to her. I'm available all day to discuss.

I set the phone down, but it buzzes before I let go.

I jump, and Logan raises an eyebrow at me from where he's pouring boiling water over coffee grounds.

I pick the phone back up.

On my way now.

"Detective Hanratty is coming," I say.

I stare at his text longer than is necessary.

"You still get that weird feeling about him?" Logan asks.

"Weird feeling about who?" Aunt Janine asks from the doorway.

"That state police detective I was telling you about."

Aunt Janine finds a tray above the fridge and starts pulling mugs from the cupboard. "The one who seems haunted?"

I pull the twig from her hair as she passes me. "The very one. You can go use our shower if you'd like. I really am sorry for what I put you through."

She sets down the mugs on the tray as Logan finishes pouring the boiling water over the grounds.

She cups my face in her hands. "Moon Pie, I wouldn't miss it for the world." She adds the cream and sugar caddy Logan put on the counter earlier, pulls a package of cheese from the fridge, and picks up her tray, headed back to the living room. "Besides," she says over her shoulder. "It's not every day I get to see someone get possessed."

She slips back into the discussion about exorcism before I can make a rebuttal.

————

A knock at the back door comes just as my mother launches into another recital of the menu she is having for her retirement party. Domingo's is setting up a taco bar, and Matt from Matt's Meats is doing his famous pig roast, the same one we host at the lodge at the end of every summer. She's also rented the pavilion at the town beach, which is good because I think she's invited most of the town.

I slip out of the living room and go back through the kitchen.

"It's open," I call before I reach it, aware of the patter of rain on the roof.

Detective Hanratty is wearing a raincoat today over his

black polo, and his shoulders are damp as he steps into the kitchen.

He smiles though as he says, "Busy morning. Do you ever sleep in?"

I shake my head. "No rest for the wicked. Isn't that what they say?"

He shrugs. "I wouldn't know." He holds up two fingers in a kind of salute. "Certified Goody-Two-shoes here."

"I thought we were going to be friends." I frown.

"I'm sorry to break it to you this way."

"It's all right. I have enough friends." I start back toward the living room and stop.

"Something wrong?" Detective Hanratty asks.

I turn back to him. "There's a gathering in there that might either school you on the details of exorcism or invite you to a retirement party complete with pig roast. We can stay out here if you'd rather."

Logan comes in from the living room then as Detective Hanratty's gaze drops. If I didn't know better, I'd say he was giving me the once-over. I feel a flush creep up my cheeks that I've been caught in this awkward position with this state police detective by my husband, which is absolutely ridiculous but also very much happening.

"Good morning, Detective," Logan says, but Hanratty doesn't respond.

The detective doesn't even look up from where he's staring at my...butt?

I look down.

I don't know why it's taken me this long to realize I'm in worse shape than Aunt Janine or Logan. My jeans are torn across one knee, mud splatters both of my thighs, crawling up my legs until—

I twist to see the mud splattered all over my butt.

I look at my husband.

He winces. "We dropped you." He pauses. "A few times."

I look back at the detective who is trying very hard and failing to hide a grin.

"More adventures on the island I take it?" he asks, but I know he's already guessed the answer.

"Something like that," I mutter.

"Coffee, Detective?" Logan asks, already moving to refill the tea kettle to make another pot.

"Please don't go to the trouble for me," Hanratty answers, holding up one hand in protest.

"It's no trouble. The Bellegrave Exorcism Club is just getting started. I'm sure they'll go another round."

Hanratty's expression turns bleak. "You weren't kidding about that."

"I wasn't." I gesture to his jacket. "Let me take your jacket and hang it up so it can dry."

I feel Logan's gaze on the side of my face, but I don't acknowledge it. He knows perfectly well I'm looking for an excuse to touch something of Hanratty's to see if I can get a better read on the unsettling energy he emits.

But when he hands me his rain jacket I feel nothing. The wash of despair that had followed him that first day is alarmingly absent. I hold his jacket for perhaps a second longer than I should, and I catch the detective watching me. It's not the consideration he gave my muddy butt, but something deeper. Knowing.

I look away.

"How is the investigation going?" Logan saves me, and I retreat to the mudroom to hang the detective's jacket on one of the hooks by the back door.

"Still early days," Hanratty says, and by the sound of his voice, I know he's watching me.

"Well, I hope what I have to tell you helps," I say, smiling as best I can on so little sleep and with the headache a gentle ache now behind my eyes.

"I hope so too," Hanratty says.

I gesture to the dining alcove. "We can talk here or..." I trail off as I turn in the direction of the archway that leads into the living room.

"I've always wanted to learn about exorcism," Hanratty says and strolls past me through the archway. "Hello, everyone," I hear him call out in greeting as he disappears through the door.

I stare at the spot where he was just standing.

"The man is a masochist," Logan murmurs behind me.

We finish replenishing the coffee tray and carry it into the living room along with a box of baked goods from Cake & Cookie Logan had picked up the day before when he and Henry had gone on their cheeseburger run.

By the time Logan carries in the coffee tray, and I follow with the box of goodies, Aunt Janine has made a spot in the middle of the couch for Detective Hanratty, and my mother is inviting him to her retirement party.

"Mom," I say sharply.

She looks at me innocently. "What? I'm just getting to know Detective Hanratty."

"He does not want to come to your retirement party. He's investigating a murder."

"You don't know that." She looks back at Detective Hanratty as she slips onto the arm of the couch by his side. "I like to decoupage and scrapbook. I also do yoga in the park every Saturday. I'm hoping to expand my practice in retirement. Do you have any hobbies, Detective? Or perhaps a sister who happens to be single?"

"You don't have to answer that," I tell the detective as I set the bakery box down on the coffee table in front of the couch.

His smile is slow and warm, and I understand then that

it's infectious, his friendly personality, but there's still something that warns me to keep him just slightly away. I don't know where the feeling of despair has gone, but perhaps it's just ebbing like echoes sometimes do.

"I think it would be helpful if you could tell me what happened this morning," he says. He looks round the room. "I take it most of you, if not all, were somehow involved."

There's a general murmur of affirmation that circles the room and ends at Carmen.

"I'm afraid I only came in later, Detective. I won't be able to verify Della's or her aunt's statements."

Hanratty nods. "That's fine. Della, why don't we start with you?"

I take the chair across from the couch so I can focus on Detective Hanratty's questions, but before I can speak, my father pulls a chair into the living room from the kitchen and settles onto it, a legal notepad appearing in one hand.

"Aunt Janine calls to tell you I might be possessed, and you stop for a legal pad?" I ask.

He pushes up his tortoiseshell glasses. "Of course," he replies.

I can only shake my head and return my attention to the detective.

I gesture to Aunt Janine. "You've met my aunt, Janine. She has the same abilities I do."

He glances in Aunt Janine's direction, and other than a polite smile, he makes no reaction to my statement.

"Early this morning I was awakened by screaming coming from the island," I start.

"Did you call the police?" Detective Hanratty looks at Carmen who is mid-bite on a cinnamon scone.

"It wasn't that kind of screaming, Detective," Aunt Janine says with a gentle smile.

The detective's brows go up. "Supernatural screaming?"

I nod. "The ghost of the victim in the oil barrel woke up. I confirmed this when we got out on the island, and I was able to see her. I've often found new ghosts panic when they realize the state they are in, and often times, screaming is the only thing they can muster at first."

"Woke up?" The detective shakes his head. "The victim was in that barrel for quite some time. Why is she only manifesting now?"

He's used that word again. Manifest. I file that away.

"I think it's probably something to do with the barrel. Especially if it contained iron."

"Iron?" He glances between me and Aunt Janine.

Aunt Janine holds her coffee mug between both of her hands. "There's a theory iron keeps ghosts contained."

He looks back at me, and for the first time since he's learned of my abilities, his expression is incredulous. "You're joking."

I shake my head. "I'm not. Removing her from the barrel likely made it possible for her energy to pool, she was able to manifest as you said, and she started screaming. She's very powerful, Detective Hanratty. And she's angry. Angry ghosts can make a lot happen."

Hanratty shifts on the couch and pulls out a small notebook from his pocket. He plucks a pen from its spiral binding and flips it open. "Why would you say she's angry?"

"It's twofold. The power she pushed toward me was agitated and restless. Something was stopped or prevented because of her death, and she's angry about it."

"And the second part?"

"She told me two words. Save them."

His pen stills over his notebook. "Save them?"

I nod. "Save them. She held up her arm as she said the words, and I think she was trying to show me her charm bracelet. The one with the bee on it." I touch my wrist where I saw the bracelet. "Am I allowed to ask you a question about the investigation, Detective?"

He stops writing to look at me. "You can always ask. I can't always answer."

"The charm bracelet isn't made of some kind of metal. It's homemade, isn't it? Like something teenage girls would have made." I encircle my wrist with my fingers and thumb. "The band was made of something like string or maybe leather. I couldn't see it very well in the barrel because it was coated in oil, but when she showed it to me in spirit form, I could see right away it wasn't something intrinsically valuable but rather perhaps sentimentally valuable." I pause, considering my words. "The bee charm." I tap my wrist, organizing my thoughts into words. "It looked carved," I finally say with a shrug. "Like someone had carved it out of wood."

Hanratty's pen falls to the notebook he's balanced on his knee.

"Dr. James, I thought you said you didn't touch the body in the barrel," Hanratty says, his voice softer than normal.

I can feel my father stiffen across the room. I hold up a hand to him and straighten in my seat.

"I didn't touch the body, Detective Hanratty," I say. "The ghost showed me the bracelet."

"Is that what happened." He says it like a statement instead of a question.

His words sound innocent, but for the first time, the charm he exudes has slipped a little.

"The victim is about five foot six or seven," I go on. "She was slightly taller than me. Probably somewhere between one fifteen and one twenty when she had a body. Her hair was long and big like they wore it then. It was a light color. Blonde or maybe red with gold tones. She wore a yellow jumpsuit with pockets down each side and a lighter shirt underneath that was soaked in blood from a wound right here." I demonstrate where I'd seen the wound using my own torso for measure. "There was the bee charm bracelet, of course, and then white socks pulled high, her pant legs tucked into them, and the outfit was finished off with some killer white high tops."

Detective Hanratty has not moved through my entire recitation, his pen flat and useless against his notebook.

Finally he turns to Logan.

"Mr. James, can you confirm you and your wife did not touch the body in the barrel when you discovered it?"

"We didn't touch it." Even just answering the question has made the color drain from Logan's face, and instinctively I reach out to take his hand.

Detective Hanratty studies me before saying, "Dr. James, it's a crime to tamper with evidence in an active crime scene—"

"Oh, pish posh," Aunt Janine interjects. "That crime scene is as old as the Reagan administration. Try that on someone else, Detective."

Hanratty's gaze slides from Aunt Janine to my father who is still holding his pen above the notepad balanced on his knee.

"Janine—" The detective pauses, waiting for Aunt Janine to fill in her last name.

"Hopewell," she says with a disturbing gyration of eyebrows. "Never married. Never saw the point."

"Janine Hopewell," the detective says carefully around a smile he is trying to suppress. "Can you corroborate Della's story?"

"I sure can't," she says, slapping one hand against her knee.

Hanratty had picked up his pen again but stops at this. "I'm sorry?"

Aunt Janine shakes her head. "I can't. The spirits on the island—not your dead girl, the other ones—separated us telepathically. They messed with our minds and made us think the other one wasn't there. It's a common tactic. I didn't see anything that happened to Della until—" She stops and looks at me.

"Until?" the detective prompts.

"Until she glowed," Aunt Janine finishes succinctly.

Hanratty looks between me and my aunt, his smile slowly growing now.

"Ah, hence the call for an exorcism," he says, glancing at Father Patrick who is perched next to Carmen, the Cake & Cookie box held between them now.

Father Patrick waves shyly.

Hanratty looks back at Aunt Janine. "Do you believe the evidence of glowing is a sign of possession?"

Aunt Janine shrugs. "Hell if I know. I've just never seen anybody do that in the presence of so many mischievous spirits. I don't know what else to think."

Hanratty looks at me now. "Do you think you're possessed?"

"No," I say flatly, daring my mother or Aunt Janine to oppose me.

Neither of them looks away from my pointed stare, but also neither of them speaks.

Hanratty goes on. "Did the ghost of the woman in the barrel say anything else?"

"No," I answer. "She disappeared before I could ask her anything."

I don't offer anything more than what is needed to answer the detective's question, but his eyes have changed again. He's watching me the way he did when I hung up his rain jacket.

"Do you think she had spent her energy by then? You did say she was screaming. I imagine that took something out of her."

His question isn't one that could possibly help the investigation, and I wonder what he's truly trying to discover by asking it.

"Maybe," I hedge. "There are a lot of spirits on the island all vying for the same energy. It's hard to know what might have happened. I bet the storms that passed through in the night helped them."

He looks at Aunt Janine as if asking the same question.

She shakes her head. "Detective, I've been doing this for seventy-six years, and I still don't know how it works." She shrugs now, the collar of her jean jacket pushing against her one remaining hoop earring. "It's anyone's guess what might have happened."

Hanratty makes a few more notes on his notepad, but his smile is noticeably absent. If anything, I would say concern has crawled across his brow.

"Detective Neil," Hanratty says then.

I look over to find Carmen has just split a chocolate croissant like a wishbone with Father Patrick. She freezes, guiltily.

"Yes?" she says around a mouthful of whatever she has just finished.

"Do I need to worry about Dr. James looking into this matter on her own?"

My gaze swings back to the state police detective, indignation clogging my throat.

"No," I manage at the same time Carmen, my father, Logan, and Aunt Janine all say, "Yes."

Father Patrick looks around skeptically, and I pity the man for getting drawn into this. My mother pats Detective Hanratty's shoulders.

"Don't worry. Della and I have an agreement. She's promised me she won't interfere."

Carmen points with her half of the chocolate croissant. "She promised me she wouldn't shoot Marty Pruitt."

"I didn't promise that," I say much too quickly and shut my mouth before someone brings up Becky Brewer.

My mother's lips purse before saying, "I suppose she did."

Detective Hanratty's usual smile is entirely gone when he looks at me again. "You shot someone?"

"Castle Doctrine," I say. "She was trying to kill me."

"Yeah, because you exposed her as a murderer," Carmen adds. "Allegedly," she adds. "Trial's set for September," she adds for Detective Hanratty's sake.

His lips don't quite meet as he processes this. Then he flips his notebook shut, slips the pen back into the spiral, and stands.

"Dr. James, I suppose I don't need to lecture you about contaminating evidence that may need to be used by the DA in order to secure a conviction."

I stand as well.

"No, you don—" But I can't finish the sentence.

The wave of despair hits me then, and I buckle from the sensation. I reach out, trying to find the chair behind me, but Logan catches me instead.

"Hey, you okay?" he asks as my mother, Detective Hanratty, and Aunt Janine reach for me, ready to catch me if Logan can't.

I shake my head. "I'm fine," I assure them. "Just stood too fast." I force a smile. "I promise, Detective. I'm not going to do anything to jeopardize your case."

He doesn't respond to this, just continues to watch me in that careful, quiet way he has. My mother breaks the silence by reminding him when her party is and adds an invitation to yoga in the park on Saturday as well.

When the mudroom door bangs shut behind the state police detective, Aunt Janine puts her arm around my shoulder, pulling me close to her. "I think I'd better stick around for a few days, Moon Pie. You've got a lot going on here."

I don't turn to look at her, but instead, watch the detective retreat to his car in the rain while the rest of my concerned family, friend, and priest return to their discussion about exorcism in modern cinema somewhere behind me in the living room.

"You felt it too, huh?" I ask.

"I felt it too," she answers. "Something is haunting that man, Moon Pie. But I don't think it's a ghost."

TEN

Logan doesn't want me to go to work, and well, he's right. The bruise on my back side is already forming into what looks like a map of Siberia, and my headache doesn't quite go away. I text Frances and Allie, simply saying I need a sick day. Frances acknowledges my text, but Allie sends me another private one.

Ghost dog?

I text her back.

I'll tell you tomorrow.

After a long, scalding shower, I spend the rest of the day on the couch watching every *Thin Man* movie with Henry curled against me. Logan filters in and out from the dining alcove in the kitchen where he's set up his office for the day. I tell him he can go to work, but he insists on staying. I'm not too stubborn to admit I'm glad he's there.

The first thing I do when I get to my office the next morning is find a blank piece of notebook paper to write down everything I know so far. After the events of the previous day, I don't bother pretending I'm not going to investigate. The girl in the barrel was clearly stopped from saving someone or someones, and I'm the only one who can find out who. And maybe, if it's possible, try to save them now.

I've written down a couple of names when Frances darkens my door.

"Mr. Fairchild called this morning," she says in her usual brusque monotone. "He wants to speak with you about putting in a projection system on the grounds so we can show movies on the lawn during the summer."

Arnold Fairchild is the last of the Fairchilds, the original owners of Lady Josephine Lodge, and although the Lodge was donated to the Bellegrave Historical Society before he was even born, he still feels the need to give us his input on the running of it.

"The lodge is a historically protected structure. We can't change the outside of it or alter the grounds in substantially destructive ways. He knows that," I say.

"I sent him to Diana," Frances goes on. "She's still on the phone with him. The last I heard she's reminding him we still need to raise funds for blown-in insulation after the pipe rupture this past spring, and priorities need to be addressed."

Frances hasn't shown an emotion since Watergate, so I smile smugly for the both of us.

"Thank you, Frances."

She retreats, and I go back to my notes.

The exercise helps me to focus, but I still can't shake the encounter with Detective Hanratty the previous day. I'm worried it's clouding my judgment of the case, but it's odd how he was the one to show up when we found the girl in the barrel. Are they connected? Is that why my other sense is so triggered by his presence?

When I've finished with my notes, I pull up the digital archive of the *Bellegrave Bulletin*, the local newspaper, on my laptop. I'm about to type in Sadie Beaumont's name when I stop, a sense of déjà vu washing over me. The last time I'd done this, I'd uncovered some dangerous secrets, and I'm not dumb enough to walk into such a perilous situation again without some forethought.

Instead I type in Donald Carmichael.

I'm not surprised when the first two returns are property transfers. The Carmichaels are not locals. Even when I was growing up, they were still known in town as the wealthy family from the shipping legacy. The Carmichaels in Bellegrave were the same ones with the shipyard on the Hudson that outfitted canal boats for the Erie Canal when it first opened. From there, the business grew into an international conglomerate out of New York.

But it seemed one branch of the Carmichael family had found its way here to Bellegrave and purchased two properties, a parcel outside of the village that must be the post and beam house Chief Wise had mentioned and the island on which the girls camp was erected.

The next hit is an advertisement for Camp Carmichael someone has scanned and uploaded to a blog about the cultural history of the Adirondacks. I click on the link, and the image of the advertisement expands. It takes several seconds of me studying it to realize I'm looking at the island from the vantage point of my cottage. Except the image I'm seeing looks nothing like what it is today.

The trees at the top of the plateau are trimmed back, leaving the ridge open to the sky above. The rocky hill I clambered up twice in the past few days is cleared of brush, and a trail of switchbacks winds its way up the steep slope, providing an easier and smoother route to the top. At the bottom of the image is a series of docks populated by a crowd of young women sporting shorts and matching tops with little Peter Pan collars. They're all in various poses of waving at the photographer, long limbs flashing in the summer sun, their smiles contagious.

Come to Camp Carmichael blazes across the top of the photo.

I wonder if any of those girls is Sadie Beaumont. Unlikely, I think. Why would they have the caretaker's daughter pose in a publicity photo?

I click out of the ad and return to the search results. The next one stops me, and it isn't until the article opens that I can make sense of the headline.

Local Shipping Magnate Seriously Injured in Hit-and-Run.

Chief Wise had mentioned something about the Carmichaels moving out to their Bellegrave home full time after Mr. Carmichael's accident. Is this what he had been talking about?

I scan the article quickly, absorbing the facts, before going back through more slowly to understand the details.

Donald Carmichael, the patriarch of the Carmichael family, had been seriously injured in a hit-and-run accident when he had been out for his morning run near his home in Kingston, New York. The shipping magnate had been medevaced to Albany where he remained in critical condition.

I checked the date of the article. May 19, 1999.

More than twenty years ago.

The remainder of the article is about the Carmichaels' contributions to Bellegrave over the years as proprietors of Camp Carmichael and then as benefactors of the local art community.

Chief Wise mentioned the Carmichaels' daughter, Ashley, and how she might have still attended the camp after her mother died. So by rough estimation Donald Carmichael most likely was about ten or so years older than my parents. He would have been in his mid-fifties at the time of the accident, and as I didn't see a result for an obituary he's likely in his mid-seventies now.

I close out of the *Bellegrave Bulletin* and open a browser window. I navigate to a search engine and type in Miriam Carmichael. It's likely her obituary is also in the *Bulletin*, but I'm curious to see what regional or even national coverage there might be on the wife of a shipping magnate.

The first search result is one I'm not expecting.

Son of Shipping Magnate Killed in Alpine Climbing Accident.

I click on the article. Donald III, son of Donald and Miriam Carmichael of the Carmichael Shipping Company, died in a tragic fall on October 9, 1998. Only eight months before his father's accident. I sit back and take in the photo that accompanies the article of Donald III. It shows a man in his late twenties or early thirties wearing skiing googles, bright sunshine reflecting off the lenses. He's smiling at whoever is taking the photo. He is the kind of handsome money tends to breed, but I can't help but think of the tragedy the Carmichaels have been through. Wealthy doesn't always mean lucky.

I click out of the article and return to the search result. I need to scroll down a ways before finding the one for which I'd been looking.

Miriam Carmichael, crusader for young women's advancement, dead at 58.

The article is a human interest piece from a major outfit in New York. Not only does it list the goodwill contributions and major achievements of what appears to be the grande dame of New York society in the late sixties, but it includes several photos. The first is a picture of Miriam herself. If I didn't know better I would have said the photo was a marketing tactic for a country club. From her perfectly teased pageboy to her seersucker, sleeveless dress to her string of pearls, Miriam Carmichael screams poise, elegance, and money. The background in the photo is blurred, but in the caption, I discover where it was taken.

Miriam at her beloved camp in Bellegrave, New York.

I study the photo again, but the background is simply too blurred to orient it. It could have been taken anywhere on the island. Perhaps in the mess hall or one of the cabins if the faint lines behind her were beams or paneling.

Another photo is a family affair. Miriam beside a tall, striking man with hair and teeth that look like they came from a Sears catalog model. There are two children with them, a boy and a girl. The boy is a replica of his father in waiting, and my stomach clenches knowing what happens to him. The hair and teeth are already present. He only needs to sprout up. The girl though looks nothing like her mother. She has long curly hair tamed into pigtails, and her shoulders slouch forward. It's hard to tell in the photo, but it looks like she's wearing braces.

The caption below reads *Miriam with her husband, Donald, and children. Daughter, Ashley, and son, Donald III.*

So that is Ashley Carmichael.

I can only hope she grew into her looks because having a mother that beautiful would have been intolerable otherwise.

I open the donor database next and type in the name Carmichael. It gives no return, but I wasn't really expecting one.

I roll back in my chair until I can reach the drawers of my desk. Pulling open the deep one on the right, I flip through the file folders until I find the one labeled *Donor Directory*. I pull out the most recent one and hold it between two hands as if studying an artifact. Mostly because I am.

Back before donor databases, everything was done by paper, and once, long before I came to the society, a donor directory was handed out at every Founder's Day gala to the attendees. The idea, I had been told, was to allow donors to contact one another in support of the Historical Society and organize fundraising efforts together. A quaint, if unrealistic, idea, one that stopped when privacy concerns were raised.

The directory I held in my hands had turned brown with age, but the words *Founder's Day Gala 1996* still shone in gold across the cover. It was a long shot, but if the Carmichaels were so philanthropic, maybe they'd given to the society back then. When records were transferred to the new database, not all of them made it, and I knew if the Carmichaels had ever given to the society, this was my only chance of finding their contact information. The alternative was showing up at their door unannounced, and I was hoping to avoid that.

I flip to the Cs. Halfway down the first page I find it.

Donald Carmichael with an address on Byre Road and most importantly a phone number.

I pick up the receiver of my desk phone and dial the number. The chances it still works are slim, but I have to try.

On the third ring, someone picks up.

"Carmichael residence."

For a second, shock steals my voice. "This is Dr. Della James, the executive director of the Bellegrave Historical Society. We are looking to do an exhibit on Camp Carmichael, and I was hoping to speak with Ashley Carmichael."

It isn't the first time I have lied for an investigation, but maybe someday we *would* do an exhibit on the camp. Who was I to say?

There is a pause in which I hold my breath, and then, "One moment please, Dr. James."

There is a click as if I've been put on hold.

The human interest piece is still open behind the window of the donor database, and while I wait, I study the smiling faces of the Carmichaels before tragedy began to tiptoe through their lives.

It isn't long before there is another click, and a crisp, clear voice says, "This is Ashley Carmichael."

"Hello," I say, slightly too breathless. "This is Dr. Della James—"

"I understand you're interested in the history of the camp," Ms. Carmichael cuts me off.

"Yes, that's correct."

There's another pause in which I think she's going to hang up on me, and I suddenly regret not launching a sneak attack and showing up at their house.

"It's probably easier if you come here," Ms. Carmichael finally says, a slight annoyance in her tone as if I've put her out. "You'll probably want to see the camp yearbooks and things?"

Yearbooks?

"Yes," I say quickly before she can change her mind.

"Does tomorrow at two work for you?"

I agree that it does. She gives me the address even though I already have it, and we say our goodbyes. I hang up the phone and stare at it. It really can't be that easy.

"Wifi in the conference room is down again."

I jolt back to awareness at the sound of Frances's voice. I look up to find her in the doorway, arms full of a stack of binders. "Steve's on it, but the natives are getting restless. Thought you might want to talk to them."

There's a Ladies Auxiliary retreat in the conference center today. Just walking past it and into my office that morning had been like walking into every perfume sample in every magazine ever.

"Great," I say.

This is an easy problem, one for which I have a ready solution. The lodge is split in two with the offices in one wing and the conference spaces in the other. I leave my office and head in the direction of the other side of the building where the conference room is, which used to be the great room when the lodge was a summer residence. It's a sweeping, double-story affair with a fireplace at one end, dressed pink and gray granite at the bottom that morphs into river rock at the top, stretching to the vaulted ceilings. The traditional twig and branch decor remains along with the diamond pane windows overlooking Bear Lake.

I gather the attendees' attention and introduce myself before launching into the story of the namesake of Lady Josephine Lodge. It is a beautiful story of love and valor about a woman who did great work in the last half of the nineteenth century and whose husband memorialized her in the naming of the lodge. The Ladies Auxiliary eat it up and don't even notice when Steve gets the wifi back up. I leave the conference room to exclamations of thanks and endearing smiles to find Allie along with our Director of Development Diana Milton already in my office for our eleven o'clock programming debrief.

"No one showed for Marjorie Heywood's talk on Tatting Patterns of the Edwardian Period, and she's pissed. She's threatening to revoke her bequest," Diana says before I've even closed my office door.

Allie snorts. "Nobody attended because nobody tats anymore." She looks to me. "What is tatting even?"

"It's weaving lace," I say.

Allie's eyebrows go up. "People do that? By hand?"

"They used to." I grab a notebook and pen from my desk before joining them at the conference table in the corner of my office. "All right, let's get into it," I say as I flip my notebook to a blank page.

Every week we go through the previous week's programming, what worked, what didn't, determine what can be tweaked for the remainder of the season and what needs a rethink for next year. A good deal of our programming is donor driven, hence Diana's participation in this weekly debrief.

It's after lunch by the time we wrap, and I head back to my desk to find my email inbox has exploded. Before I attempt to clear it, I go in search of coffee. I really should find something to eat, but there's no time for it.

I've gotten through my email in time for my porch chat on the importance of architectural features in keeping Victorian homes cool in the summer and make it back to my desk to find a bag from Shelly's Diner there and my husband reclined in my desk chair.

He looks as smug as I felt after talking to Frances that morning.

I shake my head. "You'd feel pretty stupid right now if I ate lunch."

"I would, but I know you haven't." He stands and opens the bag. "Your mom is having a barbecue at the Hopewell Mansion tonight. She wanted me to tell you."

"Why didn't she just text me?" I take the Reuben he hands me.

"She's afraid the cell phone will irritate the ghost that's possessed you."

I stop unwrapping my Reuben. "You are joking."

"I am not." He takes out another sandwich wrapped in wax paper and without having to look I know it's chicken parm. "She looked it up on the internet. Ghosts don't like cell phones."

"That's entirely made up," I say.

"How do you know?" he shoots back. "You're just making this up as you go along as far as I can tell." He takes his sandwich and plucks one of the fountain sodas from the paper tray on the desk next to the greasy bag. "I've got a three o'clock, so I've gotta run. I just wanted to feed you and let you know about tonight."

Before I know what he's doing, he leans in and kisses me.

I'm too stunned to move, although I kiss him back, some muscle memory kicking in before I tell it not to. I can tell by the shocked expression on his face when he pulls back that he didn't mean to do it either. It wasn't intentional. It was something of habit but not recent habit. It's something he would have done before before. Before Heather Russo. Before the accident. Before everything.

We stare at each other, neither moving, and I know we're both trying to figure out what happens next. Whether we acknowledge it or ignore it. Whichever it is, there is one thing I can't ignore.

Something inside of me lit up at his kiss.

"I'll see you tonight," I manage far too loudly before this realization can rob me of breath.

"Yeah, tonight," he says and only barely doesn't run for the door.

I sit down at my desk and rest my forehead against its wooden surface. I give myself five seconds to think about what just happened before I sit up, rip open my Reuben, and go back to my email.

I shamelessly use work to distract me from my real life for the next hour before Frances intrudes, reminding me the Board of Directors quarterly meeting is only six weeks away, and she needs to put a planning meeting on the calendar. The summer board meeting is the only one of the year where the directors can tour the lodge, and we try to make it a special occasion to thank them for their service to the historical society.

This sidetracks me from my donor reports and from there the afternoon spirals. I spend too much time with Hannah, our social media coordinator, going through candids she's taken during the summer camps to use for a social media campaign next spring to up enrollments, and then we're all called to the conference room to find a lost hearing aid.

By the time I manage to get back to my desk it's after four, and my inbox is flooded again. I sit down and start over.

When I've answered the last email, the lodge has grown quiet. The Ladies Auxiliary have left for the day, and I heard Diana shut and lock her office some time ago.

Allie steps into the doorway of my office. "You good?" she asks. "Anything weird I should know about?"

She's already changed into running shorts and a tank top, her backpack slung over one shoulder. I know she wants to know why I didn't come in yesterday, but I can't bring myself to dampen her day, so I shake my head.

"Just still not right after Saturday. Ya know?" I hedge. I nod at her getup. "Hiking?"

"Kayaking," Allie says with a grimace.

I hold back my smile. Allie's wife, Phoebe, has been trying to get Allie to enjoy the lake more. Allie didn't grow up around water, and she doesn't have the pull to it. Her last kayaking experience with her wife hadn't gone well or at all. Allie had flipped the kayak simply trying to get into it from the dock at the boat launch.

"You're a good sport for giving it another try," I say.

Allie's grimace remains affixed. "A book never tried to kill me. That's all I'm saying."

I wish her good luck, and the lodge becomes even quieter.

It's late, and I know I need to get to my mother's for dinner, but I can't stop myself from returning to my laptop. I minimize the email client and open a browser window. I navigate to a search engine and type in Maurice Beaumont. The first return is a listing for a camp-turned-retreat on Raquette Lake. It looks like Maurice is still a caretaker there just as Chief Wise had mentioned. I add the address of the camp to my notes and move on to my next search query.

Lionel Melrose.

I try both a search engine and *Bellegrave Bulletin* query, but the results provide very little insight. It looks like it's going to be harder to track him down than the rest. I make a mental note to swing by Shelly's sometime this week to see if any of the DPW guys who usually have lunch there remember Melrose or might now how I can find him.

My phone pings just as I'm packing up. Picking it up, I find a text from Aunt Janine. It's a photo of my dog, sitting on a grassy hillside, the lake spread out behind him. I recognize the giant oak tree to the right of Henry in the background, its spread arms casting shade over a series of docks that spill out into the water.

Holding your dog hostage. Ransom: one New York Strip. Rare.

Aunt Janine has kidnapped my dog and taken him to the B&B where she's checked herself in.

I type back.

Keep him. He drools.

I hit send and rethink it.

And farts, I add.

See you at the Hopewell Mansion, she texts back.

I toss my phone in my bag, shut off the lights in my office, and close and lock the door behind me.

I just hope barbecuing doesn't upset possessive ghosts.

ELEVEN

Dinner at the Hopewell Mansion is thankfully uneventful. Logan and I pretend the kiss in my office didn't happen, and Aunt Janine distracts everyone with pictures from her Croatian bike trip. It's late when we get home, and Henry goes straight up to bed, exhausted from having played with his favorite person in the world—my father—all night.

When my alarm goes off for my swim the next morning, I almost ignore it. While my body has recovered from the ordeal of the past few days, my mind has not, and the idea of getting into the lake feels dangerous. It's too close to the island, leaving me vulnerable to another attack.

I force myself out of bed, habit more than anything driving me. When I walk into the aquatic center twenty minutes later, Bethany smiles knowingly from behind the front desk, and I wonder if she's heard only the mass grave version or the mass grave with sex cult version of the story.

My swim is blissfully dull, and I give myself a few minutes to just float when I'm done.

Logan is waiting for me in the kitchen when I get home.

He hands me a mug of coffee with an understanding smile I refuse to acknowledge.

I leave my office a little before two that afternoon. The Carmichael home is a post and beam structure set high into the hill on the west end of the lake not more than a mile and a half from Peter Bellegrave's hotel, Bellegrave Manor, which was constructed in the latter part of the nineteenth century and abandoned sometime in the middle of the twentieth.

I pass it on my way up Byre Road and studiously avert my gaze from the empty, black windows, the peeling white paint that too closely resembles overgrown fingernails curling back on themselves, and the brown and green vines that crawl up its face as the forest reclaims the land Peter Bellegrave stole.

I knock on the Carmichaels' door at exactly two. The house is situated to look out over the valley and the lake, and the side door off the driveway is sheltered in a small porch. I stand there for a couple of minutes before the door is wrenched open so quickly the person on the other side bounces with the force of it.

If this is Ashley Carmichael, she is not what I was expecting from the tight voice on the phone the previous day. For one, she's barefoot, her toenails covered in chipped red paint. Her long tanned legs are bare as well and disappear into cutoffs. She has a faded t-shirt tucked into the shorts, remnants of what looks to be some heavy metal rock band's name splattered across her chest. Her clearly dyed blonde hair flops at the top of her head in a messy bun, pieces of hair sticking out from her head, giving her the appearance of a 1960s Russian satellite.

"You must be Della," she says, extending a hand. "I'm Ashley Carmichael."

Her eyes are warm behind dark-framed glasses, and her smile exposes teeth that must be veneers.

I hesitate, reality catching up with my expectations, and I wonder if I had just caught her at a bad time yesterday.

"Thank you so much for seeing me. I appreciate you taking the time for the Historical Society."

Ashley's smile brightens, her head tilting to the side in a gesture suited to someone much younger. "Of course. Anything for Bellegrave. Come on in."

I follow Ashley into a foyer that is clearly designed to mimic the old camps similar to Lady Josephine Lodge. The walls are wood slats in their natural state, and the doors are trimmed in cut pieces to resemble the notched corners of camps. There are warm accents that offset the wood—a plush green carpet running the length of the hallway we're in and tasteful antique pieces along the walls. There are even small watercolors in a gallery along the right of the foyer giving the space color.

And it smells *divine*.

"I'm so sorry, but I've got food on the stove. Would you mind chatting in the kitchen while I finish up?" She's already trotting—*trotting*—down the hall in front of me, so I follow.

I pass more watercolors, a framed print of a theater festival, and an oil painting of the house itself, the perspective of which is from the road below. There are no family photos. I pass what looks to be a sitting room on one side and a bigger space on the other completely furnished with what looks to be original twig and branch designed furniture. My step falters as I try to calculate the amount of money sitting in the silent room.

Ashley has disappeared in front of me though, and I'm forced to quicken my step.

The kitchen takes up nearly the entire rear of the house. I pause just inside the threshold, confusion clouding my judgment.

Ashley looks up from where she's perched over a stainless

steel work surface. She's chopping something leafy and green, the knife barely moving yet a rhythmic *chop chop chop* fills the air.

"Come on in. Do you like gumbo? I'm trying a new recipe."

I think I got lost somewhere between here and the door because I've clearly stepped into a commercial kitchen. The surfaces are vast, stainless, and immaculate. The range looks more expensive than my car, and I'm fairly sure all the members of MENSA could fit in the subzero freezer.

"I've never had gumbo."

"Really? Ah, you're missing out, girl."

I stop my perusal of the kitchen, my gaze flying back to the woman who must be somewhere over fifty. She flits over to the stove and the industrial-sized pot that sits there. Even from where I'm standing I can see the steam rising from it. If it tastes half as good as it smells, it must be something divine indeed.

"I tend to subsist on peanut butter straight from the jar," I say.

Ashley laughs, perhaps too loud, perhaps not. Maybe she just genuinely thought what I'd said is funny.

She turns off the burner under the pot and using oven mitts the size of Rhode Island slides the pot to another burner.

"Just give me a second to get some bowls," Ashley says and disappears through a door beside the refrigerator. I can see shelves with various dishes stacked like soldiers waiting for inspection, a butler's pantry maybe.

"I'm sorry if I was curt with you on the phone yesterday. We've been getting so many phone calls since they found that poor girl," she calls from the pantry.

I continue my scan of the kitchen, pausing at a frame on the wall just to my left. It's one of those shadow box types that has depth to it. There's a tightly rolled piece of leather with a tie in the middle nestled inside an ivory satin pillow. There's no other indication of what it might be.

"Oh." Ashley's self-conscious laugh pulls me from my inspection of the frame. "Those were from Daddy." Ashley gestures to the frame with the stack of pasta bowls she holds in her hands. They look weighty as she's using both hands to carry them. "He gave them to me just before I left for Paris to apprentice under Chef Theroux." She puts the stack of bowls on the stainless worktop.

"Chef Theroux?" I ask.

Ashley blinks at me a time or two as though she doesn't understand the confusion. Then she gives that same self-deprecating laugh. "Oh, I forget sometimes normal people don't know who he is." She pushes her bun up higher on the back of her head as it tumbles every time she tilts her head, which is a lot. "Chef Theroux was one of the greatest French chefs of the last century. He only ever accepted four apprentices in the whole of his career. I was one of them." She gives a shrug as if this is no big deal. "Those are the set of knives Daddy gave me as a congratulations present." She shakes her head, her expression suddenly wistful. "Those were good times," she finally says and starts unstacking the bowls.

Daddy. Huh.

"Phone calls?" I try to sound casual.

"Reporters mostly." She dismisses this with a wave of her hand. "A few busybodies. You know how it is." Her tone has changed, the edge of steel entering it, and I change the subject.

"When did you go to France?" I ask.

Ashley looks over her shoulder from where she's ladling the thick mixture from the pot into a bowl.

"Fall of '84," she says. "You afraid of spicy things?"

"I'm not sure anyone has ever asked me that. I don't think so," I reply as I make my way farther into the kitchen.

She sets a bowl on the stainless worktop and slides it

toward me. I stop it with the palm of one hand and stare into its depths. The smallest amount of gumbo congeals at the bottom, and the salad I had for lunch from Shelly's Diner turns over in my stomach.

"It looks hot," I say.

Ashley laughs as she tugs out a drawer that gives off the tinkling sound of cutlery. She tosses a spoon into my bowl, and it makes a clang against the pottery.

"It better be," she says. "Try it."

I take the smallest bite possible. It's like a nuclear warhead has gone off in my mouth. I open my lips, huffing to cool the burning of my mouth when a glass of milk appears on the worktop next to the bowl. I down it.

"What is in that?" I choke when I can finally manage words.

"Nuh uh," Ashley says with that same laugh. "A chef never tells her secrets."

She washes her hands in the sink and dries them on her cutoffs.

I poke at the gumbo. "This is quite a nice kitchen you have."

She leans on the worktop, her hands spread along its edge and takes in her surroundings with an assessing eye.

"It's not bad," she says with a shrug. "I'm just lucky Daddy decided to make some changes after Donnie died." Her gaze turns to me, and for the first time since I've met her, it turns serious. "This house has really been the best place for Daddy since his accident." She shakes her head, and the next she speaks her voice has softened. "It's fortunate yet sad that Donnie's death made Daddy put his affairs in order. It's made things easier for us."

"I'm very sorry. I understand your life has been riddled with tragedy."

I couldn't fathom being Ashley, her mother and brother

gone too soon and left with an ailing father to care for. Ashley tilts her head again, her bun flopping to the side. Her smile is sad, but only for a second. She straightens with a bounce and pats my arm.

"Come on," she says, and I realize she says that a lot. "I pulled out the camp albums and yearbooks from Mama's office. They're on the table on the sun porch."

She skips out of the kitchen before I can say anything, and I follow her. Two steps lead down into the sun porch off the kitchen that runs along the south side of the house. The windows at this hour are filled with light, and Ashley moves along them, adjusting the shades to prevent burning our retinas. The space is cooler than the rest of the house. The windows are all open, and the smell of pine and damp invades, nearly overpowering the spicy scent from the kitchen.

There's a long table taking up most of the room, and it's here that I see the stacks of photo albums. There are benches on either side, and Ashley hops over one, patting the seat next to her.

"Come. Sit." She pulls an album toward her. "There is some good stuff in here."

I clamber over the bench next to her, decidedly less graceful at probably fifteen years younger than her, and my bag bumps against the bench awkwardly. I set it down next to me.

Ashley stabs a finger at the page. "That's Mama," she says. "Look at that hair. She looks like she stepped out of an ad in *Harper's Bazaar*."

I lean over to see the photo Ashley indicates, and it's similar to the ones I'd seen online of Miriam Carmichael, only here she's wearing a camp shirt instead of a sleeveless dress. It's a polo style shirt with a collar she's buttoned up entirely. On someone else, it would have looked awkward, but on Miriam Carmichael, it frames her face perfectly.

"I don't remember a time before camp," Ashley says, her finger stroking the bubbling cellophane on the album page absently. "Mama was always happiest at camp."

I look swiftly at Ashley. It's the first time I've heard her use a sincere tone. Even when speaking of her father's accident and her brother's death, she sounded sad but not sincere. When I take in her expression, I see shadows in her eyes. Is it sadness? Regret? Longing? Maybe a little of all three.

She reaches over and taps a photo on the opposite page. "One of the rare appearances of Daddy at the camp."

I look where she's pointed to find a young Donald Carmichael. He's standing on a dock, waving at the photographer.

"Your father didn't stay at Camp Carmichael?"

Ashley snorts a laugh. "No, the camp was Mama's thing. Daddy was always busy with work in New York." She holds up one finger. "But Daddy always came up one weekend a summer for Mama." She drops her finger to trace the edge of the photograph. "Daddy always did what Mama asked. He just loved her that much." There's a pause before she says softly, almost childlike. "We all did."

She flips the page before I can say anything, and I get the sense she's flipping away painful memories as well.

The next few pages are taken up with photographs of girls in canoes, girls sunbathing on docks, girls surrounding a campfire, the flames shooting up to the edge of the photo. Ashley keeps flipping pages and although the girls in the photos change, the activities don't vary much.

"Camp Carmichael had a pretty set activity schedule," I mention.

Ashley nods. "Mama did that. She liked order and routine, and even after she died, I kept things just as she liked them." Her smile fades. "Until Daddy decided to shut down the camp, that is."

"Why did he decide to do that?" I hedge my question, not wanting to seem too nosy.

Ashley shakes her head and flips the page. "I think it reminded him of Mama too much. Having to always do for the camp when it was hers and not his. There was just too much of Mama on that island."

I scan another page of girls sitting around picnic tables, girls teaching other girls how to dive off the docks, girls braiding each other's hair. In every photo, I see smiling faces and silent laughter. There isn't a single thing that could tell me why so many spirits haunt the island today.

"Nothing happened at the camp that turned him off from running it, did it?"

Ashley turns to look at me so swiftly I back up.

"Why? What have you heard?"

I stare at her. "I haven't heard anything." I tap the photo album. "The camp shut down the year I was born. I don't know much about it except what I've heard from some of the older volunteers at the society. I just thought there might be a more personal and deeper reason for your father's decision to shut it down." I adjust on the bench, the hard surface uncomfortable. "It sometimes helps us tell the story of a place if we can find a deeper, human connection," I explain.

Ashley's eyes sweep back and forth across my face, watchful, considering. I don't move. I can't.

It looks as though she's made a decision when a voice behind us startles me.

"Miss Carmichael."

I turn to find a woman in nurse's scrubs standing in the doorway to the kitchen. She's an older woman, thick about the middle so her scrub smock pulls, with short black hair cut around her ears revealing large gold earrings.

"Your father needs you."

I turn back to see Ashley's frown. It's a frown tinged with worry, and she scoots off the bench.

"Will you excuse me for just a tick?" she asks. "Daddy can sometimes become agitated. I'm the only one who can settle him. Feel free to look through the albums while I'm gone."

She disappears through the door at a much more sedate walk than how she'd entered the sun porch. The nurse remains in the doorway a second longer than necessary, her eyes boring into me. Her mouth pinches as though she might say something, but she slips silently back through the door.

I don't waste any time in finding the albums from the eighties. I pass through '81, '82, and '83 at speed. Ashley isn't hard to pick out among the campers in the photos. It helps that these later albums have the names of everyone pictured written in small black letters beneath each photo. I wonder if Ashley took over making the albums after her mother died, and if it's her handwriting there.

Finally I find '84. The photos are much the same as all the previous ones. Canoeing, diving, swimming, arts and crafts, campfires. The camp really didn't change after Miriam died. Ashley had been right.

I'm nearly halfway through the album from '84 when a picture stops me. It's unlike the monotonous scroll of canoes and campfires. It's a picture of four girls standing on a dock, the sun behind them, their arms looped over each other's shoulders. Ashley is the second from left, and standing next to her is the girl from the barrel.

Shock spreads through me like ice water, and I jerk back, upsetting the album so it skids across the table. I struggle to stand, my legs trapped in the ridiculous bench. I try to push back against it at the same time as reaching for the album on the other side of the table. The bench is too heavy to move. I stop, regroup, shove my palms down on the table and leverage myself out from between table and bench.

I reach across the table now and pull the album back to me. I check the photo again, certain I was just seeing things. But I'm not. The girl from the barrel stands next to Ashley Carmichael. They have their arms around each other. They're smiling, happy, and I can almost feel the photo. Feel what it was like to be eighteen, the whole world spread out before you as you stand on the brink of the rest of your life.

My eyes drop to the caption below the photo, one, two, three, four names. The third name. The girl from the barrel is standing third from the left. My eyes double as I'm straining too hard, and I blink, try to read it again. The third name from the left.

Sadie Beaumont.

TWELVE

My phone gets stuck in my pocket, and I wrench it free, sending my knees painfully into the bench. I'm shaking so badly it takes me several tries to take a photo of the photo. I stuff my phone back into my pocket and shut the album with a little too much force. I slip it back in with the others and pull one at random from the middle of the pile I hadn't looked through yet.

I don't see anything as I turn page after page, my mind suddenly blank, overwhelmed by the discovery that the girl in the barrel is the same girl that was presumed drowned in the summer of 1984. I hear a rustling and realize my hands are still shaking. I shove them into my pockets just as I hear footsteps approach the door.

Ashley stands there, her hands in her pockets. "I'm so sorry. Daddy's having one of his bad days. I'm going to have to reschedule this."

I look back at the photo albums. It takes all my resolve not to look at the one concealing the photo of Ashley and Sadie Beaumont.

I force a smile. "Of course. I understand completely."

Ashley's head tilts, but she pulls one hand free of a pocket and rubs at the skin on her neck. "I sure appreciate it."

I try not to run for the front door, and I trip on the hunter green runner in the hallway. Ashley is walking ahead of me and luckily doesn't see.

She opens the door. The sun has shifted since I came in, and the driveway is mostly in shadow now.

"I'll be in touch to reschedule." Her shoulders slump. "I just never know when Daddy is going to have a good day or a bad day."

I say something comforting—I hope—and head for my SUV. I drop my bag in the passenger seat, start the car, and back out of the driveway, trying to buckle my seatbelt at the same time. I don't see the road. I can't hear the engine. My heart is thumping, my mind racing with possibilities.

I'm almost two miles down the road when I see a turnoff large enough to fit my SUV. I slow and pull over. I have my phone out of my pocket before I get the SUV in park.

I bring up the photo of Sadie Beaumont. A tremor spreads through me. The last time I'd seen her she was a ghost, hovering in front of me, imploring.

Save them.

I tap the phone and send the photo to a text message. I hit Detective Hanratty's contact and type in a message below the photo.

The girl in the barrel is Sadie Beaumont.

I hit send. The message hesitates. I'm deep into the woods that line the hills around Bear Lake, and the reception here is spotty. It seems like years before the message finally goes through.

I stare at the phone, unable to move my limbs, unable to put the car in drive and return to the village, the lodge, and my office. I'm supposed to lead a four o'clock chat on the porch about the importance of boat houses in the Gilded Age, but I can't move.

I stare at Sadie Beaumont on my phone. Her smile. Her bright eyes. The warmth that exudes from the photo. I glance at the other girls, the ones on each end. The girl on the left has short hair, a pixie cut. It suits her sharp cheekbones and impish smile. The girl all the way to the right has long, straight hair that appears almost black in the photo. She's braided the front of it, and it curves over her forehead, accentuating her big eyes.

I read the caption again. The girl on the left is Debbie Fraser. The one on the right is Monica Davies.

I'm not sure how long I'm sitting there when I register the noise in my ears.

At first, I think it's my SUV. I've left it running while I'm parked there, and I think at first something must have gone wrong with the engine. But the sound I'm hearing isn't mechanical. It sounds like running water maybe or...

I look up and around, thinking I'm closer to the Bellegrave River that exits the lake near here before curving along the county highway. But all I see is a curtain of trees, craggy trunks and diaphanous green leaves, melting together in an impenetrable cloak.

Almost impenetrable.

Through the curve of trees and bend of branch, the straight lines of a building stand out. They don't belong in the contours of nature, and it's as though the forest is calling my attention to them, the interloper, the stranger, the one that doesn't belong.

Suddenly the forest surrounding me comes into focus, and Bellegrave Manor sits not more than ten yards from where I've parked my car. I look around, my ears filling with the sound of static, growing louder as my eyes search. I must have turned into the old driveway of the manor, now largely overgrown and forgotten.

The static swells, morphing, flexing, until—

Come.

The word comes out of the static, clear and crisp. I recoil, my head hitting the headrest behind me.

The noise returns to static, nonsense, but my breathing is still shallow, rushed.

Then—

Come with us.

Join us.

The words are garbled, like words that might come through when you're tuning a radio, before disappearing back into static. I concentrate, push my focus, and the static grows louder, more indistinct.

I should get out of there. I should put the car in drive and leave, but instead I undo my seatbelt and slip from the car.

The loose gravel and dirt crunches under my feet, and I slide, the driveway being at a slight incline as it reaches up into the hill. I catch myself on the open door, my gaze never moving from the dissected lines of the abandoned manor through the trees.

I can feel the voices. They are just there, just beyond my reach.

But they shouldn't be. I should hear them. I should see them. But it's as though something is standing between us, something that didn't use to be there. My breath quickens, my heart rabbits, but not out of fear. At least, not fear for the dead.

Something is different.

Something has changed.

Something isn't right.

I take a step forward, and my phone beeps in my hand.

The sound cuts the static, and in a flash, it disappears

entirely. There's only the wind rustling leaves, the hollow, echoing sound of insects, and the abbreviated chirp of a warbler.

I forgot my phone was still in my hand, and I peer at it, trying to remember why it's there, my brain foggy from the dead.

The dead I couldn't reach.

There's a text. A response from Detective Hanratty.

Where are you?

I know what he's really asking and type back a reply.

I'll be at Lady Josephine Lodge in five minutes. You can find me in my office.

I take one last look at the manor, but it remains silent.

I get back in my car, pull out onto the road, and head toward the village.

———

I drop my bag beside my desk and open my laptop.

The lodge buzzes around me. I'd passed Diana on the way in with a group of older women, one with actual blue hair. Diana was giving her donor speech, why history is important, and why historical preservation is even more important, and I wonder if they were prospective donors.

Allie was in Hannah's office as I passed, and I vaguely heard words referring to click through and social media ads targeting program registrations.

Frances, thankfully, was nowhere in sight. I love the woman, but she has a knack for throwing my day completely off course.

I'm barely in my desk chair when I pull up a search engine and type quickly. I'm not sure how long it will take Detective Hanratty to get here, but I can't stop the feeling of urgency he invokes. It's as though I need to be two steps ahead of him at all times.

I type in the name Debbie Fraser.

Nothing.

Deborah Fraser.

Nothing.

Debra Fraser.

An article about a financial advisor in Plattsburg. I click through. The photo shows a young woman in a bright pink blazer. Not pixie Debbie from the photo.

I click out of the article.

I try adding search terms like New York, Albany, Hudson Valley, but either I don't have the right combination, or Debbie Fraser no longer exists. The idea leaves a cold feeling in the pit of my stomach.

"Della's office is at the end on the left." Steve's voice travels down the corridor and through my office door.

I close the browser and click on the donor database. It fills my laptop screen. I click blindly on the first donor record.

I have my smile firmly in place when Detectives Hanratty and Perez step through the door.

Hanratty's expression isn't friendly.

"Dr. James," he says. "I trust you're having a nice afternoon."

I check my watch as I stand. "I have a lecture I'm leading at four, so I hope it's all right if we skip the pleasantries. The girl in the barrel is Sadie Beaumont. She was presumed drowned in July of 1984. You can check with the Bellegrave Police Department for specifics."

Perez's lips part as he studies me. Hanratty's expression worsens.

"How is it that you got this photo?" Hanratty holds up his phone, the photo of the photo on the screen.

"I was meeting with Ashley Carmichael about a possible

exhibit on her family's camp. The photo was in one of the photo albums she shared with me."

Hanratty lowers his phone, but his gaze doesn't move from my face.

"Interfering in a police investigation is a crime, Dr. James. I'm sure in this small town your assistance is sometimes overlooked, but I won't be making such concessions."

His tone is flat but not unfriendly. Still his words grate.

"I'm not interfering, Detective," I say. "I was meeting with Ashley Carmichael on Historical Society business. The fact that I found a photograph of the victim in the case you're investigating is coincidental."

Hanratty's jaw tightens. "Coincidental?"

"Yes," I say.

That is not entirely true, but it's not like I had set out that morning to find the identity of the victim.

Hanratty shifts, putting more weight on his left leg. "You're telling me you happened to have a meeting with—" He lifts his eyebrows.

"Ashley Carmichael. The Carmichael family owns the island on which the body was found. I'm sure you've spoken with her already."

Perez smacks his lips shut, the sound reverberating through my office.

Hanratty's smile is annoyed. "We have notified the Carmichaels of our discovery, but our priority is identifying the victim."

"Great," I say, gesturing to the phone still in his hand. "You've identified her. Now the investigation can move forward."

Hanratty rubs the back of his neck and lets out a harsh breath of air. "That's not quite how this works, Dr. James." He meets my gaze. "This meeting with Ashley Carmichael. You said it was for an exhibit?"

I nod. "I regularly meet with citizens of Bellegrave who may have an interesting story the Historical Society wishes to capture." I turn to the credenza behind my desk and the stand of brochures there. I pluck one from its plastic slot. "We have a grant for capturing oral histories of the Bellegrave area. It's a fascinating—"

Hanratty holds up the hand without the phone, his eyes wide. "That's all right. I trust it's...fascinating," he finishes.

I put the brochure back. My stomach roils again, concern growing for how easily I'm lying now.

Hanratty looks at the photo on his phone again. "So you're telling me this girl, Sadie Beaumont, was presumed drowned."

I nod again. "Yes. In July 1984."

"Why was she believed to have drowned?"

I shrug. "I can't say. I was only a newborn at the time."

Hanratty blinks. "Really?"

I tilt my head like I'd seen Ashley Carmichael do. "I'm sorry, Detective. I'm not an officer of the Bellegrave Police Department. I don't have any more information."

The line between us becomes finer. The feeling of despair isn't haunting him today, but I still remember to keep Detective Hanratty at a distance until I figure out what his deal is.

Hanratty lets out a harsh laugh. "Oh, I see. All right," he says with a shake of his head, the usual jovial tone of his voice returning. "I see how we're going to do this." He shakes his head, his lips press flat. "I knew you were going to be trouble, Dr. James. Detective Neil warned me."

I smile. "I'm never any trouble, Detective. I assure you."

"Della, do you have a minute to—"

Lisa stops in the doorway, her hands full of what looks to be sheet music. Her eyes go to Detective Hanratty then Detective Perez where her gaze hesitates, likely because Detective Perez wears his badge on a chain around his neck.

"Is this a bad time?" she asks, her attention coming back to me.

"Not at all," I say. "This is Detective Hanratty and Detective Perez. They are here about the body Logan and I found."

Lisa waves awkwardly over the stack of sheet music. "Hi." She looks at each of the detectives in turn. "Detective Perez. Detective Hanratty."

"It's Daniel," Hanratty says, and I about fall on the floor. *Daniel?*

He's never invited me to call him Daniel.

Hanratty approaches Lisa and shakes her one free hand. "Nice to meet you..."

"Lisa," she says, her eyes darting to me.

I shrug.

"Are you a volunteer here?" Hanratty asks.

I sink one hip against my desk and cross my arms. I take in Detective Perez, but he's watching his partner. I don't know the man well, but his expression is almost a scowl. A protective one.

"I'm teaching music classes here before I start at the school in the fall. I'm a music teacher," Lisa explains.

Again her eyes dart to me.

Again I shrug.

Detective Perez follows the line of Lisa's gaze, and I give him a shrug too.

"Music teacher? Wow. Voice or instrument?"

"Voice," she says. She shakes her head. "I just need to run through the choral selections for the school groups coming at the end of the month. Should we set up a time for that?"

A part of me wants to keep this going to see how it plays out, but the other part of me, the one that values Lisa's friendship, capitulates.

"Yeah, we can do that. Want to send me some times that work for you?"

"Sure," Lisa says. She nods at each of the detectives. "Nice to meet you both."

"I hope we run into each other again," Hanratty says.

I plant a hand on my desk to keep myself steady.

Lisa's smile wavers as though she's flustered. When she runs into the doorjamb as she tries to back out of the doorway, I *know* she's flustered.

My smile is more of a grin when Hanratty turns back to me.

He clears his throat. "You'll stay out of this investigation, Dr. James. I have your word?"

I hold up both hands. "I was never in this investigation, Detective."

His expression tells me he doesn't believe me, but still he and Perez leave.

I wait until I can no longer hear their footsteps in the hallway before I sit back down at my computer.

I minimize the donor database and open a new search window.

I type in Monica Davies.

The first return is a mugshot.

I move my mouse to click into the search field and type new terms until I stop, the cursor hovering over the picture.

Straight black hair, lanky with grease, accentuating wide eyes.

Dread pools in my stomach as I click on the mugshot.

Monica Davies of Clifton Falls was arrested for possession. I study the photo. I don't want it to be her.

I click back and go to the next link. It's a news article about a drug sting. I click again.

This mugshot is clearer, and there's no denying it's the same Monica Davies from the photos of the girls.

I sit back in my chair, unable to take my eyes off the photo. She could be anywhere from twenty to fifty, and I look at the date. It's from four years ago. I think of Ashley that morning, perky, bouncy, tanned, and healthy.

Monica looks as though life has dried her out, leaving only a shriveled husk of a person left. Her gorgeous, thick, straight hair has thinned, and it's obviously dyed, the roots showing a mile wide down the middle of her head. Her face is pock-marked and red. I can make out the peeling, dried skin even in the terrible mugshot photo.

But it's her eyes I can't stop looking at.

It's not anger there or resentment at having been arrested. It's a much harsher emotion, one with which I'm too familiar.

It's fear.

THIRTEEN

Henry is upside down on the couch in the living room when I finally get home a little after five that evening. His tails thumps against the cushions when he sees me, but he doesn't get up. I go to him and sink my face in the softness of his belly.

"It was a long day, bud," I murmur into his fur. "Let's hit the water."

At the word *water*, he flips, nearly knocking me off the couch. He gives one shouting bark and races to the glass doors off the kitchen that lead to the patio and the boat dock beyond.

"Let me get changed," I protest feebly and run upstairs.

Once I'm in cutoffs, a tank top, and flip-flops, I open the glass door. Henry runs straight for the dock.

"Go pee first!" I call after him.

He pivots, lifting his leg against a poor rhododendron. He wastes all of five seconds tending to business before his paws hit the dock. I grab my floppy hat from where I'd tossed it on the table in the dining nook. My sunglasses take a little longer to find. Henry had knocked them off my head with his couch flip, and they've sailed under one of the chairs in the living room.

I grab a bottle of water from the fridge and Henry's collapsible dish before heading out the door.

By the time I get down to the dock, Henry is already in my little boat. He's in the bow, his head hanging over the side as he peers into the water. I pull the mooring lines loose and hop into the boat. The engine starts with a single pull, and in moments, we're away from the dock.

Henry doesn't change position, his head still hung over the side. I admire his confidence, as though he's really going to catch a fish if we pass one.

I can't stop myself from looking at the island as we pass it, my hand turning on the throttle just a little to get us past it faster. It's dark and silent today, the evening sun lighting the western side and leaving the other half in shadow.

I turn my gaze away. When we reach open water, I open the throttle completely, and the boat planes, carrying us with it. It's the closest feeling to flying I've ever had, sitting in my boat, the water splitting in a curtain before us, the wind whipping against my cheeks. Henry has lifted his head, his nose in the air, his face serene even as his ears flap against his head. I wonder if he feels like he's flying too.

We do a lap around the entire lake. I wave to people on their docks and passing boaters. There's something calming about taking a lap around the lake, and I feel the shock of my discovery today recede into something manageable. From my vantage point, I can see the more private pieces of people's lives as they're out on their decks and patios along the water's edge. I see fathers lighting grills in preparation for dinner. I see teenagers lounging on rafts and swimming platforms. I see friends gathering around fire pits, cocktails in hand. I see the most important parts of life.

Henry has resumed his hunt for fish over the side of the

boat as we make the last turn into the cove where our cottage sits. I'm nearly to the dock when a reflection of light makes me look up. Someone is opening the glass doors of our patio. For a moment, the peace the lap around the lake gave me vanishes, the events of the past few days sending me straight to trepidation, when I see Logan emerging from the house, his hands full of takeout boxes.

I glance at my watch. It's only half six. My husband is home, and he's brought dinner.

The trepidation vanishes, replaced by a slight uncertainty.

I cut the throttle, and my little boat bobs in the water just off our dock. I'm just like my little boat, buffeted by the things I can't control, unsure where to go from where I am. Things have changed between us, between Logan and me, and not when I expected them to nor how I wanted them to. But I'm wondering if this is something really in my control or if change is inevitable, maybe even good.

Logan looks up from where he's put dinner on the patio table. I raise a hand, turn the throttle up enough to guide the boat back along the dock. Henry is out before the bow bumps the buoys that hang down the sides of the dock, and he takes off toward his dad.

I tie up the boat at a much slower pace and follow him up the hill.

"Bad day?" Logan asks from where he's seated on the patio pavers, petting Henry as the dog squirms between his legs.

"The girl in the barrel is Sadie Beaumont," I say.

Logan stops petting Henry. "How do you know that?"

I pull out my phone and show him the photo of the photo.

"Damn," he breathes. He looks up at me. "What does this mean?"

I put my phone away and glance at the table. He's brought BBQ from Thelma's, and I want to melt in happiness.

"I saw Ashley Carmichael today. The photo was in one of the photo albums she likely made about the camp. I gave the information to Detective Hanratty." I shrug. "That's all I can do there."

"That's not all you're going to do though, is it?"

"Hanratty told me to stay out of it."

I look down at my husband. Henry has curled himself into his lap. Logan is still wearing his dress slacks and button-down shirt he wore to the office. My chest tightens, and I look away.

"She asked you to save them," Logan says.

"Save who?" I ask the island.

"You know what will help with that?" Logan says, and I look back down at him. "Ribs," he says with such conviction I laugh.

Henry bounces up at the mention of meat.

"No," I say, pointing my finger in his face. "It's kibble for you," I pronounce in my best cursing voice.

Henry barks excitedly like I've just promised him filet mignon. I get his kibble while Logan gets plates, silverware, and napkins. Henry gobbles down his dinner like I really have just given him a prime cut of meat before scampering out the door in pursuit of Dad. I grab a couple of bottles of beer from the fridge and follow him.

The sun is setting along the western ridge over the lake, but the sky is still lit with orange, lavender, and fading blue. I can just make it out along the horizon as I take a seat at the patio table. Logan hands me the container of ribs. There's a thump, and something soft and bulky lands on my feet under the table. I nearly drop the container of ribs as Henry settles against my legs.

"So the girl in the barrel is Sadie Beaumont. She told you to save them. Who are they? Who was she referring to?" Logan asks.

I take a healthy portion of ribs and trade them for Logan's coleslaw. "I think there's a more immediate concern."

Logan looks up from getting his own ribs. "What's that?"

"Someone killed Sadie Beaumont and made it look like an accident. They wanted everyone to think she'd drowned. That takes some doing."

"Didn't you say they found a capsized canoe?"

I nod and take my first bite of ribs. The meat practically melts in my mouth.

"It takes a lot to capsize a canoe," Logan says, considering potato salad and cornbread.

He takes a little of both.

"Not unless you're my mother and Mel," I remind him.

My mom and her best friend, Mel, capsized a paddleboat during the previous summer's Old Home Days paddleboat race. A paddleboat is nearly impossible to flip. It's too wide. Yet somehow my mother and Mel managed to do it. They had to be rescued by Elmer McQuiggan and his launch.

"I forgot about that," Logan mutters. "That was spectacular."

I snort. "My mother didn't think so."

"Why would someone want to kill Sadie?" Logan asks, sobering.

"Chief Wise mentioned a few things I want to look into." I take the potato salad from Logan. "Sadie allegedly started seeing some boy the summer she died. I don't have a name yet, but Chief Wise and Lisa both remember rumors Sadie had changed. She apparently got into a fight with her father the afternoon of the day she died. I wonder if this boy she was dating had something to do with that."

"Her dad didn't like her dating him?"

"Or he didn't like how Sadie was changing because of him," I add.

"And no one remembers his name?"

"No." I rummage in the takeout bags for more cornbread. "And I couldn't find anything about someone named Lionel Melrose when I searched for him." I explain about Lionel Melrose, his junkyard, and how Sadie got it shut down.

"She was a real crusader," Logan says when I'm done.

"I know." I poke at my potato salad. "I'm worried she got into something no one has mentioned yet, maybe didn't even realize she had gotten caught up in. It seems like she wasn't afraid to stick her nose in where it didn't belong."

"And that's what got her killed," Logan says.

Henry rolls over, and I shift my foot to pillow his head.

"I can't forget about the bracelet. She showed it to me for a reason." I glance up at the water. The sun has sunk behind the western hills now, and the lake is dark and unmoving. "Chief Wise said it sounded like something her father might have whittled. If her father had made that bracelet for her and she was wearing it when she died, it was important to her."

"Even if they had fought that day?"

I take a sip of my beer before answering. "Not if what they were fighting about didn't have to do with their own relationship."

"But something Sadie had gotten involved in? Like the boy she was dating?" Logan asks.

I sit back in my chair. "What if the boy is a red herring? Everyone keeps talking about him, but no one remembers his name."

"What if he was helping her in whatever quest she had found herself entangled in when she died?" Logan asks.

"Maybe," I say. "Did you ever meet any of the Carmichaels?"

"No," he says, wiping his hands with a wet towel. "What was Ashley like?"

"You know when people overcompensate when something terrible happens? I think Ashley is like that. She seemed deter-

mined to keep things going no matter what and try to be positive." I pull apart a piece of cornbread even though I'm nearly
bursting at this point. "Donald Carmichael the elder was
injured in a hit-and-run while out running one morning in
Kingston. Donald Carmichael the junior died the year before
in a climbing accident. And Miriam Carmichael died of lung
cancer when Ashley was young. That's a lot for one person to
carry. Now she's up at that house trying to take care of her
dad. There's a nurse there, but it seems like a lot is relying on
Ashley. I wonder if his situation has deteriorated over the
years."

"Is Ashley one of the girls in that photo?"

I take my phone out again and pass it to him. "Yeah, she
has her arm around Sadie. I think she's one of the friends
Chief Wise mentioned told the police Sadie took the canoe
out. I'll need to go back and question Ashley. I wasn't able to
this time because she was already on edge from all the
reporters calling after the story about finding the body broke."

Logan studies my phone but glances up at this. "From
what you've said, a lot has happened to that family. It would
make anyone defensive."

"I suppose so," I say and start gathering up our dishes.
"Still, I have plenty of other places to start first."

"Such as?" Logan asks.

"I need to find Maurice Beaumont."

Fourteen

S trangely Maurice Beaumont finds me.

It's Friday afternoon, and I'm looking forward to a full two days away from the lodge and the tourists demanding the wifi password. Aunt Janine and I have somehow gotten sucked into retirement party planning, a scheme I think my mother has concocted to keep me from investigating Sadie Beaumont's murder, and I find myself on Church Street in the village a little after five.

My mother has decided to not only have the traditional pig roast, but she wants kebobs for appetizers, and I stopped into Matt's Meats to confirm everything.

I'm on my way up Church Street to Main Street and the Cow Patty Parlor where my mother has placed an order for individual ice cream cakes. Something extravagant and absurd as she's planning on about a hundred guests. I'm about to stop in to see if they can recommend something better, like a sundae buffet, when I see Maurice Beaumont come up the steps from the Bellegrave Police Department, which is housed beneath the renovated Opera House.

I only know it's him because I've been studying the

website for the camp-turned-retreat he manages on Raquette Lake, trying to find an excuse to make my way there for an interview with him. He's thin, his cheeks concave, his already sharp features bordering on severe. His gray hair is thinning on top, and he wears it swept back from his forehead. He's wearing jeans and a work shirt rolled up at the sleeves. His expression would cow a Catholic school nun, but I decide to approach him.

"Mr. Beaumont?" I call out after him as he rounds the iron railing of the police department stairs.

He doesn't stop. He is fixated on the line of cars parked head in at an angle along the road.

"Mr. Beaumont? Can I speak to you a moment? It's about Sadie."

Now he stops. He not only stops, he swings around, and those sharp features are seething.

"Who are you? I'm not talking to any reporters." His voice is low with just the hint of a faded accent.

"I'm not a reporter," I assure him quickly. "My name is Dr. Della James. I'm the executive director of the Bellegrave Historical Society."

His eyes narrow. "What do you want?"

"Mr. Beaumont, I'm afraid there isn't a delicate way to say this, so I'm going to say it. I can see and communicate with the dead, and I spoke to your daughter."

He says something then too low for me to hear, but I'm fairly certain it's foul. He turns away, his attention once more focused on the parked cars.

"She showed me her bracelet. The one with the bee charm on it. It was important to her," I call after him.

He stops.

His thin body is like a tightly wound spring, and I watch him as he coils there on the sidewalk. I wonder if he'll turn back to me or go forward, likely to a car he's left parked along the street.

"What do you know about the bracelet?" He doesn't move forward or back. He speaks these words over his shoulder.

"It's a bee. Carved from wood. On a leather strap. She was wearing a yellow jumpsuit when she died and probably a white shirt."

When he turns this time, his movements are glacial.

"You've been speaking to that state police detective." He points at the stairwell leading down to the basement of the Opera House.

"Detective Hanratty?" I clarify.

The state police must be using the Bellegrave Police Department for their investigation.

"That's the one. You tell him you saw my daughter?"

I can see the defiance in his eyes. He wants to catch me in a lie, but there isn't one.

I raise my chin. "Yes. I'm cooperating fully with Detective Hanratty and the state police." I pause, draw a steadying breath, and take a step closer to him. He doesn't retreat. "This isn't my first investigation, Mr. Beaumont. Sometimes the dead tell me their secrets, so I can set right a wrong from their past. Your daughter wants me to help her."

Beaumont scoffs and looks away, but he doesn't retreat.

"What did she say? She tell you who killed her? I bet it was that rich snake from the Tomahawk Camp."

This must be the boy Sadie was dating at the time of her death. I want to ask Mr. Beaumont the kid's name, but he's striding toward me.

"I don't know what your game is." He spits the words with each step until he's nearly in my face. "But there's no money to gain from me. I had nothing then, and I have less now. If you think you can—"

"Sadie had a dog," I interrupt his rant. "A medium-sized dog. Black wearing a faded red collar. A stocky dog, probably a mix of pit bull and Lab."

Beaumont has gone completely still at my words, the hardness of his face vanishing as he stares at me.

"You know that dog, don't you?" I say, the words hardly a whisper.

He swallows. "How do you know about Atticus?"

The hardness has left his voice too.

"Atticus found me. He brought me to your daughter's body. He crossed over once he was certain we had found her."

He looks away again, but this time the noise he makes is one of pain. He turns his body just enough, and I think he's going to walk away again.

"He stopped eating when she didn't come home. I tried everything. Sweet potatoes. Carrots. Cooked him hamburger. That was his favorite. Picked up some scraps from the butcher. He wouldn't touch them." He stops speaking as his voice turns rough. He swallows, and when he looks down at the sidewalk, I swear I see unshed tears in his eyes. "One day he crawled under the porch and died. Vet said he probably died of a broken heart. I buried him under the oak tree behind the house where I'd hung a swing for Sadie when she was just a little girl." He looks up. "The state police didn't mention Atticus."

"I saw Atticus. He led me to her. And now I need to help her."

He shakes his head and drags his arm across his face. "There's nothing you can do. Her killer is probably long gone or—" He makes another scoffing noise and watches a truck pass on the street in front of us, its windows down, a few notes of a tinny guitar coming from within. "The bastard is protected by money and political red tape."

Again, I want to ask about this, but he stops me with a sudden look. "You said you saw her. Was she...is she..."

"She wasn't in pain. Not the physical kind. I think once we leave our bodies we don't feel pain like that anymore."

Pain is usually the first concern of the living. Pain is always a concern when one has a physical body, but that kind of pain is no longer a worry for the dead.

"Mr. Beaumont, I'm trying to understand Sadie's life at the time of her death. What is this about the boy at Tomahawk? I've heard him mentioned a few times."

He shakes his head, his expression righting itself. "That damn kid," he says, but I can't be sure of whom he speaks because next he says, "I told her not to get involved. She had no business doing what she did. I told her to stay out of it. But that wasn't her way. She was always stirring things up. I knew it would get her into trouble, and it did."

"Stir what up? What did Sadie get involved in that might have gotten her killed?"

When Sadie appears behind her father, it's so sudden I jump, falling back a step into the iron railing around the opening to the basement door of the police department.

Mr. Beaumont is talking, answering my question, with a hand gesture and a nod, but I can't hear him. There's a roaring in my ears like a television left on late in the night when broadcasting used to end. The static fills my ears until I think I can feel it, like static cascading down my arms. I want to brush it away, but somehow I know it's not real.

Sadie is talking, her mouth moving, her hands waving wildly at her father, but I can't hear any of it. I can't understand her. The static grows, and it's like I'm back in the lake, the motorboat speeding by me, the waves coming up over my head, the blackness creeping in at the sides of my vision.

Then Sadie is gone, and the world snaps back into place. I steady myself against the iron railing, and it's a few seconds before I realize I'm gripping it so tightly my hands have turned white.

"And that's it," Mr. Beaumont is saying when the roar fades from my ears. "That's what happened, and that's all I know about it. That's it. I can't help you anymore. Sadie was always her own person, and she was her own person in her death. I just didn't know who she was anymore. Not at the end. That's all."

I don't understand what he's saying, but I can't ask him to clarify. He's already turned, striding away until he stops at an older model truck and gets in on the driver's side. The engine rumbles to life, and he backs out of the spot, pulls down Church Street without sparing me a glance.

I look back at the sidewalk, but Sadie is gone.

I don't know how long I'm standing there. I can't feel my legs, but my heart feels like the bass drum of a marching band. I try to slow my breath, but I can't concentrate. I'm shaking too hard.

"Del?" There are footsteps on the stairs. I can hear the ring of the metal treads on the edge of each stair as someone climbs them. "Del? What the heck? What's wrong?"

It's Carmen. She's touching me, holding me, holding me up.

"I can't hear them," I say.

"Can't hear who? Della, are you all right? If you die on my watch, your mother is going to kill me."

Carmen's nails are the color of sunflowers, and they match the print of her wide-leg pants.

"Sadie was right there, and I couldn't hear her. She was trying to tell me something. Something about her dad. She looked so upset, and I couldn't hear her."

I try to remember Sadie's face. The way she looked at her dad, her features pinched, her manner agitated. What was she trying to tell me? Had her father something to do with her death?

"Honey, do you need a doctor? Should I call the boys at the firehouse?"

I shake my head. "No, I'm fine."

I mean it. The feeling has returned to my legs, and my heartbeat has slowed to a mere trot.

"I'm really fine. I'll be okay." I try to straighten from the railing and fall back against it.

"You are not fine," Carmen says, wrapping one arm around me. "C'mon. You need to sit down."

She leads me toward the police department stairs, and I lurch back.

"No." The word fires from my mouth, echoing off the bricks of the Opera House.

"No. Right. Sorry!" Carmen manages and turns me about, her arm even tighter around me as we slump back against the iron railing. "Sorry," she says again. "I forgot."

She looks around while I test my ears, prodding first one then the other, but they seem perfectly fine. I can hear the jangle of dog tags as a couple walks their French bulldogs down the sidewalk past us on the way to the lake. There's a shout of joy from the square at the top of the street as someone catches a frisbee.

But I couldn't hear her. I couldn't hear Sadie.

"Can you make it to Shelly's? We can get you something to eat. Maybe that will help."

"I don't think cheese fries are going to help me hear the dead."

Carmen steps in front of me. "What are you saying? You can't hear them anymore?"

Her eyes search my face, and I suddenly feel the scrutiny of cop Carmen and not friend Carmen.

"I can't." It's nearly a whisper. I'm too afraid to speak the words. I've spent my whole life seeing the dead, communicating with them, and to have it suddenly be gone is like I've lost a limb. "I heard Sadie on the island. I heard her perfectly. But now something's changed. I can't..."

I let my voice drift away as I remember Bellegrave Manor on the day I'd gone to see Ashley Carmichael. The static through the trees. The intermittent voices.

"I can't hear them anymore," I say more firmly now.

What I don't say is I can't hear them anymore since I glowed on the island.

"Maybe you need something sweeter. Like ice cream," Carmen says, her face a mask of worry.

I shake my head and say something I never thought I would again.

"No," I say. "I need Logan."

FIFTEEN

L ogan pushes the margarita closer to me.

"It's medicinal," he says, one side of his mouth lifting, and I know he's trying to get me to laugh or at the very least release my death grip on the chair.

We're sitting on the deck at Domingo's, the lake alive around us as Friday afternoon deepens into evening. The pontoon boats with their pleasure cruisers circulate the harbor as they pull out from the marina, headed for a spin about the lake, as the motorboats return with their loads of passengers, washed clean of sunscreen and filled with the happy tiredness of a day spent on the lake.

Domingo's is busy as it usually is at this hour, but we were able to get a table in the corner, far enough away from the happy hour crowd that is slowly turning over into the dinner crowd. Carmen had called Logan. I'd been unable to let go of the iron railing, the confusion of what just happened with the ghost of Sadie Beaumont causing a sudden onset of paralysis.

The police station isn't far from his offices off the square, and he'd been there within minutes. It wasn't until he took me in his arms that I deflated, the terror at not being able to hear Sadie, at the abrupt and nonsensical disappearance of my gift, flooding through me like the aftershock of an adrenaline rush. I'd trembled, shook, and let him hold me.

I heard Carmen tell him what she had managed to glean from me. She'd been on her way to pick up the girls from rec camp and had been about to call Raymond to have him pick them up, but I'd waved her off with reassurances I was fine. There was a minor squabble in which she insisted I talk to Father Patrick about my possible possession, but in the end, she went to pick up her girls and Logan walked me down the hill to Domingo's and medicinal margaritas.

He'd called Aunt Janine on the way, and she was going to meet us there after she was done picking out the centerpieces for the tables with my mother at Lorna Hiddles's house. Lorna was the president of the Bellegrave Gardening Society and had offered to create centerpieces from her own garden for my mother's party. My mother was over the moon about it. Aunt Janine felt more like a hostage, I was sure.

I glance over at my husband now. "Thank you for coming so quickly. I'm sure you were busy trying to get things done before the weekend."

His expression turns confused. "Della, you're my wife. You remember that, right?"

His words rankle, but I don't know how to explain that to him. We're married, but we haven't been together for a long time, and it's hard reconciling the two.

"I know," I say instead of any of what I'm actually thinking. "It's just—"

"You really are possessed," he interjects.

Now I do laugh. "I'm not possessed," I whisper and look around at the tables that surround us, but nobody is paying attention. "Aunt Janine never should have put that in everyone's head."

Logan shakes his head and picks up his beer. "The woman has had a lot of experience with this kind of thing. I'm tempted to trust her."

I think about the day on the island when the light seemed to spread out of me.

"I don't think she's right this time. I think this is something happening to me. Something's...changed."

I look around the deck, at the groups of people crowded around the tables, sometimes five or six at a time. The pitchers of margaritas and platters of nachos. I think about the normal workweeks they might have had.

"I bet none of those people have had to worry about being possessed," I mutter.

Logan glances over at the other diners. "I bet they've had other things to worry about."

"Don't be considerate right now. We're having a pity party for me," I admonish.

He turns back and folds his hands primly in his lap. "Sorry. I didn't know this was a pity party." He nods at my drink. "Do you need something stronger?"

"I need an explanation," I say. "Why all of a sudden? Why like this? What's happening to me?"

He leans forward, elbows on the table. "I want to say this as delicately as possible." He pauses, his eyes searching my face. "You're a woman of a certain age, Della. Do you think this might have something to do with normal hormonal changes in your body?"

I stare at him. "You think I'm menopausal? I don't have a uterus, Logan. That ship has sailed."

It is as though the air has been sucked out from between the two of us. He blinks, and then I blink. I've never joked about what happened that day. About the accident, about Audrey, about my forced hysterectomy. And yet, somehow it felt really good to say that just now.

I press both of my hands to my forehead. "What is happening to me?" I say again, but this time, real concern pitches my voice higher than I intend.

Logan reaches up and pulls my hands down, cradling them in his. "Just because you are without a uterus doesn't mean other things aren't happening. Your body will continue to change as you age. Before we start jumping to conclusions, we should talk to Janine. She might have gone through something similar, and she can guide you through this just like she always has."

I frown. "But what if she hasn't?"

He shakes his head. "This isn't like you, Del. What are you really scared of?"

I tug my hands free. "I'm not scared of anything."

"Usually, no. But I think right now you're genuinely frightened."

His eyes travel over my face again, and instead of facing his scrutiny I look away.

Just in time to see Detective Hanratty step out onto the deck, his hand at the small of the back of a tall woman in a stunning red dress, her blonde hair loose about her shoulders.

I don't know what I'm doing, but I reach out and smack my husband's shoulder, too stunned to talk.

"Look," I hiss.

Logan's already looking even though I try to smack him again, and he merely catches my hand, pinning it between his own as we both stare.

"Is that Hanratty?" he asks.

"Yes. Shhh," I hiss. "He'll hear you."

"There's a mariachi band playing next to an active marina. *I* can barely hear us," he returns.

I have my rebuttal ready when the woman turns to take the seat Hanratty has pulled out for her, and instead of a rebuttal, I swear.

"Holy monkeys." I blink, sure I'm seeing things.

"Is that Lisa?" Logan asks, his voice even lower now.

"It is," I say.

"Are they...on a date?"

"Maybe?" I remember that day in my office, Hanratty's unusual interest in Lisa, Lisa's own responding befuddlement. "Probably," I amend.

Hanratty takes the seat next to her and leans in as he does so, whispers something into her ear. She smiles, maybe blushes, and tucks a piece of hair behind her ear as he leans away, a smug smile on his face.

"Wow," Logan breathes.

Inside of me, something falters, remembering what it was like to be a on date. The way the feeling of expectation expands, the excitement that frizzles through the evening. When Logan was in law school and I was in grad school, we still made time for date nights even with our busy workloads. It was the one night a week when the weight of responsibility was lifted from my shoulders, and I could remember what it was like to be free again.

I see it now in the way Lisa smiles at Hanratty, at the way she keeps touching her hair, and the way he leans on one elbow, his gaze intense as he looks at her.

"Hey."

I jump when Logan touches my arm, and I swing my eyes to his face. He's watching me with an intensity I'm not used to, and I can't look away.

There's something there. Something tangible, and it's as though if I only reach out I might grasp it. This thing that has changed. The thing that is different. The reason why my ability is suddenly stifled.

But it's gone with the snap of a bark somewhere nearby, and I look away to find my dog careening across the deck to me.

Domingo's deck is dog friendly, and Henry is not the only canine on it at the moment. His leash dangles behind him as he scoots through tables in as direct a path as possible toward me. Aunt Janine trails behind, her flip-flops slapping the wooden boards of the deck as she waves at a table on the other side of the deck.

Henry falls at my feet, tongue lolling to one side.

"Did you have fun today with Grammy and Aunt Jan Jan?"

He lets his head fall back in ecstasy as I scratch his neck. When Aunt Janine reaches us, I look up.

"All right, Moon Pie. Spill it," she says as she takes a seat opposite us. "What's this about not being able to hear them?"

I go through it again. My encounter with Maurice Beaumont, Sadie appearing behind him, my inability to hear her, the roaring of static in my ears.

"It's not the first time," I admit when I've finished my story.

Aunt Janine raises her eyebrows over the rim of her smoked margarita the waiter brought her.

She sets down the drink without taking a sip. "When was the first time?"

I glance at Logan, who is pretending not to slip Henry a tortilla chip.

"Up at the old Bellegrave Manor." I explain about my visit to Ashley Carmichael and my unexpected stop at the manor on my way back into town.

I'd already filled Aunt Janine in on the identity of the girl in the barrel, but she sits back at my recounting of the story about the manor.

"You're sure the sound wasn't real? It was definitely supernatural?" she asks when I'm done.

I nod and finally take a sip of my margarita. I feel steadier, having Henry nestled against my legs and Logan sitting next to me, Aunt Janine picking through her plate of nachos for the good bits. Everything feels normal again, but I know something isn't quite the same. It's there again, just out of reach. But like a shadow, when I turn to it, it disappears.

I answer Aunt Janine. "I'm sure. It was like someone changed the channel on the TV. It just stopped. It wasn't natural."

Aunt Janine chews for a minute before pointing at me with a tortilla chip. "You noticing any other changes about your body? Physical changes, I mean."

Logan sits up and gives me a knowing look. I resolutely look away.

"Not that I can tell," I say with a shrug. "Just the usual aches and pains of being in my forties."

Aunt Janine shakes her head. "When I went menopausal, I kept hearing Elvis."

"Elvis?" Logan asks.

"The cat, not the singer," Aunt Janine clarifies. "Elvis was an orange tabby I had in college. Died when I moved out to San Francisco. I miss that little son of a bitch. He would bite me every time I tried to pet him, but if I left the room, he would wail." She gestures with another tortilla chip. "That's what I kept hearing when I went through the change." She says these last two words with exaggerated gravitas. "I was in Seattle by then. The damn cat must have left an echo on my stuff. That's the only explanation I could come up with." She gives a shrug and shoves the tortilla chip into her mouth. "But when my hormones started careening out of control, that mournful cat was the only thing I could hear."

"Do you think that's it? I'm hormonal?"

Aunt Janine shakes her head. "Menopause didn't make me glow, Moon Pie. There's something else going on with you."

"So what do I do?" I ask.

Aunt Janine leans her elbows on the table. "You're not left with much choice, Moon Pie. If you can't hear the dead, you're going to have to talk to the living."

Sixteen

By Monday morning, I've abandoned all pretense of sticking to the agreement I made with my mother. Hopefully Aunt Janine will keep her busy enough with party planning to allow me to investigate. And if I'm going to investigate properly, I'm not going to mess about any longer. I'm going right to Bellegrave's most valuable historical source.

The bell above the door at Shelly's Diner jingles softly as I enter. It's that slightly hushed time between the morning and lunch rushes where the counter is occupied by retired DPW workers, and the booths host the Silver Sneakers Walking Club after their morning rounds about the village, and occasionally, the village volunteers who man the information booths in the square during the summer as well as posts in the Opera House and the library.

One such volunteer is just about to take a bite of a carefully stacked pile of pancakes when I slip into the booth across from her.

"Dottie," I say.

Dottie Uttin eyes me through the triple-thick lenses of her

glasses. Her lip curls ever so slightly before she sets down her bite of pancakes uneaten.

"I knew you'd come find me when you got your head on straight," she says. Her fork clatters softly against her plate, and she reaches for her coffee mug. "Heard you found our poor girl, Sadie Beaumont."

"I did," I say.

Shelly herself stops at our booth and pours a cup of coffee for me without asking.

She gives a nod. "Elmer McQuiggan's been in here every day talking about the mass grave you found. The counter's even busier than normal. Can I get you a cinnamon roll? On the house," she says with a smile and a wink.

It seems my encounters with the dead might have an economic impact.

"Thanks," I reply, taking the cup of coffee. "I'd love one."

When she's gone, I gesture to Dottie with my cup of coffee. "So tell me what I need to know about Sadie."

Dottie Uttin is well on the other side of eighty, but like most good octogenarians, she doesn't let it slow her down.

"Sadie shoveled our driveway the winter Joe had his knee surgery," Dottie says. "She was a good girl. That's the only reason I'll tell you anything about her. You know I don't like gossiping."

Dottie is one of the best sources of village gossip, but as the product of a gentler time, she would never call it gossiping.

"Understood," I say.

Shelly delivers my cinnamon roll then. I thank her with a smile and tuck into it while Dottie tells me about Sadie Beaumont.

"Sadie Beaumont was a good girl. Her whole life. I don't care what her daddy might say about her. Maurice was a good father, but teenage girls and their dads are like oil and water. They just don't mix."

"I heard Sadie's mother died when she was young," I say between bites of cinnamon roll.

Dottie nods. "Sylvia. Nice woman. A bit quiet. The Beaumonts weren't locals, you know. They came from a house in Saratoga. One of those big ones. Horse money, you know? Maurice was caretaker there until the family sold it. He took the caretaking position out on the island when the Carmichaels bought the camp."

"Do you remember when that was?" I ask.

"Oh, sure," Dottie says, her fingernails tapping on her coffee cup. "It was a tuberculosis retreat at the beginning of last century. It wasn't used much after the war, and folks were happy to see it bought up and brought back to life."

It takes me a second to realize she's referring to the Second World War.

"Were the villagers excited to have a camp put in at the lake?" I question.

Bellegrave is a tight-knit community that relies on tourist dollars, but a summer camp can be a robust operation whose presence can ripple into a place. Sometimes not always in welcomed ways.

"Yes, ma'am," Dottie assures me. "I remember because I'd just had Marilyn in April, and they hired Joe's crew to dig the new well out there. They needed three of them to run the whole island. It was good for business, and we needed money for the baby." She shakes her head. "Marilyn was so fussy. Wouldn't take to my breast milk, and I had to resort to evaporated milk. How embarrassing. But I couldn't have done it without the money from the camp."

Marilyn is Dottie's oldest, and I try to picture it. Dottie as a young mother and new wife, happy to see her husband working so she can afford diapers.

Marilyn is now a human rights lawyer in New York.

"What were the Beaumonts like?" I try to steer the conversation back to Sadie.

Dottie looks up. "I suppose like any other family. They tended to keep to themselves, but Sylvia always said hi when I ran into her at the Super Duper, and you always saw them at Sunday services. That kind of thing. I think just living on the island kept them separate from everyone else by virtue of where they were." She shrugs and meets my gaze again. "I wouldn't say they were standoffish. Nothing like that."

There's a polite quiet to her words, and I know she's holding something back.

"But they did something that left you weary of them in the end," I say.

Dottie blinks, her eyelashes rubbing against her thick glasses. "I wouldn't say weary. Just surprised is all."

"What was it?"

She wraps both hands around her coffee mug now. "Well, this was after Sylvia had died, of course," she begins. "Maurice was on his own with Sadie, and we all thought that would be okay on account of Sadie being such a good girl."

"Who is we?" I interrupt.

Dottie blinks again. "Me and the other mothers." She licks her lips. "I'm sorry, dear. Mothers tend to congregate in a community. I forget sometimes that you're not—"

I hold up a hand. "No apology necessary. Do you remember who any of the other mothers were?"

There may be someone else I can interview to get their perspective on the relationship between Maurice and Sadie. She'd been trying to tell me something that day on Church Street, and I knew I'd let her down. There had to be another way of finding out what she was trying to tell me.

Dottie shakes her head. "Well Tabitha and Myrtle are in Rolling Fields now. Memory care unit. Gladys went after she fell and broke her hip in eighteen, and Eleanor lives in Fort Lauderdale with her daughter."

"Go on," I encourage when her expression turns crestfallen as though she'd somehow let me down by having elderly friends.

"Well, it wasn't until May of that year that any of us even knew Maurice was struggling with Sadie. We'd still see her about town, and she was in the grade between Marilyn and Joe Junior," Dottie says. "So I saw her a lot up at the school." She shrugs. "We all thought everything was fine until Maurice showed up at the Baptist church one Sunday."

"He wasn't Baptist?"

Dottie gives one solid shake of her head. "No, ma'am. They always attended the Methodist church. We just thought he'd walked into the wrong church."

The Baptist and Methodist churches sat on the same side of Main Street, separated by a courtyard.

"Why did he suddenly change churches?"

Dottie's eyebrows go up above her frames. "That's just what we wanted to know, and Gladys finally asked him. I remember it was Gladys because it was the summer she tried a perm." Dottie wrinkles her nose. "It wasn't a good look for her. Eleanor and I still talk about it." She taps the table by her plate. "So Gladys asks him why he's there, and he says Sadie was going through a tough time, and he wanted her to have more direction in her life. He thought Pastor Philips could help."

"Pastor Philips?" I picture the girl in the killer jumpsuit and wild big hair being forced into a pew to endure Pastor Philips's spittle.

Dottie nods gravely now. "Poor girl. She overheard her father, and that's when it happened."

"When what happened?" I've forgotten my cinnamon roll, so enraptured am I by Dottie's story.

"Sadie, poor, quiet, well-behaved Sadie started yelling at her father. Said he was the one who needed help. Said it was all his fault what was happening, and he wasn't going to stop her."

Dottie's choice of words has me dropping my fork on the table next to my plate. I can picture Sadie as she was on the island, appearing before me, but even more, I can feel her. Her rage, her anger, her frustration at being *stopped*.

"Why would Maurice try to stop her?" I ask.

Dottie's shake of her head is mournful. "We never heard. Maurice pushed Sadie into their truck and off they went. Sadie stayed mostly on the island that summer, and then...well...you know what happened to her."

"Chief Wise mentioned something about Sadie getting the junkyard shut down. Was Maurice upset she was getting involved in that?"

Dottie bites her lip, leaving tiny crescent moons of mauve lipstick on her front teeth. "No, that whole thing with Lionel was years earlier. Eighty-one or eighty-two, I think." She gives another decisive shake of her head. "No, Maurice was proud of her for stopping Lionel. We all were. Who knows what he was doing to our beautiful lake the way he was running things up there."

"Do you know where Lionel is now?"

"Oh no," Dottie breathes. "Last I heard he was growing marijuana in Colorado. Never saw him in Bellegrave after the government shut down his business."

I shift in my seat, feeling the avenues of questions closing off one by one.

"I've heard Sadie was dating someone that summer. Some boy that her father might not have approved of."

Dottie's snorts. "Ha! Hardly. Maurice didn't have the breathing room to complain about Jonathan Starkley. Nobody complained about the Starkleys."

Somewhere a chime goes off in my memory.

"Why does that name sound familiar?"

"Because he's a state senator now," Dottie replies.

I sit back. "Sadie Beaumont was dating State Senator Jonathan Starkley? The man who introduced the Healthier Lunches Bill and the single stream recycling program in public schools? The one who is supposedly launching his bid for governor?"

Dottie laughs. "That's the one. He was the same as a teenager, only skinnier. He was always doing for others, and of course, with the Starkley name behind him, he achieved a lot." Her expression sours. "Sadie deserved the same recognition, but she didn't have the family name carrying her through the way Jonathan did."

"So Jonathan wasn't a bad boy from the wrong side of the tracks, so to speak?" I ask.

Dottie scoffs. "Gad, no. But I could tell Maurice didn't like it. Thought Sadie was getting above herself. She was changing, he said."

I try to recall what Maurice said the day I'd confronted him. Was this what he had been talking about? Did he not want Sadie getting involved with someone with the clout of a Starkley?

"What do you think happened to Sadie?" I ask then.

Dottie goes quiet, contemplative, before she says, "I don't know." Her words are soft, and I know she's really thinking about it. "I don't know what happened to her. I think that's the worst of it. Sadie had always been a bright part of our community. She was always *seen*, you know?" She puts her hands in her lap, fiddles with her napkin there, before she meets my eyes again. "Whatever she got into, whatever it was that got her killed, it happened on that island. Because if it had happened in the village, the rest of us would have seen it."

I think of the island, the vast number of spirits, their relentless torment of the living.

"Thank you, Dottie," I say. "I'm sorry I've interrupted your breakfast."

She waves this off. "You know I'll do anything for one of your investigations." She eyes my plate. "Joe sure likes Shelly's cinnamon rolls."

I smile and stand, already pulling my wallet from my bag. "Any idea how I can get in touch with State Senator Starkley? I doubt he's easy to reach."

Dottie looks up at me. "I heard you were up to see Ashley Carmichael the other day. You can ask her to get in touch with him."

I tilt my head. "Would Ashley know him?"

"Oh, sure," Dottie says, adding more maple syrup to her stack of pancakes. "They started dating after Sadie died."

I pay for Dottie's breakfast and have Shelly package up two cinnamon rolls for Dottie to take home for Joe before heading out of the diner, knowing I'm going to have to talk to Ashley Carmichael again sooner than expected.

———

When I get back to my desk, the first thing I do is search Ashley Carmichael's name.

I can't say that Ashley has been hiding anything from me or lying because quite frankly, I haven't asked her anything. If truth were told, it was me who was lying with my story about an exhibit on the camp.

The first search return is an old social media profile on a professional networking site. It shows a much younger Ashley. Judging by the hairstyle, one made popular by a character in a television show at the end of the last century, I would say the photo was old when Ashley set up this profile. It lists her schooling and training as a chef under Chef Theroux and then a series of positions in restaurants in New York.

The list ends with a restaurant in Kingston called Carmichael's, and I wonder at how swiftly Ashley seems to have opened her own restaurant. I thought it took years for chefs to have their own place. I wonder how much family influence affected her progress.

I close out of the profile and go back to a search bar and type in Carmichael's and Kingston. This returns a series of newspaper articles. The first is a listing for the grand opening of a new contemporary restaurant in Kingston's up-and-coming Roundout Waterfront District. The restaurant is led by Chef Ashley Carmichael trained by the renowned Chef Theroux in Paris. I pause in my skimming, realizing I'm going to need to look up this Chef Theroux guy to see if he's everything Ashley makes him out to be.

The article goes on to list the varied and exquisite offerings Carmichael's will have, including outdoor seating and live music on the weekends. There's an accompanying photo of Ashley leaning against a bar in her chef's whites.

I go back to the search results. The next few articles are the usual newspaper fare, highlighting young entrepreneurs in the region, a gimmick used to sell papers. Ashley seems to have hit every one. *Hudson Valley's Hot 40*, which seems to highlight successful individuals under forty. *Kingston's Newsmakers*, the *Catskills Capitalists*, and even *Who to Watch on the Hudson*. Ashley was by all accounts successful in her career.

I think of the woman in the house on the hill, her chipped nail polish and over-bright personality, so far from the young woman in the chef's whites that accompanies every article.

I click back to the search results and scroll farther down until I find what I'm looking for.

Restaurant to Close Following Near Death of Chef's Father.

I click through. This time the photo is of Ashley in front

of her restaurant dressed all in black as she locks what appears to be the door of the establishment with a properly aggrieved expression on her face. The article goes into detail about her father's accident and Ashley's decision to close her restaurant to focus on her father and his care. The conclusion of the article asks for privacy for the family.

I sit back and study the article. By all accounts, Ashley is the good daughter she appears to be. She made a name for herself in the culinary world and from what I can tell achieved a measure of success. But when circumstances changed, she made the ultimate selfless decision to care for her family.

Chief Wise had mentioned something similar about Ashley's mother's death. How Ashley continued to go to the camp and see to things when her father stepped back. It seemed Ashley was always left to pick up the pieces.

I began to reassess my idea of her, focusing instead on her obvious enthusiasm for her gumbo recipe, her cutoff shorts, her bouncy ponytail, and her joy at recalling her days at the family camp.

Maybe like the rest of us, she was trying to find her way somewhere between tragedy and hope.

I close my laptop and go in search of coffee.

I'm waylaid by Steve who needs to have a repair approved for the boathouse. I sign it quickly, but when I get back to my office with my coffee, Frances snatches me for a problem in the library.

My coffee is cold and forgotten on the table in my office by the time I return for lunch. The lodge is a little quieter now as the board meeting for a local architectural firm taking place in the conference area has adjourned to the grounds for a picnic lunch. Even though, I close my office door before making my way around my desk.

I wish I had gotten Ashley's cell phone number the day I saw her, but I'd been too startled by my discovery of Sadie

Beaumont in the camp's photo albums and had left without thinking.

I use my desk phone and dial the home phone number I'd found before and as before a clipped voice answers.

"Carmichael residence."

I wonder briefly if this is the nurse I saw with the big gold earrings, but the voice is drier than the one I heard the nurse use that day.

"This is Dr. Della James calling. I met with Ashley last week, but our meeting was interrupted. I'm calling to see if I can set up a new time with her to go over the potential for an exhibit on the camp at the historical society."

There's the briefest of pauses, one that wasn't there when I'd called the week before, and I take note of it.

The voice comes back. "One moment please."

I listen to the silence on the other end of the phone, my mind skipping from name to name.

Ashley Carmichael.

Jonathan Starkley.

Sadie Beaumont.

Lionel Melrose.

Maurice Beaumont.

Monica Davies.

How do they all connect?

Does Jonathan Starkley have anything to do with this at all? Or am I wasting time with the state senator? Monica Davies has a record. Could she also be a murderer?

There are too many rumors circulating about Sadie getting involved with a troublesome boy around the time she disappeared, but somehow Jonathan Starkley doesn't fit that image. The man rides a bicycle for two with his eleven-year-old son in all of his television promos, smiling with his toothy grin as he promotes his upcoming state tour before he launches his gubernatorial campaign.

Was there someone else Sadie had gotten involved with?

Is it not Starkley at all?

My thoughts have gone full circle when there's a click on the phone.

"Della?" Ashley's voice is dull.

"Ashley," I say, smiling as I do so, so she can hear it in my voice. "How are you?"

I want to ask if we can reschedule our meeting, but the strain in her voice has me slowing.

"Yeah, you know. About the same as always." She doesn't offer much, and I wonder at the change from the woman who greeted me at the door last week.

"I can imagine," I say. "I was hoping we could set up another time to talk. I was really getting into those photo albums you showed me. I think there's real potential there for an exhibit." I stop, but only a weighty silence fills the line. "An exhibit about the camp. And your mom." I add the last part as the silence grows.

I can hear Ashley draw a breath. I think she's going to respond, but then there's a rustle, as though she's moved her lips away from the phone. I press the receiver closer to my ear. There's whispering, two voices, one distinctly male. Her father? For some reason, I had thought his accident bad enough that he was now unable to communicate. Perhaps not. The person who answered the phone was female along with the nurse I saw. Who else could be in the house?

For moment, I wonder if it's Detective Hanratty or Perez, and I feel a pinch of guilt going against Hanratty's demand that I stay out of the investigation.

The whispering stops, and Ashley comes back to the phone.

"Yeah, I'm sorry. Now is not a good time. Dad's not doing well, and I really need to focus on him. Maybe another time." She says goodbye before I can respond, and the line goes dead.

Something has changed from the week before. She's closed herself off to my inquiries. Maybe Hanratty has gotten to her or the press. Elmer McQuiggan's tales at the diner are enough to get the town talking, and I wonder if she's overwhelmed by it all.

But then who was that other voice I heard?

I open my laptop and pull up a search engine to type in Jonathan Starkley's name, but I'm interrupted by a knock on my door.

"Come in," I call.

Frances pokes her head in. "Arnold Fairchild is here."

My fingers freeze on my keyboard. "Here?" I hiss. "Like in the building?"

Frances's expression could freeze the sun. "I put him in the library."

I close my laptop on Jonathan Starkley. "All right. Let's go."

SEVENTEEN

I've barely gotten my bathing suit on for my swim the next morning when my phone lights up with a text.

I glance over at Logan and Henry still asleep on the bed, snatch up my phone, and switch it to silent before opening it to the text. It's Phoebe, Allie's wife. It appears Allie has been hit with extremely bad food poisoning, and Phoebe had to take her into Saranac and the medical clinic there. She's on an IV because of dehydration, and they're keeping her for the foreseeable future.

Allie is scheduled to lead a three-day immersive course at the lodge on Adirondack camp life starting that morning.

I type Phoebe back, letting her know I've got it, and Allie needn't worry.

She texts back to assure me worrying is the only thing distracting Allie from the gas station sushi that caused this whole thing.

I stare at my phone, thinking about gas station sushi, before shaking my head and putting my phone away. I shed the bathing suit and head for the shower.

I get to the lodge a little before seven, Henry in tow.

Frances opens the door for me. "I take it something's happened," she says, taking Henry's leash from me without asking.

Henry goggles at her, tongue hanging out the side of his mouth.

I explain about Allie.

"You set up the conference space. I'll get the course materials," Frances says, and she and Henry disappear in the direction of the offices.

My dad shows up just before eight to collect Henry, and the next I look up it's Sunday morning, and I'm at the waterfront park setting up my mom's retirement party.

With running the Adirondack camp life program and trying to keep Allie from coming back into work until she could hold down solid food, running errands for my mom, and managing my regular job, I'd had little time for anything else. I felt a niggling sense of guilt that I was letting the investigation wallow, but I knew after today, life would resume some more normal pace, and I could continue following the leads I'd left untouched.

My phone call with Ashley still haunts me, and so I jump when Carmen touches my elbow, my mind elsewhere.

"Whoa," she says, stepping back with both hands raised. "It's just me. The living."

I set down the recycled napkins I'd been fanning out by the biodegradable plasticware and frown at my best friend.

"I'm sorry," I say with a shake of my head. "I haven't been a good friend. I've barely—"

Carmen shakes one finger at me.

"Nah uh," she says. "No apology. You got some weird stuff going on, and you needn't report to me." She settles a hip against the table and crosses her arms. "But spill. What's going on with you, and have you seen Sean Connery? With or without hair. Doesn't matter."

I smile, feeling my thoughts clear. "No Mr. Connery. Sorry. But I'll keep looking."

Carmen swears under her breath. "I can't catch a break."

"I can't hear the ghosts." I speak the words quickly, suddenly feeling like I don't want them touching my lips.

Carmen stills. "You can't hear them? Like at all?"

I lean back against the table next to her and peer out across the park down to the water. My mother is directing Logan and Raymond in setting up more folding tables even though a fleet of them have already been deployed. My dad is bent over the pig roast with Matt from Matt's Meats. He's had the roaster set up since yesterday morning, manning the pig overnight in shifts with his brother who helps out with the roasts. Aunt Janine is getting Henry's input on the centerpieces.

"I don't think so. I've only had a couple of encounters since it started, but both times the voices are blocked out by what sounds like static."

"Static? Like white noise?" Carmen asks.

I nod. "Something like that."

"Is that what happened that day outside the station?" Her words are careful, and I hate that she feels the need to be cautious.

I meet her gaze. "Yep. Sadie was there. She was trying to tell me something, and I couldn't hear her. She looked really upset." I shake my head. "Not like she was that night on the island. It was a different kind of agitated energy she was sending to me, but I couldn't hear her."

"You sure she was trying to say something?"

I picture Sadie that day, her lips moving on words I couldn't hear, the agitation rolling off of her.

"I'm sure," I reply.

"What are you going to do?"

I glance away and back. "You sure you want to hear?

Detective Hanratty asked me to stay out of the investigation. I don't want to implicate you."

Carmen straightens and glances in the direction of our husbands trying to figure out how to extend the legs of the folding table while my mother gestures unhelpfully.

"Hanratty and Perez have taken over my conference room for their investigation and keep stealing the good donuts before I get in." She turns her attention back to me. "You can tell me anything. Maybe I hear it. Maybe I don't."

I grin and tell her about my conversations with Ashley Carmichael, Chief Wise, and Dottie Uttin, relaying every detail of the investigation I have so far.

When I finish, she draws a steady breath.

"You really telling me you're going to look into a state senator?" she asks.

I shrug and go back to arranging the napkins before my mother sees me standing there.

"I'm not afraid to question him, but from the little I've seen of him on TV and the way Dottie talked about him, I don't know how he could be involved. He seems a little…"

"Like he needs a hot dog bun because he's a little weenie?" Carmen offers.

"Something like that," I say.

"I can't say I picture State Senator Starkley killing a teenage girl. How did he do it? With his electric motorcycle?"

I turn to her. "He drives an electric motorcycle?"

Carmen's eyebrows go up. "You didn't see that? He drove one to the Egg as part of a publicity stunt for electric vehicles. Said they could still be cool. I wonder if he'll drive it when he comes up here in two weeks for his campaign stop."

"A motorcycle?" I ask again.

"He was wearing plaid pants when he did it."

"No," I breathe.

"As sure as I'm standing here."

I frown at the plasticware, wondering if we need more. "I just can't picture a guy like that doing anything to harm someone."

"But you're right," Carmen says, reaching under the table to pull out the boxes of compostable paper plates. "Maybe he knows something about what happened that summer." She pulls a stack of plates out, and we begin arranging them on the table. "What about Ashley Carmichael? You going to try her again?"

"I have to," I say, taking a stack of plates from Carmen. "She's the best person to ask about what really happened that summer."

"Good luck trying to get her to talk," Carmen says. "I've always heard she tends to keep her own company."

"She does?" I try to imagine the woman I'd met that day shutting herself off from the world.

Carmen gives a one-shouldered shrug. "That's at least my impression. She doesn't come into the village often, and you don't see her at any functions."

"That's true," I say. "But Bellegrave does tend to keep to its own. Ashley's an outsider."

"Since the 1960s?" Carmen asks.

"Bellegrave has a long memory."

Our conversation dead-ends with the arrival of my mother and Aunt Janine with the first of the aluminum pans of potato and macaroni salad from Thelma's.

The guests start to arrive shortly after noon. Domingo's taco bar is immediately overrun, and he has to refill twice before the pig comes off the spit. By three the park is at capacity, and the band kicks off its first set. Aunt Janine, Dad, Logan, Carmen, Raymond, and I try to manage behind the scenes so Mom can enjoy her guests.

While she had attempted to invite the whole town, it feels more like the entire county has shown up to celebrate the career of Maxine Hopewell. It was nice to see old friends who had moved away and made the trip back to see Mom. Joan and Joyce made it in from San Diego. Father Patrick is being plied with snow cones by Catholic moms hoping for blessings for their children. I even spot Lisa with Detective Hanratty as they slip through the crowd in the direction of the bandstand.

I'm not able to follow them and tactfully interrogate Lisa on what the heck is going on between her and the detective before there's a shout from behind me.

"Yoohoo!"

Even now, probably ten years since Poppy Mayfield moved to Boca Raton with her dermatologist husband, I still recognize her greeting without having to lay eyes on her. I turn from tossing recycling into the correct bins, and there she is.

Poppy Mayfield is tall, slender, and manicured in all the places that matter. Her hair never deviates from a warm blonde, and she always wears fitted white button-downs with a popped collar and long knit pants in bright colors that usually match her sandals. She finishes it off with all the jewelry her husband bought her over the years.

Close behind Poppy is Maeve.

Maeve Robbins is short to Poppy's tall, round to Poppy's slender, and her hair resembles a ball of steel wool. She has a robust way of walking, and she marches alongside Poppy in her orthopedic sandals, her elastic capris showcasing her very white shins.

"Delia Ann!" Maeve calls when I make eye contact.

I smile. "Hi, guys," I say, genuinely pleased to see them.

While Poppy married straight out of high school and has a couple of children, Maeve remained unmarried and childfree. From what I've gathered, it's by choice. She became a flight attendant when they were still called stewardesses and spent thirty years flying out of Albany three days a week before retiring and building her knitfluencer empire.

Maeve was an inspiration to me while Poppy's just-older-than-me-to-be-annoying children were a nuisance. Still, they knew Mom before she was Mom, and like any child, I enjoyed hearing how my mom was really human after all.

Poppy leans down as she tends to when speaking to people. I always figured it was because she's so tall, and the evidence of how it has rounded her shoulders can be seen under her tailored shirt.

"Your mother tells us you're investigating Sadie Beaumont's murder," Poppy says without preamble.

Poppy has a large jaw, and it's always made her smile a little mischievous as it does now.

"I leave the investigating to the police, Mrs. Mayfield," I say.

"Oh, stocking stitch," Maeve says. "Give us the details. Did you see her? Did you see Sadie?"

I blame reality TV for how people talk about the dead. It makes it seem glamorous or at least scandalous, and I think that's what makes people talk about the dead with such carelessness.

"Yes, I saw Sadie," I say. "She was screaming in agony."

My words dampen their eager expressions, but Poppy straightens, crossing her arms over her starched shirt.

"I'm not surprised," she says, giving the side eye to Maeve.

"How's that?" I ask, watching the exchange of glances.

Maeve shakes her head. "That place always was trouble." She says this with a little salute and takes a swig from her energy drink.

"Trouble?" I look between the two of them. "I haven't heard anything about trouble at the camp."

Poppy scoffs. "Please. That place was a viper's nest. All those posh kids getting sent there for the summer." She shakes her head slowly. "What did they think was going to happen? Especially after Miriam died."

"What are you talking about?"

This image of the camp contradicts everything I've heard so far, both from Ashley Carmichael and Chief Wise and even Lisa. I picture the advertisement I found in my initial search, the photo of the girls on the docks, all sunshine and peppy collars.

"That place was bad news," Maeve says. "Sometimes the girls would come into the village to use the payphone. This is when the Wine and Dine on Water Street was Abbots Pharmacy. They had a phone booth in there." She flinches. "The things you would hear the girls say when they called their parents begging to go home."

"What did they say?" I look to Poppy who is nodding along with Maeve.

"The usual teenage stuff, but because it was girls, it was probably a thousand times worse," Poppy says.

"A thousand times," Maeve agrees. "Girls are the worst, especially to each other."

"There was apparently a ritual hazing," Poppy says. "It wasn't called that then. I think they called it a rite of passage or something. It was all pretty mild until Miriam died. I think she kept those girls reined in a bit."

"Hazing? At summer camp?" I ask.

"Oh, sure. I think every summer camp used to have a little bit of it. That's how you assimilated to the group, you know? But not that camp. Bad stuff was going on there," Poppy says again.

"Sometimes the girls would have bruises. They tried to hide them by popping their collars and wearing those white sweaters draped over their shoulders to cover their arms. But you could still see them. Chief Wise couldn't do anything about it. The camp had their own medical staff, and every time one of the villagers brought it up he just said his hands were tied. Nobody had reported any crime."

"There was a crime all right," Poppy says with a pointed finger. "Those boys from Tomahawk would come over and things...well..." She licks her lips. "There were rumors, you know," she finishes.

"Rumors?" This is not at all the idyllic scene everyone else had painted of Camp Carmichael.

"A couple girls got pregnant. Not by choice, if you know what I mean," Maeve says.

"They were raped?" I ask bluntly.

Poppy and Maeve both shift uncomfortably.

"Now you would call it rape," Poppy says. "Back then a girl was accused of not being careful."

"This is awful," I say. "Why didn't Chief Wise ever do anything?"

"No girl was going to report it," Maeve says with a snort. "No one would believe her." She gestures to the water and the island somewhere beyond. "All of those kids had money. Money makes things disappear real quick."

I follow the direction of Maeve's hand and think about all the spirits on the island, the unusual number of them and the power of their agitation.

"Those girls went to summer camp and were tortured, even so much as being raped, and no adult did anything about it?"

Poppy nods. "No one touched Camp Carmichael. Do you know the kind of money the Carmichaels had?"

"It was a different time then," Maeve adds. "There was a lot of girls will be girls, boys will be boys thinking." She bares her teeth. "Disgusting."

"My mom has never mentioned this."

Poppy snorts. "Of course, she wouldn't. Your mom was in Plattsburgh at college when things got really bad. We were still here in Bellegrave. I don't think she was ever in the gossip mill like we were."

Maeve gestures with her can of energy drink. "Besides the camp shut down in eighty-four after Sadie drowned. Then everyone seemed to forget what happened there."

I look between the two of them. "So all these girls spent their summers being tortured? And they kept coming back? I thought the camp was successful."

"Oh, it was," Poppy says. "The camp was hugely popular when Miriam ran it. I think that's what kept the girls coming back. But she died in seventy-nine. That first summer without her was rocky, I think. Don Carmichael kept showing up in the village, having to sort things out." She looks to Maeve. "I don't think it was ever mentioned what was going on, but by the next summer, things seemed to be back to usual."

"Except for the hazing," I remind her.

"Except for that," she agrees. "All those summers lost for those poor girls. What a terrible thing."

"Did you two know Miriam?"

"Of course, we did," Poppy says. "She was an icon around here. Wearing all those fancy clothes she got in New York."

"I never saw the woman in anything but a heel," Maeve adds. "She's the one who inspired me to be a stewardess. I thought a woman who can do anything in heels is invincible."

"I can't imagine how that family dealt with her death. She was such a force, you know?" Poppy says.

We're interrupted when my husband slips up beside me.

"Hi, ladies," he says to Poppy and Maeve with a nod. "I'm sorry to butt in here, but the face painter is asking where she should set up."

I stare at him. "My mother hired a face painter?"

He grimaces. "It would appear so."

"Would you excuse me?" I say to my mom's childhood best friends and follow Logan.

Impossibly, the crowd seems to grow. The band keeps

playing, there's a line for the face painter almost immediately, and a corn hole tournament sprouts up beside the taco bar.

There's so much buzz and chaos I hoped to forget about Sheila Wise's warnings of the Buck Moon, but still, I can't shake the feeling of being watched. I catch myself looking behind me more than once and scold myself. I can still see the dead. I'm just having a little trouble hearing them.

It's dusk when Aunt Janine appears beside me.

"Hold on to your hat," she mutters. "I hear your mother is doing fireworks."

I blink at her over the fifth pan of potato salad I've swapped out that afternoon. "Fireworks?"

"Should start any minute," she mutters.

I look around frantically.

"Logan took Henry back to the cottage a little while ago. I warned him early."

I give her a look of relief. "Thank you."

Her eyes narrow. "You okay, Moon Pie? You've been a little jumpy today."

"Just a lot going on," I try to assure her.

I take the empty potato salad pan in the direction of the rubbish bins but only make it a few steps when the first firework cracks through the sky. I jump, dropping the pan into the grass. Aunt Janine picks it up before I can reach it.

"Geez, Moon Pie. It's like you've seen a ghost."

I force a smile. "No ghost," I say over the crack of another firework.

The darkening sky lights with a starburst of golds and reds and blues, and the party crowd suddenly stills, seeming to drift as one toward the front of the park and the water's edge where the fireworks erupt over the lake.

But I don't see any more fireworks because Sadie Beaumont has appeared not five feet in front of me, her face contorted, her chest bright with red blood.

"Aunt Janine," I say softly.

She's watching the fireworks like everyone else, and slowly her head drifts down. I know the moment she sees Sadie. The potato pan jolts against us, we're standing so close.

"Moon Pie," she whispers.

The roaring is so loud, so sudden, I flinch. The explosion of fireworks like a breeze in the far-off distance. Sadie is talking. Her mouth is moving. Her expression is anguished.

"What is she saying?" I manage.

Aunt Janine has a hold of my arm now, the potato salad pan forgotten in her other hand.

"She's saying—" She stops, her voice rough. She tries again. "She's saying she's coming. Save her."

"Who's coming?" I don't know how loud my voice is.

The roaring of static in my ears grows. The fireworks explode in the sky overhead.

"Who is coming?" I try again.

I think of what Poppy and Maeve have just revealed to me, about the level of evil suffered at the camp all those summers.

Aunt Janine is so still beside me. "I don't know. She just says she's coming."

Sadie Beaumont disappears as quickly as she arrived, taking the roar of static with her like a vacuum. It's in that sudden silence, between the explosions of fireworks, the muted ringing in the absence of noise, that the shout comes from behind me.

"Boo!"

Instead of jumping and slightly peeing myself like a normal forty-something-year-old woman, I spin, fist already coming up.

And I punch my little brother right in the face.

Eighteen

Ryan makes a noise he once made in grade school when we decided to see if a pop bottle would really shatter if you hit someone over the head with it.

We learned two things that day. The bottle did not shatter, and Ryan can make some really weird noises.

"Ryan?" Aunt Janine says at the same time I grab my fist, pain radiating up every single digit through my wrist into my elbow.

"Cheese and crust, Ryan!" I yell back at him. "Do you really think it's a good idea to sneak up on people who see the dead?"

Ryan holds his nose when he eventually straightens, and even in the dim light, I see the blood coating his fingers.

"Do you make a habit of punching ghosts, Del? Because that doesn't make sense," he whines into the palm of his hand.

"Ryan? Ryan?" My mother's voice is high-pitched with worry as she scurries onto the scene. "Ryan, what are you doing here?" She reaches for him but stops to turn a glare on me. "Delia Ann, what did you do?"

"He started it," I cry childishly, my finger pointing at him accusingly, which I immediately regret as the pain spirals up my joints.

Dad comes to me and pulls me toward the barrels of ice and soda cans. He stuffs my hand into them, and the relief is almost immediate.

"Nice swing, slugger," he says. "You even kept your thumb out."

"I don't know what that means," I say.

He shrugs. "Let's pretend you do. It's more impressive."

"Ryan, you're supposed to be recording in Nashville this weekend," Mom says, gingerly moving him to one of the picnic tables and forcing him to sit.

Aunt Janine has somehow acquired a wet rag and peels Ryan's hands from his nose.

"Head back," she says as she eases the rag onto his nose. "Pinch."

He obeys, tilting his head back.

"We finished early." His voice is nasally. "I thought I would surprise you."

"Well, it's a wonderful surprise, dear, but really, we all know better than to sneak up on your sister." My mom's expression is very mom-like, a little disappointed, a little not surprised.

"When did you learn to throw a punch like that?" Ryan asks.

"About a minute ago," I return.

"Huh." He tries a laugh, but it's half gurgle, half nasal. "Never knew you had it in you. Could have used that in high school to fend off the bullies."

"You were never bullied, golden child," I reply.

He thinks about this for a second. "Nah, I wasn't."

Ryan and his golden boy good looks would fit right in in the hills of Hollywood but instead he chose a recording studio in Nashville and New York.

He gestures to Aunt Janine.

"AJ," he coos. "Didn't know you would be here. I would have changed my recording schedule."

He tries to gyrate his eyebrows over his pinched nose, but the effect isn't quite right, and it just looks like he has something in his eye.

Aunt Janine gives him a look I think might have originated in a bar in SoHo in 1973.

"You're batting up, sugar," she says and switches out the bloody rag for a new one.

Ryan turns his attention to Mom. "Happy retirement, Mom. I hope your party was everything you wanted it to be."

Mom turns her attention to me. "I knew this was going to happen."

I gesture with the hand that isn't submerged in ice. "He's not dead."

"He might have permanent brain damage," Mom protests.

I frown. "You mean more permanent brain damage," I mutter after Mom looks away.

Ryan sticks his tongue out at me. I stick mine out in return.

"Kids," Dad says, but he's not successful at keeping the laugh out of his voice.

Mom kneels in front of Ryan. "Sweetheart, I'm so glad you came tonight. I'm sorry your sister is the way she is. We're all trying to cope. Do you want to get your face painted? Would that make you feel better?"

Ryan looks sideways at her as he's trying to keep his head back. "Can I have a pony ride afterward?"

"I'll see what I can do," Mom says and stands, brushing the grass from her knees as she does.

"I think I'm going to call it a night," I say.

I pluck my hand from the ice, and the throbbing returns almost immediately.

"So soon?" Mom says. "Ryan just got here."

"Logan took Henry home a while ago because of the fireworks. I want to check on them."

Mom's face blanks. "Oh no, the fireworks. I forgot."

"Maxine, what have you done to our grandson?" Now Dad's voice is properly scolding.

Mom presses a hand to her neck. "Oh, Greg, how am I supposed to remember everything?" She turns her attention to me. "Will you please let us know if he's okay?"

"Of course, I will," I say.

I press a kiss to her cheek. "Happy retirement, Mom. Aunt Janine will stay here and keep the ghouls away."

Aunt Janine snorts. "No promises."

We exchange a glance, the latest encounter with the ghost of Sadie Beaumont still crawling along my skin.

I give my goodbyes and punch Ryan on the shoulder as I leave. I roll down the windows in my SUV and turn up the music, hoping to shake the feeling of unease that crept over me as I watched Sadie Beaumont, her lips moving without sound, the static pulsating in my ears.

The cottage is quiet when I get home, and I go straight for the half bath tucked under the stairs where Henry prefers to hide during loud noises, but I find it empty.

"Up here."

I look up to the ceiling where Logan's voice has emanated and stare, confused. I shake myself loose of my confusion and head for the stairs, but I only make it halfway up, my hand tightening to stone along the handrail.

The door across the landing from our bedroom is open.

I stare at the crack between the door and the door jamb, a soft light spilling through it. My stomach turns, and for one moment, I think of not going any farther.

"You don't need to come in here," Logan says as if sensing my thoughts, and it's just enough to have me moving again.

I reach the door and push it open before I can change my mind.

The crib is the first thing I see. Aunt Janine got it for us as soon as she heard the news. It's a light oak, the hue of which is only just discernible against the white curtains that drape behind it. I'd forgotten the lovely pale green of the walls, the plush carpet I'd found to cover the hardwood. I'd been too eager to turn this room into the nursery and had started fixing it up before we knew if it was a boy or girl. Green had seemed the perfect color.

I don't know how long I stand there, my eyes drifting around the room. The changing table we never unpacked and assembled, still in its box in the corner. The small shelf of books my mom had brought over and set up with copies of *The Hungry Caterpillar* and *How Do Dinosaurs Say Good Night?* The empty crib, the blanket my mom had been crocheting for our baby girl long forgotten somewhere, unfinished.

It's a second before I realize what I'm seeing. A pair of legs and a brown tail emerge from beneath the crib.

Slowly, I ease to the floor, my palms sinking into the plush carpet as I lower myself all the way down.

Henry and Logan are under the crib. Henry has managed to get all the way under, nearly to the back wall. He lounges happily and gives his tail a series of happy thumps when he sees me but doesn't bother to get up. His ears are flat against his head, his face relaxed. He looks nothing like a dog who just survived a fireworks show.

Logan looks less comfortable, crammed halfway under, his head pillowed on one bent elbow, a tablet propped up in front of him, the glow of its screen illuminating the strange tableau.

"Hello," Logan says as though it's every day I find him under our dead daughter's crib with the dog. "How were the fireworks?"

I blink. "Fine. Ryan showed up."

Logan raises both eyebrows. "Really? I thought he was recording this weekend."

"He said he finished early." I nod. "What's happening here?"

"I don't know," Logan says, his voice low. "When the fireworks started, I thought he'd go for the bathroom like he usually does. But he—"

He stops so abruptly, I look at him. He licks his lips.

"He looked up the stairs like someone was calling him," Logan finishes. "He went up the stairs, so I followed him. I thought maybe he was going to try to hide under our bed, but he stopped on the landing and pawed at the door to this room."

I look back at Henry who has rested his head against his paws, his lip already vibrating with his snores.

"He pawed at the door until I let him in. He went straight for the crib as if he knew it was here," Logan says.

"He's never been in this room." My voice is as quiet as Logan's.

"I know."

I meet my husband's eyes again. I'm not sure what passes between us, but it's heavy with sorrow and lost hope. It was only too late that I realized Logan lost his daughter that day too. For so long, I'd been alone in my grief, thinking no one could possibly understand what I was feeling, no one could possibly have *felt* what I was feeling.

But Logan had been there, right beside me, feeling the same things, and he was the one person I'd pushed away the most.

I regretted that now, and it was this that had me reaching beneath the crib, clutching my husband's hand in mine. Our gazes remain on each other, the heaviness lifting, before I move my eyes to our dog, peacefully asleep.

"Do you think he can sense her?" Logan asks after a while. "Like not her ghost. That other stuff you talk about. The way we leave an impression behind. Can he feel she was here?"

I watch our dog sleep for several seconds because I don't know the answer. Audrey died in my womb. She never got to live in the outside world, not even for a moment. There was nowhere for her to have left an imprint.

Eventually, I say, "I don't know."

But I don't move. I don't get up and walk away. I hold my husband's hand and lie there beneath a crib that's never been used.

Nineteen

Ryan shows up at my office the next morning with a box from Cake & Cookie.

He knocks on my door. Loudly.

"Hi, sis!" he says with false cheer, his smile accentuating the growing bruises on either side of his nose.

I had left my hand in ice for an hour before falling asleep the night before, so I don't feel a lot of guilt about his nose.

I lean back in my chair. "Your recording session didn't end early. AJ called you."

It had taken me a while to piece everything together. Ryan had always been Aunt Janine's, or AJ as he liked to call her, favorite, and after our conversation at Domingo's that night, I was almost certain now, she had called Ryan.

Ryan, the good little brother that he was, had come home to save his big sister.

Ryan's smile fades. "Maybe," he says, looking left and right. He shrugs and enters my office. "Either way I have sugar, and I've come to say hello to my sister and let her know I'll be in town for the week. Maybe two."

I snap my laptop closed just to have something to do.

"Ryan, that's entirely unnecessary. You don't need to upend your life for me."

His expression is serious, and it unsettles me. I'm not sure I've ever seen golden child Ryan serious in the whole of his life.

"AJ says you can't hear them anymore." His voice is as serious as his face.

I eye the Cake & Cookie box. A part of me wants to hold my own and stay mad at him for doing caring things like leaving behind his very busy professional life to swoop into the backcountry of the Adirondacks to save his big sister. The other part of me really likes cookies.

He sees the direction of my gaze and pulls open the lid of the box as he sets it on my desk.

Four black and white cookies stare back at me.

"You don't play fair," I mumble and take a cookie.

I've just poured myself a fresh cup of coffee and for a moment I let myself sink into the bliss that is sugar and caffeine. Ryan pulls a double fudge brownie from the box and plops into one of the chairs in front of my desk.

"So you can't hear the dead people anymore, but you can see them. AJ said some things have been changing for you." His voice wobbles a little at the end, and I think he already knows what's changed for me.

"You mean the part where I thought Logan was having an affair and I finally told him why I've been mad at him for thirteen years or the part where I shot a revered member of the Bellegrave community in the foot because she was trying to kill me."

Ryan pauses in the act of breaking the brownie in half. "You've been mad at Logan for thirteen years?" His face shows his utter bafflement.

"I sometimes forget you don't live here anymore."

He leans forward in earnest now. "For real, Moon Pie, you were mad at him? Is this about the accident?"

I wave off his concern with my cookie. "Yes, but we talked about it and have reached a different place in our relationship. That's not why AJ summoned you here." I set my cookie down on a napkin from Shelly's that's lingering on my desk. "There's this ghost."

"Sadie Beaumont," Ryan says, nonplussed.

I blink. "AJ told you or you've been making the rounds this morning." I sit back and cross my arms over my chest, fixing an aggrieved expression on my face. "I'm not your first visit this morning, am I?" I sit forward abruptly, elbows on my desk, eyes narrowed. I tap the Cake & Cookie box with one finger. "How many of these boxes do you have?"

He slows in his chewing. "Four," he says around a mouthful of brownie. He chews, swallows. "Two now."

"You went to see Logan." I sit up with a dramatic gasp. "You brought him lemon danish."

"And chocolate dipped Madeleines." Ryan's smile is quite pleased.

"You're diabolical." I shake my head slowly. "So you know about Sadie Beaumont then?"

Ryan nods. "Yeah, so you think she's the reason you can't hear ghosts?"

I think about that afternoon on the hill outside the abandoned manor. The static in my ears, the wavering voices through the trees.

"I think it's all ghosts, and I don't think it's because of her. She doesn't want to stop me. She asked for my help."

"Is that all she said?" Ryan's tone has that knowing quality to it again.

"You did talk to Logan."

Ryan looks around theatrically. "I don't see Henry. Didn't Logan tell you to take him with you?"

While we were under the crib last night, I told Logan about Sadie's visit, her warning that she was coming, whoever she is. He'd asked me to keep Henry with me during the day.

"He's in Frances's office," I reply.

He snorts. "Some guard dog."

"I don't need protecting. I can handle this myself."

"So that's why your husband has asked you to take your dog with you everywhere and why Aunt Janine is living at the B&B, and she called me for reinforcements."

I wrinkle my nose. "You're not reinforcements. You can't even see the dead people."

"No, but I can see the living. And if this is a live person who is coming for you, then I'd better be here."

"And do what? Adjust their audio levels?"

"Ha ha," he mutters, brushing the last of the brownie crumbs from his fingers. "I just want you to know I'm here. Maybe this time you won't have to shoot someone in the foot." He stands. "I'm staying at the Hopewell Mansion. Mom asked me to clean out my room. She wants to turn it into a pottery room?" He says this with a tilt of his head.

"Ah, yeah," I say. "Dad wouldn't let her take over the shed."

He grimaces. "I don't know how Dad is going to get through this."

"He'll find a way. If anyone can manage Mom, it's him."

Ryan plucks another brownie from the box before turning to the door.

"I don't know," he says over his shoulder. "People change. Retirement is going to be an adjustment for Mom."

He turns back to me, and I smile reassuringly.

"Mom can handle change. She's pretty resilient." I frown. "I just hope she realizes that."

"I guess we'll see," he says. "Later, sis." He salutes me with his brownie and slips out the door.

I open my laptop again and return to the emails that have

piled up in my inbox over the weekend. The end of the month looms, and there's an email from Diana saying we're slightly off our donation targets for the month, but she's hoping the free concert Lisa has planned for the coming weekend will help spur one-time donations. I make a note to meet with her about giving goals and her strategy for targets through the end of the year before I'm pulled away from my desk because of a problem with the wifi in the conference space yet again.

The end of July and early August before school resumes are our busiest weeks. I'll be working at least one day a weekend from now until Labor Day, and Sadie Beaumont and her fierce expression press me with guilt. I try to remind myself that my day job comes first and then investigations into the dead, but it's difficult to remain focused when I'm struggling with my own problems.

Namely my sudden inability to hear the dead. At least I haven't glowed again, I suppose.

It's Wednesday before I know it.

Ryan was a pleasant, if entirely unhelpful, addition to our trivia team the night before at Domingo's. It was heartwarming to watch him catch up with friends and villagers he hadn't seen in a while as his demanding job keeps him in the city. So although he hadn't contributed much to the actual game, it was a much-needed break from everything.

It didn't mean my thoughts slowed down. My last phone call with Ashley Carmichael still haunted me. Who was the male voice I'd heard in the background? Was it her father? Or was it someone else?

A quiet part of me wondered if it could be Maurice Beaumont. After hearing the news of his daughter's murder had he confronted the last of the Carmichael family? Or did he know something about his own daughter's murder? Was there more to the fight Dottie Uttin had heard that day outside the Baptist church?

How did Jonathan Starkley fit into all of this, and how was I going to reach him? Was there any chance I could speak to him when he made his campaign stop in Bellegrave?

And finally, who was the woman who was supposedly coming? How was I supposed to save her?

These were the thoughts that bounced around my head while trying to run Lady Josephine Lodge and why on that sticky Wednesday afternoon I found myself in the shadowy recesses of the lodge's back porch, the lake breeze teasing me with its cool caress, my lunch from Shelly's open on my lap in its biodegradable container while Allie grilled Lisa on her love life.

"Spill it," Allie says. "I want to know every sordid detail."

Lisa makes a noise of embarrassment as she pushes coleslaw around her to-go container. "I don't kiss and tell," she says.

"You do now," Allie says.

She's having a yogurt parfait she's brought from home as she's still a little gun-shy from the gas station sushi, a situation she refuses to explain.

Lisa shrugs and pushes off from the porch with one foot, setting her rocking chair to rocking.

"I don't know what there is to say. We've only been on a couple of dates." She pokes at the container with her fork undecidedly. "He's...nice."

"Nice?" I nearly squawk. "He's a good Midwestern boy if I ever saw one. He has a stable job he seems to be good at, he's intelligent, and he has an unholy way of being kind."

I prod my fries for a particularly greasy one so it's a second before I realize they're both staring at me.

"What?" I say around a French fry.

"Are *you* dating him?" Allie asks.

I frown. "No. I've just unfortunately had reasons to run into him." I pause. "A lot."

Lisa's lips thin before she says, "Still Sadie Beaumont?"

Despite their desire to have me tell them everything about the investigation, I don't. I need to remember it's an active police investigation, and I don't want to jeopardize a court conviction.

So I just smile. "Maybe." I gesture with a fry. "Have you told him about..."

I still don't know how to delicately bring up the fact that Lisa's mother is a murderer, but Allie seems to have no such compunction.

"That your mom killed a beloved schoolteacher?" Allie says.

Lisa nods almost enthusiastically. "Of course. I told him straightaway. With Mom awaiting trial, Dad's health the way it is, and everything I bring to the table, I wanted to be as honest as possible before things went anywhere."

Allie's mouth doesn't quite close as she stares at Lisa. "How did you tell him? Like how did it come up?"

Lisa shrugs. "I just told him. Flat out." She swipes her hand in front of her. "As soon as he asked if I'd like to have dinner, I dumped everything on him."

"And?" I'm as transfixed as I was when she told me about the summer Sadie Beaumont disappeared.

"He told me he watched his mother get murdered. They never caught the killer."

She says this so plainly I don't process it straightaway. Allie nearly dumps her parfait onto the porch, only catching it at the last second.

"He what?" Allie blurts.

Lisa nods gravely. "Watched his mother get murdered. They never caught the killer. Daniel had to go live with a great-aunt in Batavia. That's how he ended up in the New York State police."

My heart hammers in my chest, and I try to slow my breathing, sure they can see it, wonder at my reaction.

"She was murdered?" Allie blinks, holding her parfait in both hands until her knuckles pale, and I'm worried she's going to crush the cup it's in.

"Yeah, he was too young to understand what was happening, and he never saw the face of the person who did it. He's since requested the case file from the Manhattan police. Gone over the evidence. Talked to the detectives involved. It all suggests a random act of violence apparently, but Daniel doesn't believe it. He remembers his mom being worried the days before she was killed." She glances toward the lake as a speedboat zips by. "Remember how you could feel it as a kid? When your parents' energy was off?"

I nod. "My mom's first attempt at wallpaper. There's nothing scarier than a mom whose DIY project goes badly."

Lisa nods. "Or your mom kills your favorite teacher."

"Or that," I admit.

———

I'm not surprised when I find everyone on our patio when I get home that evening.

Henry makes a beeline for Dad who has just enough time to crouch to catch the catapult of brown fur. If I overheard correctly, my mother is trying to convince Aunt Janine to let her bedazzle her jean jacket, and Ryan and Logan are doing something down on the dock that looks like bro stuff. I squint, trying to see what they're doing, but Aunt Janine spots me then.

"Moon Pie, good. You're here. We need to talk."

I drop my bag down on an empty chair at the table and raise an eyebrow.

"I'm trying to convince your mother to go on my next trip with me," Aunt Janine goes on.

Mom is sitting slightly behind her, and as soon as Aunt Janine starts talking, her eyes go wide in alarm.

"It's a walking tour of Cork. She would love it. It's just a wee thing. Only ten miles a day. You'd hardly notice. Help me convince her."

Mom's eyes are about to fall out of her face, and she moves her chin just a little left and right.

"Mom's allergic," I say.

Mom closes her eyes, her expression one of abject disappointment.

Aunt Janine taps a fingernail on the arm of her chair. "To what?"

"All of that," I say and turn to Dad. "I'm guessing you brought something for the grill."

Dad's smile lifts his glasses until they hit his eyebrows. "It's in the fridge."

"I'm just going to change, and I'll start dinner."

"Allergic to what?" Aunt Janine calls after me as I go into the house.

I find the package of steaks from Matt's Meats in the fridge and take them out to come to room temperature before I head upstairs to find cutoffs and a tank top. I stop on the landing, my eyes going to the door across the way. It's slightly open.

I touch it before I realize I'm going to and wonder if Logan forgot to close it but no. It was closed that morning when I went out for my swim. The door shivers against my touch, swaying just enough so I see the scalloped curve of my grandmother's rocking chair, the first thing my mom brought over when she heard I was pregnant.

I think about my conversation earlier that day with Lisa and Allie. I think about Daniel Hanratty.

I shove the door open and step inside.

My feet sink into the pale green carpet. The drapes are pulled across the double window on the opposite side, but light still leaks through at the cracks. It casts the room in a surreal glow. I can make out shapes and edges and muted colors, but it's like a room in a dream, not quite real even though it feels real.

I want to say her name, but I can't. Suddenly I'm afraid. Afraid of the warmth that spread through me that day on the island, the light that erupted around me, the feeling that it's coming from inside of me.

Audrey.

I don't speak her name and yet it still skitters across my mind.

I step back into the hall and close the door, pushing against it to ensure it's shut.

My flip-flops smack against the wooden stair treads as I make my way back down to the kitchen. I unwrap the steaks and arrange them on a platter to prep. The screen door to the patio is open, and I can hear what sounds like protestations from my mother. I finish the steak prep, grab a beer, and head out to the patio.

My dad has already started the grill, but he's halfway down the lawn toward the lake where he's watching Ryan try to get my mother on a swim platform. A swim platform that wasn't there earlier.

I eye Aunt Janine. "Did they just make that swim platform?"

Aunt Janine holds up both hands, the bangles on one arm clinking as she does so. "I had nothing to do with it."

"Was it Ryan's idea?"

"Yes."

"It's going to sink."

I arrange the steaks on the grill before returning to the

table with Aunt Janine. I take one of the empty chairs and a long swig of my beer before I get right into it.

"I think I'm being haunted by my dead baby."

Aunt Janine slowly turns her head. "Come again."

"You remember Lisa Reynolds? I shot her mother, Marty."

Aunt Janine nods.

"She's started dating our Detective Hanratty."

Aunt Janine coos, her eyebrows lifting. "Well, good for her. He's a sweetheart."

"Lisa told me today he witnessed his mother's murder."

Aunt Janine's eyebrows fall, and her mouth opens on a silent *Oh*.

I wait for her to connect the dots. When she does, she sits up and wraps both hands around her mason jar of iced chardonnay.

"You think that's why he has that haunted aura about him," she says.

"And how he knew those kids were coming around that corner." I watch Ryan catch my mother before she topples off the swim platform but only just barely. "I think his dead mother is someone still connected to him."

"But neither of us has seen her with him. I mean, in some sort of manifestation."

I shake my head. "I don't think it's like that. You know how some objects contain the energy of their owners or an event that once happened to them? Do you think the same thing can happen to humans?"

Aunt Janine fiddles with the straw in her chardonnay as she considers this.

"I don't think it's impossible. Humans contain mass just like anything. It would stand to reason an echo could imprint on one."

This time Ryan doesn't catch my mother, and she topples

into the lake with a hearty screech. Henry thinks she's playing, and with a happy bark, plunges into the water after her while Logan tosses an inner tube in her direction. Dad trots down the hill as though concerned, but I can hear his laughter from here.

"Do you think Audrey was the reason you glowed on the island? Was she somehow protecting you?" Aunt Janine asks.

My mother has gotten hold of the float, her stream of admonishments toward Ryan unbroken even as lake water pours off her head.

"I think so," I say. "But it's more than that."

I explain about the night I came home to find Henry under her crib, about the open door just now, and the day I felt her presence in the kitchen, the presence that was coming from inside of me.

Aunt Janine doesn't speak for a while. She sips her chardonnay, and we both watch my mother emerge from the lake, water streaming off her white capris and billowy tunic top that's now plastered to her body. She marches directly over to her son and shoves him off the dock into the water.

Henry gives another happy bark from where he's returned to the dock, his own trail of water marking the boards before once again he dives into the water after Uncle Ryan. Logan has retrieved a towel for my mother, which she takes before shoving him off the dock too. She's too weak to actually make him move, but he falls dramatically backward, earning a laugh from my mother and a happy bark from Henry.

"Audrey isn't here, right? I've never felt her. She's passed over."

I nod slowly. "I felt her go. Even when I was unconscious, I felt her leave me. It was...oddly peaceful."

Aunt Janine has gone still, and when I look over I see her eyes are glassy with tears.

"Then why is her energy coming through now? After all this time?"

Ryan pulls himself up on the dock then. He has a golden tan even though he spends so much time in a recording studio, and somehow that's just like him. He throws back his head to get the hair out of his eyes and goes straight for my mother.

"None of them have their phones on them right?" I say.

Aunt Janine follows my gaze. "I hope not."

I look back at Aunt Janine. "I think it's because I finally told Logan how I feel about what he did."

"You mean saving your life?"

Aunt Janine's retort is a familiar one, one I ignored for too long.

"Yes, that. I spent too long thinking I was the only one who lost Audrey. I'm sharing my grief with someone else for the first time, and I think it's...changed something." I shake my head, the words not making sense to me even as I speak them. "Something's different. I can feel it in here." I touch my chest. "And here." I touch my head. I meet Aunt Janine's eyes directly. "I think that's why I can't hear them anymore."

"Audrey's blocking them?"

"No, it's not that. It feels like somewhere there's a clog inside of me. I opened a floodgate without checking downstream, and now all the energy inside of me is stopped up against something. Something I can't seem to move."

"What are you going to do?"

"I don't know."

I get up to turn the steaks. Henry appears at my side as soon as I lift the lid on the grill. When I've finished, I bend and scratch the spot under his neck that sends his back leg wild.

"Soon, buddy," I say. "I promise."

Mollified, he trots back down the hill to my dad who is still somehow mercifully dry.

I go back to my chair, take another long pull of my beer.

"Are you sure you aren't the clog?" Aunt Janine asks.

"Me?"

Her expression is thoughtful. "Are you sure you aren't holding Audrey back? Maybe she's here for a reason. Maybe she left behind just enough of herself to give you strength. Strength you're going to need."

"How is that even possible?" I ask.

Aunt Janine laughs. "How is any of this possible?"

She has a point. A good one.

"So you're saying I need to get out of my own way?"

"Maybe," she says with a shrug.

She gets up and sheds her jean jacket, placing her cell phone carefully on the table.

"If you'll excuse me, my nephew seems a little too dry."

I watch her stroll innocently down the hill. She's too focused on my dad and doesn't see Ryan come up behind her. She's in the water before her scream leaves her mouth, and I smile.

TWENTY

After a week of nothing, Logan finally agrees to let me leave Henry home.

As much as he enjoys the lodge, home is far better. It has a couch, peanut butter, and the possibility of Grandpa showing up to spring him from the joint. This is far superior to any treats or pets from people at the lodge.

While I miss having him around, I am far more productive than I had been, and things are coming together for the board meeting next month. Without Mom's retirement party to distract me, Sadie Beaumont takes center stage in my thoughts while I go over email campaigns and attendance reports.

I'd seen Hanratty around the village, but luckily, he hadn't been looking for me. I was hoping to keep it that way for a while. It wasn't that I wouldn't cooperate with the police should I discover anything useful. It was more I was still caught up in what Aunt Janine said. About Hanratty's mother, about me, about my daughter.

It was safer to think about the dead for now.

While Victoria Gustafson had led me to her killer, Sadie's energy seemed to be pushing in the other direction. She wanted me to save them. Maybe in saving them I would find her killer, but it wasn't the primary feeling I was getting from her. Sadie wasn't looking for justice. Sadie wanted me to finish what she had been unable to.

It's late when my phone pings, the lodge quiet around me. It's a picture of a sad Henry sitting on the patio and a caption from Logan.

World's saddest dog misses Mommy.

I'm surprised to see it's after six. The grounds close at five on Mondays, and most of the staff have left nearly an hour ago. I text back that I'm leaving now and toss my phone into my bag. I gather my things, turning off lights and checking windows and doors as I make my way to the front of the lodge.

It's when I'm in the conference space that I see it through the diamond pane windows overlooking the lake.

The door to the boathouse is open. It swings gently in the evening breeze, and I watch it for a few seconds, letting my senses open.

But there's nothing there. All is quiet around me and—thankfully—in me. Someone has probably forgotten to lock the door after them.

I toss my bag into my car before I make my way around the lodge and down the hill to the boathouse. It's only when I've inserted my key into the door's deadbolt that I hear the crunch of footsteps behind me.

I spin, stupidly letting go of my keys still in the lock. They're my only weapon, and now I'm without them, my bag useless in the car in the parking lot at the top of the hill.

I'm not sure why fear isn't the first thing I feel when I see the woman standing there, a long knife fixed between her hands. A knife she has pointed at me. Instead, I'm annoyed. This isn't the first time someone has threatened me with a knife, and it's getting old.

The sun has drifted far enough west most of the light is blocked by the trees that surround the boathouse, but there's just enough for me to make out the woman's features. Her long, greasy dark hair is pulled back in a ponytail that accentuates her gaunt features and the streak of white down her center part. Her dark eyes are lifeless. Her lips thinned and pale. Her clothes are worn but clean. There are scabs along her forearms where her sleeves have ridden up, angry red lines that look self-inflicted.

"Della James?" The woman's voice shakes, but again, I don't sense fear.

It's something else. Something with more intent, more edge.

"I'm at a disadvantage," I say. "You know my name, and I don't know yours."

She blinks, and the knife wobbles in her grip. She shifts uncertainly, and for a second, her face dips into the dying sunlight.

I recognize her, and that recognition slices through me, a healthy, clean fear finally drifting up. Fear because the reason I know this woman is because I've seen her mugshot.

She looks around, her eyes skating left and right. I've made her unsure of herself, and I wonder if she's really intent on hurting me at all.

"You're Monica Davies, aren't you?" I say.

This brings her eyes back to me. The fear in them is obvious now. The knife wobbles just a little bit more.

"How do you know that?" She licks her chapped lips, and her eyes dart back and forth.

"I've seen a photo of you. A couple photos actually. You went to Camp Carmichael as a teen, didn't you?"

Her eyes are back on me again, but they've widened, the fear palpable now.

"Don't talk about the camp." Her voice has dropped, strained.

"Why not?" I press.

The knife has sunk, but I don't think she realizes that. It's pointed somewhere around my stomach now instead of my throat, but it still wobbles ever so much.

She moves her head slowly back and forth. "Don't ever talk about what happened at camp."

I still, my arms relaxing at my sides. She sounds like a child. A terrified child.

"Why?" I press again. "Do you not want anyone to know what happened to Sadie Beaumont?"

I know I've made a mistake before I finish speaking Sadie's name. Monica lunges, the knife arcing toward me. I fall back on instinct, but Monica is already there. My back connects with the boathouse, my head bouncing painfully against the wooden shingles.

She's in my face now, so close I can't see the knife without lowering my chin, and I'm afraid if I do that I'll stab myself.

The fear is gone from her eyes when she says, "Don't you dare talk about Sadie." Spit flies from her mouth, and I feel it land on my cheeks in moist flecks. "Don't ever talk about Sadie. I tried—" Her voice is lost on a hiccup of air, her lips opening and closing against silence.

She shifts, and suddenly there's a sharp coldness against my neck. I slow my breathing, willing my muscles to relax.

Monica regains her voice. "I tried to warn her. She was pushing too hard. She was going—" Again her voice is lost in a gulp of air. "She always wanted to change things." These last words are spoken with agitation, and the knife moves against my neck.

Monica doesn't know she's doing it. Her eyes are trained on my face, the muscles of her jaw taut. I'm the only thing she sees, not the knife.

Will I feel it when the knife slices through my neck? Will it hurt?

"She always wanted to change things," Monica repeats, softly this time. "I warned her. I warned her not to do it. I warned her she would—"

Tears appear in her eyes, flood them, streak down her cheeks. The knife falters against my neck as Monica looks down. I try to ease to the side, out from under the weapon. The metal skitters against the metal buttons of my jacket before I can feel it no longer. I know it's there though. Monica stands too close to me, and I daren't move any farther. She stands there, tears falling silently down her cheeks as she shakes with a feeling the depths of which I will never understand.

"What about Debbie Fraser?" I ask, hoping to draw her attention back to me.

It works. Her eyes snap to mine, and although they are wet with tears, a new emotion is there.

Anger.

"Debbie is dead," she spits.

The knife suddenly appears in my vision, and I shrink back. Monica holds the knife awkwardly at my face.

"Debbie couldn't take it," she breathes. "Debbie couldn't handle what happened."

Something changes then. It flashes across her eyes, and she lurches. I'm already moving, dodging to the side as the knife clatters uselessly against the boathouse wall. She hasn't dropped it though. It hangs, waiting, in her fingers.

"You could be dead too if you keep asking questions." Her voice is rough with anger. "You need to stop asking questions."

Again she lurches, and I realize now she's not doing it out of aggression. Her body is twitching uncontrollably, and instead of moving with ease, her body lurches and pulsates.

"Sadie asked questions and look what happened to her," she says quietly.

I let silence fall then as Monica's eyes drift to the ground. She sways, and the light fades around her. Her voice and emotions are a roller coaster, and I can't imagine how much it must drain her.

"What about Ashley Carmichael?"

Her head lifts slowly, and I know I'll be treated to yet another emotion. I'm not disappointed when I see her lip curl, her expression turn feral.

"Ashley Carmichael is a nobody." She scoffs and looks around as though Ashley might be there. "She got sent home for not having the right knife."

She says this last part under her breath, and I can't stop myself from looking at the knife she still holds.

Did Monica Davies stab Sadie Beaumont to death? Is that why she's chosen to threaten me with it now?

I want to ask her. I want to push her just that much further, but I fear it may be too much. I have no way of calling for help if she does decide to truly hurt me, and I know I wouldn't make it back up the hill. I'm not strong enough.

But I need to know, so I ask.

"Did you kill Sadie Beaumont?"

The words hang in the air, and I know I've lit a fuse.

But Monica's expression goes curiously blank. She's as still and lifeless as the lake on a calm day.

So when she lunges, I'm not ready. I have no time to react.

She screams. Both of her hands swing up, the knife flashing as she barrels toward me.

Just as suddenly as she starts she stops.

She isn't looking at me. She's looking behind me, through the still open door of the boathouse.

The first thing to happen is the knife slips from her

fingers. It rings sharply against the concrete of the walkway. The next is her eyes grow slowly, painfully.

This time her scream is not one of rage.

It's one of absolute terror.

She turns so quickly she trips, falling hard against the concrete. I wince in pain and reach for her, the need to render aid instinctual. But she's already gained her feet and is running clumsily up the hill, her screams never-ending as she disappears into the fading light.

I turn, fully expecting to find Sadie Beaumont in the doorway of the boathouse.

But it's not Sadie.

It's a man.

I have only a second to take him in before he vanishes.

———

"Dr. James, can you please confirm if this is the woman who threatened you?"

I sit on one of the benches scattered along the hillside between the lodge and the lake. My eyes are fixed on the door of the boathouse, my keys still dangling from the lock.

Night has fallen completely now, and the darkness pulses with the lights of emergency vehicles at the top of the hill. Red and blue paint the night sky like a morbid fireworks show, and Detective Daniel Hanratty of the New York State Police holds his phone in my face, the image of Monica Davies's mugshot on the screen.

I balk at the word *threaten* and say, "That is the woman with whom I had a conversation this evening, yes."

Detective Hanratty raises both eyebrows instead of saying anything.

"Monica Davies," Detective Perez recites from his place on the other side of me. "She's got a record longer than a basset hound, but it's all petty stuff. Drug possession mostly." He looks up from his phone. "Nothing violent."

I look between the detectives.

"I told you," I repeat. "I don't think she meant to hurt me. I think she was just trying to warn me."

"To stay out of an investigation I already told you to stay out of?" Hanratty asks.

I frown. "I was staying out of it, Detective."

"And that's how you recognized a grown-up Monica Davies. By staying out of it."

I know he's caught me, so I smile.

"She looks just like she did when she was eighteen."

"Uh huh." Hanratty is not amused.

"Detective."

Carmen's voice stops our conversation, and I glance up the hill to find my husband running full tilt in my direction, my best friend behind him.

I have just enough time to stand before he reaches me, yanking me into his arms. When he cups my face in his hands and kisses me, it's not as unexpected or awkward as the last time he kissed me.

"Are you okay?" His eyes zoom across my face as though he can take in all of me in one glance.

I cover his hands with my own. "I'm fine. I was never really in danger."

His eyes don't stop their search even at my reassurance.

Carmen has reached us then, and she addresses Hanratty. "Detective, Dr. James is a Bellegrave resident, and this assault happened in our jurisdiction."

Hanratty doesn't flinch at Carmen's direct tone. "The suspect in this incident is of particular interest to us in regard to the Beaumont investigation."

Carmen swings her gaze to me, her second-grade-teacher face firmly in place.

I once more have that sensation of having neglected my best friend.

"I didn't seek her out." Logan still holds my face, and my words come out mushed.

He lets go, but the motion only draws his attention to my neck.

"Della." My name sounds like ice on his lips.

"I'm okay," I try to reassure him yet again.

"Why is your neck wrapped in gauze?"

Instead of waiting for my answer, his eyes flick to Detective Hanratty as if this is his fault.

"The suspect had a knife," Hanratty says unhelpfully.

I raise both of my hands to stop the barrage I know is coming from my husband and from my best friend.

"I'm fine. She didn't intend to hurt me. She..." I picture Monica's face, the roller coaster of emotions that passed through her. "I think she was trying to warn me."

Again Logan addresses Hanratty. "What does this suspect have to do with the case?"

"I'm afraid I can't tell you that, Mr. James. It's part of an ongoing investigation," Hanratty says.

"I'll tell you later," I say.

Hanratty glares.

I touch Logan's arm. "I'm tired, and I'd like to go home." I turn my attention to Hanratty. "Are you almost done here? I need to secure the grounds."

I'm not sure how long it's been since the emergency crews arrived, but surely it's been long enough to have gathered whatever evidence they might want. I've been checked by paramedics but refused to go to the hospital. Monica's knife left a few dings in my neck is all. I'll be fine after a nightcap of ibuprofen and peanut butter cup ice cream.

Hanratty checks in with Perez.

"Team's almost done here," Perez confirms. He flicks his thumb over his shoulder. "What's in the boathouse?"

I frown. "What do you mean?"

Perez taps the notebook he's been holding in his hand with one finger. "Ever since we got here you keep looking at the boathouse. Someone in there?"

Hanratty looks fully toward the boathouse now before turning a suspicious expression on me.

I hadn't told them about the man in the doorway. I just said Monica finished what she came to say and left in a hurry, dropping her knife in the process.

"It's nothing," I say.

"You saw a ghost," Carmen says, her tone as direct as the one she used on Hanratty.

It's my turn to glare.

"Who was it?" I'm not surprised when Hanratty asks this.

"I don't know," I answer honestly. "I'm not even sure Monica saw him, but something spooked her when she looked at the boathouse, and that's when she ran." I shrug. "I don't know who the man is. All the time I've worked here no one has tried to contact me in there."

This was the truth. Weird things happened in the boathouse for sure, but no spirits had tried communication.

Hanratty studies me like he doesn't believe me.

"Is it someone connected to Sadie Beaumont's death?" Logan asks.

I shake my head, my gaze caught by the still open door of the boathouse. "No," I say softly. "I got the sense that he was..." I swallow. "That he was protecting me."

Hanratty's face has gone blank when I turn my attention back to him.

A small woman in one of those Tyvek suits approaches.

"We're all set here, Detective," she says.

Hanratty nods. "Thanks, Dom." He gives me a weak smile. "You're free to lock up."

"We'll process the evidence, and if we have any further questions for you, Dr. James, we'll be in touch," Perez says rather formally.

Carmen gestures to the hill. "Mind if I see you out, Detective?"

I can't imagine how difficult it is to have someone stepping into your play pool without your permission, and I admire Carmen for her ability to share what I'm sure she feels is her responsibility.

Carmen's a transplant from New York, but she's taken to Bellegrave like a duck to water, and her desire to see justice done for its citizens is strong.

I don't envy Hanratty for the questioning he's about to endure. He not only has to deal with a good detective. He also has to deal with my best friend.

She gives me a small wave and follows Hanratty up the hill.

I find Logan watching the boathouse.

"Jealous of my ghost lover?"

My attempt at a joke breaks his stoic expression, and he almost laughs.

"No," he replies. "Just know I'm taking Henry."

My jaw drops in mock surprise. "How dare you."

He shrugs, his expression nonplussed. "I know a good lawyer."

"They'd never give you custody."

"Henry would choose me," he insists.

"No, he wouldn't."

Logan takes my hand, and it feels suddenly like a first date. I've forgotten how his hand is big enough to cup mine, his palm calloused and warm.

"He would if I stuffed my pockets full of peanut butter." He draws me close to him. "You sure you're okay?"

I nod. "Nothing a little self-pity won't cure."

He glances at the boathouse and then back at me. "What are you going to do now?"

"Ashley Carmichael is stonewalling me, and I don't want to push her in case I close off that avenue entirely. Maurice Beaumont is in Raquette Lake, and I could go question him again except I didn't hear what he said the first time he talked to me because the spirit of his dead daughter put static in my ears, so I'm avoiding that interview out of embarrassment, and I still haven't figured out how to get in touch with our dear state senator." I glance back at the boathouse. "That only leaves me with one person."

A person whose name has kept popping up since this whole damn thing started.

TWENTY-ONE

I find Elmer McQuiggan at the boat launch early the following morning.

Once again I'd had to forgo my morning swim because I woke up unable to move my neck. The dark impressions I found along my chest and collar were not welcome either, but compared to the white gauze bandage still plastered along my neck, they were at least easier to hide. As it was, I had to dig out an old, collared dress I think I last wore to a conference in grad school.

"You look like you teach Sunday school."

I stop, my cork sandals scuffing along the pavement of the launch, and eye my little brother.

"No, she doesn't," Aunt Janine comes to my defense, but then she gives me the once-over. "I'd say someone high up in a multi-level marketing scheme who wants to talk to you about your kitchen knives."

I touch the gauze on my neck and give a shocked expression.

"What?" Aunt Janine says. "Too soon?"

After the incident the previous night, Henry has been

replaced with Ryan as my security and Aunt Janine as my
connection with the dead. I was against this, but as it often is
when it comes to my safety, it's not my choice.

"Baptist or Methodist?" I ignore Aunt Janine's comment.

He gives me another quick up and down. "Catholic."

I wince. "Ouch. I do not."

"Mrs. Wazowski," he says.

I gasp and make a grab for the pearls I'm not wearing.
"That was mean."

Mrs. Wazowski was ancient when we were kids, and by
some strange twist of nature is still alive, still wearing her
patterned dresses with knee socks, saddle shoes, and stretched-
out cardigans. It was as though she'd gotten dressed one day in
1956 and had never changed.

"Wait," Aunt Janine interjects. "Not *the* Mrs. Wazowski.
With the saddle shoes?" Aunt Janine studies my outfit again.
"Oh, I see it," she breathes.

"That's a truth train you can't dodge," Ryan says and
takes a sip of the coffee he picked up from Cuppa.

I look down at myself. "I have better feet."

"You need a pedicure," Aunt Janine says.

I look again. She's right.

I ignore them both and finish the trek down to the docks.

"Hey, Elmer," I call when we're close enough.

Elmer looks up from where he's bent over an outboard on
the back of the boat tied up at the nearest dock.

"Hey, kid," he says. "I need the crescent again." This is
directed at his brother who kneels on the dock, an open
toolbox beside him.

Elmer and Earl McQuiggan are identical twins in their late
seventies. They are each just shy of six feet in height and are
neither skinny nor plump. They are the kind of middling size
wrought of constant hard work. In summer, they sport a

perpetual tan, boat shoes, frayed, cutoff jean shorts, a trucker cap that says Farley's, and gold-plated, elastic band, digital watches they bought from a Brand Names catalog showroom while visiting their aunts in Tonawanda in 1987. I know this because they enjoy showing everyone in the village how they still work.

They've been running the launch on the lake since the 1960s. At first it was just a taxi service to the camp on the island, but it grew during the timeshare craze of the 1970s and '80s when condo developments across the lake hired the brothers to run shuttles from the developments to the marina. Business slowed once the condos were turned into private residences, but they adapted and started offering a tow and mobile outboard mechanic service.

And whether they liked it or not, the McQuiggan brothers are privy to much of the village's gossip.

Earl is deaf, and Elmer signs to him who is approaching on the dock behind him. I watch Elmer spell out the letters of a name to Earl, and I know just enough sign language to realize he's spelled the name Casper. I frown.

Earl turns and waves, giving me his usual dopey grin until he spots Ryan. Before I have time to move out of the way, Earl gains his feet and seizes Ryan in a bear hug.

When Earl releases Ryan, Earl gives the sign to ask what's happening.

"I'm on vacation, man," Ryan says with a laugh as he signs. "What better place than here!"

Earl shakes his head and signs Las Vegas.

Ryan laughs. "No way. Too expensive."

Earl points two thumbs at himself and shakes his head.

"Oh, yeah?" Ryan gives him a good-natured shoulder bump. "You money bags all of a sudden?" he says and signs.

Elmer picks up an oar from the bottom of the boat and gooses his brother with it.

When Earl turns, Elmer signs and says, "Quit pretending you've got money. You want to attract some lonely widow?"

Earl shakes his head and points to Aunt Janine who laughs uproariously.

"You're not my type, sugar," she says to Earl. "I like my men weak and biddable."

Earl laughs while Elmer shakes his head this time.

He gestures to the toolbox when Earl looks in his direction again. "I need the Philips again."

Earl goes back to the toolbox, but the grin doesn't leave his face.

"I suppose you're here about Sadie," Elmer says.

Before taking the Philips, he signs to Earl.

Earl turns to me and signs *bad news* and *poor girl*.

"Why bad news?" I sign this back to him, but he only shakes his head and points to his brother.

I look to Elmer who has pushed his Farley's cap back on his head to wipe at the sweat already on his brow so early in the morning.

"I was running the launch the night she disappeared," Elmer explains. "I was the one who took the boys from Tomahawk over there that night."

I blink between the brothers. "What do you mean you took the boys over there?"

Elmer rests the hand holding the Philips on his knee. "Don't you know what happened that night?"

"I heard Sadie got into a fight with her father and went over to the camp to cool off. She took a canoe out and disappeared, presumed drowned."

Elmer shakes his head and turns to his brother. "Nobody's told her the story," he says and signs. "Can you run up to Shelly's for a couple of sausage biscuits and coffee? This is gonna take a minute."

Earl wipes his hands on his jean shorts and stands. He tugs

at the rim of his own trucker cap as he leaves, but he gives Ryan a fist bump.

Elmer sets aside his tools and shuffles up to the gunwale where he settles in.

"It was Bonfire Night," he starts, and already I need to cut him off.

"Bonfire Night?"

Elmer nods. "Sure thing. Every summer Camp Carmichael had a Bonfire Night where they would host them boys over from Tomahawk. It was a big to-do every summer. Got to be such a thing the village joined in." He gestures up and down Water Street behind us. "All the shops stayed open late. Matt's dad did the pig roasts then, and he always put one on in the square." He shook his head side to side. "What a rumpus. You'd come to the village the next day, and it was like New Year's in Time Square. Took a week to clean up." He nods in the direction of the island. "Once the camp shut down, the town council put the kibosh on the whole thing. Too expensive in outlay and clean up."

I turn to Ryan. "Have you ever heard of this?"

He gives a shrug. "Nah, but then I'm not interested in this kind of stuff the way you are."

That was true. I'd stayed in Bellegrave while Ryan had left. I turn to Aunt Janine, but she shrugs.

"I was in London back in those days. I didn't know what was happening back here beyond Greg's letters."

I turn back to Elmer. "So it was Bonfire Night, and the boys from Tomahawk were on the island."

The implications bounce around my head. If the boys from Tomahawk were really there that night, the suspect pool for Sadie's murder has just exploded. It would also mean Jonathan Starkley had likely been there that night.

Elmer nods. "Sure thing. Took me three runs to get everyone over there." This time when he shakes his head it's with annoyance. "Those damn boys. I hated having to haul them over there, but what was I to do? Earl and I needed the money back then."

"Spoiled rich kids?" Ryan offers.

"That was only the start of it," Elmer confirms. "Back then fathers sent their sons to Tomahawk to toughen them up, make men out of them. All of that crap." He flings a hand in the direction of the island. "I don't know about turning them into men, but it sure did make bastards out of them. Always trying to sneak booze and drugs onto the island. If they chickened out, they'd dump their stash on my boat, and I had to clean it up."

"Booze and drugs?" Aunt Janine asks.

Elmer nods. "I never figured out what the deal was, but it seemed there was some kind of hierarchy. The ones with the power made the new boys do things to win approval. You know how kids are."

Elmer's words were strangely reminiscent of what I'd heard from Poppy and Maeve, only in connection with the boys camp instead of the girls.

"So like a hazing thing?" Aunt Janine clarifies.

Elmer nods again. "That's what they call it now. Back then it was some sicko way of being called a man." He shifts against the gunwale, his gaze moving hesitatingly in the direction of the island at the other end of the lake. "I don't know what happened at that camp. You know how money has a way of silencing things. But we all heard the stories."

Once again I think of Poppy and Maeve.

"Girls were hurt out there," I say. "Do you think the Tomahawk boys hurt them?"

It's a beat before Elmer answers.

"I can't say anything about the girls that hasn't already been said. People in this village at the time know about as much as I do." I think he's going to stop there, his voice going quiet, but then he looks directly at me. "But the thing I know that other people don't are about the boys from Tomahawk." He nods in the direction of the opposite end of the lake. "Tomahawk was over them hills, halfway to Saranac. So they'd go to Saranac more often. That's why I was likely the only one who really interacted with them." Again he goes quiet, and I sense he's gathering his words. "Those boys weren't just bored, rich kids looking for rebellion. They were nastier than that."

"What happened the night Sadie was murdered?" I'm not sure I can stomach hearing any more about hazing torture.

His eyes narrow, nearly disappearing in the shadow cast by the brim of his Farley's cap. "I was running the launch like I usually do. The boys always arrived here at the launch by bus, sometime around dusk, and I'd haul them over to the camp. But that night something was off."

I shift and glance at Aunt Janine, but she's absorbed in Elmer's story.

"What was off?" I prod.

He pushes his hat back and brings it forward again, adjusting it as it settles on his head. "Well, nothing so much when I took them. It seemed like every Bonfire Night I'd taken passengers from Tomahawk over to the camp. It was when they came back that I knew something was wrong."

"How so?" Ryan asks, and I see he's leaning against the dock railing now, his coffee cup held between both hands.

"See the thing is," Elmer began. "Even the rich have levels of rich, and that's before you take in a family's longevity, their social status, where there money comes from." He makes a sweeping gesture with his hand as if it's all rubbish. "And the Tomahawk boys were no exception. Now don't get me wrong. There were some good boys in that group just like any group has good and bad fish. But that night when I was bringing them back, they all seemed to be picking on the same kid."

"Who?" Aunt Janine asks, but I already know the name he's going to say.

"Jonathan Starkley," Elmer says. "You know him. He's a state senator now."

"Why were they picking on him?" Like with Monica Davies, I feel as though I'm on another roller coaster, but this one is headed straight down, the coaster gaining speed, hurtling me toward an inevitable conclusion.

"Someone tossed him in the lake over on the island," Elmer explains. "The kid was soaking wet. Apparently it was pretty funny, I guess. The way they picked on him." Elmer shakes his head. "But then they always picked on that kid. He didn't have the strongest backbone then. Not sure he really does now," Elmer adds as though it's an afterthought. "That was why I thought it was so strange. I thought the staff at the camp were stricter than they might have been at Tomahawk. Thought they would have stopped the other kids from picking on Starkley." Elmer gives a shrug. "Just seemed weird to me. Then the next morning we heard about Sadie, and I just plain forgot about that until just now, I guess."

I straighten. "Word about Sadie didn't get out until the next morning?"

Elmer shakes his head. "Nah. Maurice didn't call in to the police station until Sunday morning. Almost noon, I think." His expression closes. "He must have thought she would just come home. Poor man. Losing his wife and his daughter. Can't blame him for hanging on to hope."

"When you ferried the kids over for Bonfire Night, did you see Mr. Beaumont on the island?" I ask.

Elmer blinks, his answer already coming. "Well, sure I—" He stops abruptly, his expression changing yet again. "Well, now that you ask I don't think I did. It was just the usual counselors and that Carmichael girl. She was always on the dock when I came over, sort of like she was playing hostess.

She always did try to make up for the loss of her mother, I suppose."

Earl appears at the end of the dock just as I'm thanking Elmer for his time. As we pass Earl, he hands Ryan a sausage biscuit. There's some exchange of signs followed by a bro hug.

I wait until we're on Water Street before I ask, "Which one of you started the Casper nickname for me?"

"AJ did," Ryan says around a mouthful of sausage biscuit.

Aunt Janine doesn't miss a stride. "The movie came out just when your poor mother had to start explaining to folks what was happening to you. I suggested she use it as a way of helping people relate."

I shake my head, but I let it go because on some level what Aunt Janine did was right. I have more important things to do anyway.

Like take a drive to Raquette Lake.

Twenty-Two

Maurice Beaumont is the caretaker of Brackett House, a camp that has been turned into a wellness retreat that operates three seasons out of the year. He lives in the original caretaker's cottage that sits at the very edge of the property with a private drive thankfully. I don't want to explain my visit to some receptionist with a forehead that doesn't wrinkle and teeth whiter than a snow drift.

It's a little before noon when I get there, and I park in the gravel drive behind a truck I recognize from that day on Church Street when I'd had my embarrassing meltdown in front of Maurice Beaumont.

I put the car in park and turn to my passenger.

"You don't need to come in with me. This way if anyone asks you can honestly say you didn't interfere."

Carmen purses her lips. "If you think I came all this way to stay in the car, you don't know me very well."

She flicks off her seatbelt and gets out of the car with the kind of flair her mother taught her, and I can't help but smile.

I have given my usual guard dogs the day off as my mom wanted Ryan to teach her how to use a stand-up paddle board and Aunt Janine had some calls with Tokyo, so she'd been up late and wanted to spend the day in the luxurious bed of her B&B suite.

Carmen wasn't on shift, and I'd taken a personal day, which had caused more of a stir than I would have liked as I hadn't taken a day off during the busy summer season ever.

It was a Wednesday though, and we had no scheduled programming, so I was confident the staff would be fine without me.

The gauze on my neck was starting to leave a welt where it was irritating my skin, and it was a constant reminder that my investigation into Sadie Beaumont's death was growing murkier and murkier. I had high hopes today would finally bring me some answers.

I knock on Maurice Beaumont's door, and we wait on the small concrete stoop for someone to answer it. Instead a voice comes from the side of the house.

"Are you Mormons? I don't want any Mormons around here."

The voice is cracked with age and wobbles on every other word. Carmen and I turn as one to find an old woman perched on a walker coming along the hedge that borders the cottage.

"We're not missionaries," Carmen says with a smile. "We're just here to talk to Maurice Beaumont."

The old woman's brow grows even more wrinkled than it already was. "What do you want with Mo? He ain't done nothing wrong, you know. I don't care what that state police detective's been saying about him."

"I'm not police," I interject, holding out a hand. "My name is Della James. I'm the executive director of the Belle-grave Historical Society."

"What's that? Some internet thing?" The old woman's grip on her walker tightens. She's wearing several large rings, tarnished with age that scrape along the metal as she twists her hands. "I don't go on the internet. That's where Democrats are."

"No, it's not an internet—"

"What do you want?"

Carmen and I swing in the opposite direction to find Maurice Beaumont coming up a path that cuts off in the direction of the wellness retreat.

He stops when he sees me.

"What do you want?" he says again, this time with more force. "I already told you—"

"I think your daughter was murdered, trying to stop someone from doing something terrible, and I need to ask you some questions." I shoot the words out as quickly as possible, hoping to catch his interest before he can ask me to leave.

His body stills, and he doesn't say anything for so long I'm certain he's going to kick me off his property.

But he doesn't tell me to leave. Instead he says, "Mom, get in the house."

The old woman on the other end of the cottage makes a grumbly noise, but she ambles her way to the door. When she reaches us, she grabs Carmen's elbow.

"You got any cats?" she asks.

Carmen shakes her head. "No, I'm afraid not."

The woman's expression falls. "Oh. I was hoping you had some cute cat photos on your phone. Everyone has pictures of pets on their phones these days. Didn't have phones when I had my Archie."

"I got pictures of her dog on my phone," she offers, pointing at me.

The old woman's face lifts so far it nearly irons out the wrinkles.

"You don't say. Well, come on. I'll fix us some iced tea."

Carmen turns her attention to me. "You going to be okay if I go inside?"

I nod. "I'll be fine."

She gives Maurice Beaumont a direct stare before following who is presumably Beaumont's mother into the house.

"What is this about Sadie?" Maurice asks when the door to the cottage finally closes.

I shift on the stoop so I'm facing him more completely.

"I can see the dead," I remind him. "I can communicate with them sometimes in words but most often in feelings. Your daughter came to me, and she pressed upon me the feeling of frustration. Like she was prevented from doing something in life because of her murder. She asked me to save them. I think whoever she wants me to save are the people she couldn't when she was alive."

I don't add my newly discovered information about the camp, about the suspected hazing, about how the boys from the Tomahawk camp may have been involved in torturing the girls at Camp Carmichael every summer.

Maurice looks away, and when he brings his attention back to me, he settles his hands on his hips. "Sadie was always trying to save everyone."

His tone is one of defeat, and I wonder if the shock of hearing about his daughter's murder has settled into him now. That day on Church Street he'd been confrontational. Now he seems resigned.

"I think she tried to up until her death," I agree. "I'm trying to piece together what happened the night she died. I think it will help me to understand who she was trying to save. Then I might be able to uncover who killed her."

He thrusts his chin in my direction. "Those state police detectives I talked to. Aren't they looking into my daughter's murder?"

"They are," I admit. "But they can't communicate with your daughter the way I can."

This statement sticks a little in my throat. It isn't entirely a lie. I can see his daughter still. It's just hearing her has become slightly more difficult.

I try to remember back to that day on the sidewalk when I first told him of my ability. Had he believed me then? His lack of emotion now could be an indication of his distrust in me. Or he could be hiding the fact that the reason Elmer didn't see him that night on the island was because he was busy hiding his daughter's body in an oil drum.

"You're wrong about her wanting to save people," he says as he looks back in the direction of the wellness retreat.

"Why do you say that? From what I've heard of Sadie she was always trying to help."

He shakes his head as he brings his gaze back to me. "She might have once. But not at the end. She spent that summer over at the camp. Got involved with all those rich kids. Her attitude changed."

For a moment, it seems as if the ground shifts beneath my feet. Could Sadie have been complicit in the hazing the other girls at the camp endured? She had been a resident on the island, had grown up there. Maybe she felt entitled.

"How do you mean?" I ask instead of voicing my fears.

He scrubs the back of his neck, and I notice a glint of metal as he does. He's wearing a thick, gold band on the third finger of his left hand. His wedding ring, perhaps? From what I can tell his wife died over forty years ago.

"She started defending them. Sticking up for them," he says. He scoffs and looks away, shuffles his feet, and I brace myself, waiting for him to walk away. "She spent her whole life on that island. She knew what those kids were really like, but that summer she started saying things about them. When I said they asked for too much, she told me to go easy on them.

That they had problems of their own." His scoff this time is brittle with disgust. "She knew better than that. She let them get to her."

"Did you make her that bee charm bracelet?"

He takes a step closer to me, and the energy shifts between us. "What about it?"

"She showed it to me, remember? It was important to her. Even after death." I study him, watch the way his eyes flick over my face. "She showed me that bracelet because it means something. Why did you give her that bracelet?"

He turns completely away from me then, and my stomach drops. I know I've lost him as he paces several steps away. I think about where I might go from here if I can't get answers, but before I've finished the thought, he circles back, stopping inches in front of me.

"I don't know what kind of sick freak you are. Coming here telling me you can speak to my dead daughter, but I'm telling you right now I won't stand for it." His words are filled with venom, but his voice cracks against them, and he spins away again, the gurgle of a cry lodged in his throat. When he turns back, there are tears in his eyes. "I made those bracelets for Sadie to give to her friends. Far as I know she never gave them to anyone. She started hanging out with those rich girls and lost all her friends. And I—" He stops and wipes an angry arm across his mouth. "Do you want to know what really happened that night? Do you?"

It's my turn to take a step back. Is he going to confess to killing his daughter? Is he going to tell me how he stuffed her dead body into a barrel? All because she grew up, got caught up with the wrong crowd.

But that isn't what he does. He doesn't confess.

He says, "I wasn't there." Three simple words, words that corroborate Elmer's story. "I wasn't there the night my little girl needed me." Now his voice is flooded with anguish. "I yelled at her. I said things. Despicable things. About how she wasn't my daughter anymore. About how disappointed her mother would be in her. I told her I hated her." His voice breaks entirely, and he collapses, bending forward, hands against his knees as sobs escape him.

I want to comfort him, but just as I take a step forward, the static roars into my ears, pinning me to the spot where I stand. Instinctively, I try to cover my ears, but also instinctively, my head swings left and right, looking for Sadie.

She's there. She appears behind her father. She reaches for him, her face twisted in anguish that mirrors her father's. When she looks up, I'm hit with the full force of her grief. It rolls over me like a tsunami, and it's all I can do to keep my knees from buckling.

I force myself to lower my hands from my ears. I stare at Sadie as though my eyes can find their way through the static I'm drowning in.

Sadie is talking. Her lips are moving. I can't hear her. I stare harder.

She's trying to grab hold of her father, pull him close to her. I can see her useless motions, her mouth moving on words I cannot hear. Sadie is strong, but I know she's using so much energy. Soon she'll vanish, and I'll know nothing more.

"Sadie is here." I don't know how loud my voice is. I can't hear myself through the static. "Sadie is here, and she's trying to comfort you."

Maurice straightens so swiftly his body cuts through the spirit of his daughter. I watch it happen. The moment his body touches her energy, he jerks as if burned.

"What the—" He stares at the spot, his left hand going to the opposite arm where he touched her.

"It's cold. I know." I'm probably shouting the words. There's no way for me to tell.

He stares at the spot beside him, about where Sadie's neck

is. He looks between that spot and me. Sadie looks between her father and me, her eyes huge, imploring.

Tell him...love him.

The words filter through the static, and I latch on to them. "She says she loves you."

He jerks again at my words, stumbles back against the hedge along the cottage, his eyes never leaving the spot where he felt the intense cold of his daughter's ghost.

Sadie disappears as quickly as she appeared, and the static cuts away.

Maurice breathes heavily, his arms spread against the hedge as if to anchor himself or hold himself up. His eyes never leave the spot where he felt his daughter.

I don't know how long it is before he starts speaking.

"It was Bonfire Night. July fourteenth. July fourteenth." He says the date twice as if by speaking it, it will take him back there. "Sadie and I—" But he stops and shakes his head. "I went onto the mainland. There used to be a party in the village on Bonfire Night. Shops open late. Restaurants opened up on the sidewalks. That wasn't a thing back then. You couldn't just eat out on the sidewalk. Drink a beer with a beef on weck. It was a big deal. Everyone just let loose for one night." His voice crumbles again, but this time, I hear self-loathing in his tone. "I just wanted to get away for one night. After the fight with Sadie, I..." His voice disappears entirely. "I went to Farley's. Got drunk. Passed out in one of the booths. I didn't get back to the island until the next morning. That's when I found Sadie was gone." His words fade back into the past, and as though it's physically let go of him, he straightens and meets my eyes.

"Can someone verify your whereabouts that night?"

He laughs, a sad sound. "Yeah, Barry Wise. He wasn't chief back then. Just a deputy and the best drinking partner I had. He woke up on the other side of that same booth the next morning at Farley's. Poured me into my boat at the marina and went home to his wife and their two little kids."

His expression is a familiar one then, as though he's seeing a life he was supposed to have had and didn't. That night of July fourteenth everything changed for Maurice Beaumont, and he's had forty years to carry the weight of it.

But his expression hardens then. "I wasn't there when Sadie needed me. It was one thing when I thought she'd drowned. But now—" He swallows, hard. "Now I want whoever did this caught. I want—" His voice shakes with anger, and he swallows again. "I want her killer brought to justice."

"That's exactly what I plan to do," I say.

The door of the cottage opens behind me, and voices emerge, mid-conversation.

"And that's how I ended up in bed with Mick Jagger," Maurice Beaumont's mother says as she comes out on Carmen's arm.

I look back at Maurice, but he just shakes his head in a *don't ask* gesture.

Carmen nods even as she glances at me. "Got everything you needed?"

"Sure did," I say.

We say our goodbyes, and once we're in the car, Carmen says, "Do you know she's lived in that cottage her whole life? Her father was the caretaker of Brackett House when it was a private estate and then her husband took over and now her son. Can you believe it?"

I think of Sadie, appearing next to her father, and I nod. "Yeah, I can believe it."

TWENTY-THREE

I drop Carmen off at home, and although I promise to go straight home where Logan is waiting to take over guard duty, I make a beeline for the Victorian at the end of the village.

There's one of those moving box units in the driveway now, and Chief Wise himself is maneuvering a bag of golf clubs into the back of it when I pull up to the curb.

He lifts a hand in greeting as I get out of my car.

"You were with Maurice Beaumont the night his daughter was murdered," I say without greeting.

He stops, his arms wrapped around the golf bag.

He stares at me over a nine iron. "You're a good investigator."

"It helps when you can speak directly with the victim," I quip.

He gives a small smile and shoves the bag into the storage box. "You should join Carmen on the police force."

I shrug. "Nah. I already got a job."

He nods. "I suppose we'd better have a seat and talk about this."

He brushes off his hands as he leads the way up to the wraparound porch. Like before, there's a tray of lemonade complete with several glasses on a small table between two rockers on the porch. Chief Wise pours himself a glass and gestures to me. I shake my head. He downs half the glass as he perches a hip against the porch railing.

"I was with Maurice that night. God, that was a lifetime ago," Chief Wise says, his eyes growing distant. "Mattie was teething, and we'd just started potty training Louise." He laughs, but it's a tired sound.

I've only ever heard of Mattie referred to as Matthew. He's a geology professor at Colgate. Louise is a doctor in Albany, I think. It's funny to hear Chief Wise still talk about them like they're little kids, but then, I suppose, to him, they always will be his little kids.

"Bonfire Night. Man." Another laugh, this one more jovial. "What a night. Town council made the right choice in ending that tradition when the camp closed." Chief Wise whistles softly. "What a ruckus it could turn into. Never could get all the toilet paper out of the fountain in the square. Used to piss off Mayor Belden."

I don't remember a Mayor Belden, and I wonder how far back he or she goes.

Chief Wise sets his nearly empty lemonade glass on the porch railing next to him.

"I met Maurice at Farley's. I was off duty that night, and Belinda's mom was in town for a few weeks. She used to come stay with us during the summer when the kids were really little. It was nice. She was a good egg. The kids loved her, and Belinda got a break. Like I said, Mattie was teething and Louise was afraid of the little potty we'd gotten her. Belinda told me to go down to Farley's for the night. She'd take care of the kids with her mother. She told me I was going to have a hell of a week cleaning up after the celebration, and it would do me good to have a night off." He laughs genuinely now. "I don't think she considered the hangover I was going to inflict on myself."

"Did you really pass out in the booth with Maurice Beaumont?"

His laugh is even stronger now, and his smile travels all the way to his eyes. "Oh, yeah. Sure as I'm standing here. Farley's ran a two for one special on Bonfire Night. It's a wonder the whole town didn't get drunk. Maurice would talk about his time in Vietnam. About the crazy things he'd seen. How he got wounded and sent home before the end of sixty-seven. We'd all gather around him and listen. He was always good for one hell of a story." His voice fades as he studies his feet, lost in thought. "Maurice drank harder than usual that night. I remember that now. He was fighting with Sadie then. The whole town knew it. She got mixed up with that boy."

"Jonathan Starkley."

Chief Wise looks up sharply. "You know, I think that's it. The state senator." His eyes grow as he shakes his head in disbelief. "I'd forgotten it was him. I'll be. He's a state senator now," he finishes as if he's trying to convince himself.

"Do you know if Sadie was really involved with Jonathan Starkley? I have conflicting information on that point."

Chief Wise's eyes harden. "Well now, I can't be sure, but the rumors that summer linked the two of them."

"Wouldn't it be odd for a rich boy from Tomahawk to get involved with the caretaker's daughter?"

Chief Wise's expression falters, almost as though he internally flinches and tries to keep it from showing on his face.

"I think I'd better be honest with you, Del," he says. Before going on, he picks up his lemonade glass and drains it. "Things weren't right at Camp Carmichael. I know that. I think everyone in the village knew that. The girls would come over on Elmer's launch and line up for the payphone in

Abbots Pharmacy. Some of them looked like they'd been roughed up. Welts on their arms and legs and such. Some were just scared. You could see their fear plain as day."

"Why was nothing done about it?" I ask.

Chief Wise's expression closes. "That's the thing. We did do something about it. Every week I went over there myself. Asked around to see what was going on." The shake of his head is forlorn. "Never got anywhere. Some counselor or camp manager would run me off. I would report back to the chief at the time, and he would tell me to let it be."

There's a hardness to his eyes that tells me he didn't listen.

"You didn't stop there, did you?" I ask.

He's quiet for a minute, but finally straightens, crosses his arms over his chest. "That summer paramedics showed up at the launch asking Elmer to taking them over to the camp. Something had happened. They pulled a girl out of there and took her to the hospital in Saranac. The next day the village was overflowing with rumors."

"What happened to her?"

He takes a deep breath before saying, "She miscarried. Nearly died from blood loss." His lips open as if he's going to say more, but he stops himself.

"What else? What else aren't you telling me?" The question might be forceful, but the pieces of the puzzles are starting to come together in a way I find revolting, and I need answers.

"The rumor was the girl forced the miscarriage herself with a clothes hanger."

I look away, bile rising in my throat.

"I called Don Carmichael then at his mansion down there in Kingston. I demanded to know what was going on." Chief Wise's expression is grim. "I got blocked by his goddamn lawyers, and I got an official reprimand from my chief."

"What do you think happened?"

Chief Wise turns, wraps his hands around the porch railing as he looks down to the street. "There was talk back then about the boys over at Tomahawk. The county sheriff deputies had gotten a few calls about the camp. Some domestics. Noise. That sort of thing. When the deputies went to check it out, they always got the same rebuff we did at Camp Carmichael. Except one time a deputy overheard a conversation about some boys planning to visit Bellegrave." Chief Wise looks directly at me. "The deputy overheard them talking about date rape drugs, and he tried to intervene. The camp counselor pulled some lawyer speak on him and got the deputies removed from the property."

My breathing has grown shallow. "Do you think the boys from Tomahawk were raping the girls at Camp Carmichael?"

Chief Wise shifts his weight. This conversation is uncomfortable for him.

"I think it's worse than that. I think the boys at Tomahawk were led to believe the girls at Camp Carmichael would submit. And the ones that didn't would get drugged."

"Why didn't anyone stop them?"

"Have you ever gone after someone with money?"

I think about Martha Pruitt and all the terrible things she'd done to retain the power of illusion money gave her.

Chief Wise turns his gaze back to the road. "Every time we showed interest in that camp, we got phone calls from half a dozen parents. Senators, congressmen, industrialists, financial tycoons. You name it. They threatened us. Said if we kept upsetting their daughters, they would make sure tourism dollars stopped flowing to Bellegrave. They threatened to end the whole damn town."

"I imagine they had the power to do it, didn't they?"

Chief Wise shrugs. "Who knows? But I wasn't going to be responsible for people losing their jobs. For shuttering family businesses that had been run in Bellegrave for generations."

He digs at a splinter on the railing. "Besides. The camp shut down after Sadie disappeared, and it all just went away."

I think of the sightless eyes in the black windows of the decaying cabins on the island. I think of the bodiless laughter, the oppressive, incessant dark energy.

"Except it didn't go away." My voice is low, but I know Chief Wise has heard me when I look up and see him watching me carefully.

"Have you spoken to Detective Hanratty?" I ask.

Chief Wise shakes his head. "I assume that's the state police detective Carmen mentioned. He hasn't been to see me."

I nod. "I'm going to tell him what you've told me here."

Chief Wise straightens. "I expect you will." There's a pause, and his eyes study my face, searching. "You know what you're getting into, don't you? The people you are going up against?"

I nod again. "Yeah," I say, turning for the stairs. I call out over my shoulder as I head for my SUV. "Let's just hope I won't be forced to shoot any of them."

———

I find Logan in the kitchen when I get home.

He's digging paper plates out of the cupboard while a box from Papa's Pizza sits on the counter beside him.

"Hey," he says when he hears me come in.

I don't answer him. I just walk into his arms. He clings to me awkwardly, a stack of paper plates in one hand, a roll of paper towels in the other.

"Hey," he says again to the top of my head as Henry whines mournfully at my feet. "What happened?"

I tell him everything.

By the time I've finished, we're seated at the table in the

dining alcove, the half-finished pizza between us and Henry asleep on my feet.

I pick at the slice of pizza on my plate. "I asked Detective Hanratty to meet me here. He's in Plattsburgh, but he said he'd be here around eight."

I glance at the clock. It's just past seven.

Logan nurses a bottle of beer. "Who can prove one way or another if the Tomahawk boys targeted the girls at Camp Carmichael? Right now you have village rumor and Chief Wise's observations. You have no proof."

"I know," I acknowledge. "That's why I need Hanratty. There's still one person I haven't spoken to, and I need Hanratty's help."

"Starkley?" Logan asks.

I lean forward. "Maurice Beaumont wasn't on the island the night his daughter was murdered. From what I understand Donald Carmichael was never truly involved in the running of the camp. Chief Wise said he had to call him in Kingston. Carmichael wasn't even here that summer, yet he gets all inquiries shut down." I tug at a piece of pepperoni and pull a chunk of gooey cheese off with it. I pop the whole thing into my mouth, chew, swallow. "Ashley Carmichael thinks summer camp was a time of sunshine and roses. You should have seen her with her photo albums and her bare feet and her bouncy ponytail." I lay a hand flat on the table. "Her ponytail *bounced*."

"You think she didn't know what was really happening at the camp?" Logan's eyebrows go up in disbelief.

"Elmer said Ashley was always there to greet him when he docked. I think Ashley enjoyed playing the hostess after her mother died."

"So she ignored everything else?" Logan asks.

"It was her last summer there." I can almost hear her voice in my head, the note of pride as she talked about the camp. "I think she wanted everything to be the same. Just as her mother had it. One last time."

"And accusations of rape would have upset that," Logan says.

I unearth another piece of pepperoni. "I can only imagine any employment records for the camp are long gone. Donald Carmichael is incapacitated. Ashley is probably blind to the events that happened that summer, and Maurice Beaumont wasn't on the island. That leaves me with one person."

"Our dear state senator, probably soon to be governor."

I pop the piece of pepperoni into my mouth and take out my frustrations on it. "I can't just walk up to a state senator and ask him what he remembers about a possible rape accusation in the summer of eighty-four."

Logan shakes his head and takes another swig from his beer bottle. "Not now," he says. "You know he's supposed to be launching his gubernatorial campaign this fall. He's going to have increased security when he stops by here next week."

"I know," I say. "That's why I need Hanratty to question him."

"Do you think the detective will get to him?"

"He'll have a better shot at it than me," I say.

Logan tilts back in his chair. "So we know Sadie was murdered the night of July fourteenth. Bonfire Night. Her dad wasn't on the island, and his alibi has been confirmed by Chief Wise. This Monica person who appeared in the photo with Sadie has threatened you."

I hold up a finger. "I would like to use the language of warned me. She warned me."

Logan's eyes narrow. "I'm going to stay with the word threaten." He pauses, but I don't object. "She said Debbie is dead. Debbie being the other girl in the photo."

I nod. "I think it's important to remember what she said

about Ashley too. She said Ashley was a nobody. That reinforces what Elmer said about her and my own observations."

"So Ashley is playing host while a bunch of bored teenage boys target the other girls in the camp."

I pick up my own beer. "And Sadie found out about it and tried to stop it."

Logan drops his chair and leans against his folded arms on the tabletop. "Then the only thing left is why was Jonathan Starkley soaking wet when Elmer picked him up from the island?"

"Elmer said they were picking on him more than usual that night. What if he was pressured into doing something he didn't want to by the other boys?"

"But why was he all wet?"

A knock at the back door stops our conversation. I move to stand, but Logan holds out a hand.

"Uh uh," he says. "I'll get stabbed this time."

He comes back with Detective Hanratty and surprisingly, Lisa as well.

"Hey," I say to her.

She gestures awkwardly. "We were having dinner."

Detective Hanratty is in plain clothes, jeans and a t-shirt.

He faces me directly. "I can't tell if this is a social call or a professional one."

"Yeah," I say, my voice heavy with resignation. "That's often how it is with Carmen too. Sorry." I point to Lisa. "I'm probably going to tell her what I'm going to tell you, so it really doesn't matter if she hears this now or later." I touch the gauze at my neck. "Plus, I shot her mom. Nothing I'm going to say is going to surprise her."

Hanratty's expression is nonplussed.

"She's right," Lisa says and heads into the living room where Henry has flipped onto his belly on the couch, ready for pets.

We follow her and find seats.

"I need you to interview State Senator Jonathan Starkley," I jump right in as soon as everyone is settled.

Hanratty blinks. "What does the state senator have to do with this?"

"Starkley was on the island the night Sadie was murdered."

Hanratty looks at Lisa, who only shrugs and resumes petting Henry.

Hanratty straights and pulls his phone out of his jeans pocket.

"All right," he says. He taps his phone, and I hear the swish of a notes app opening. "You'd better explain."

So I do. I start from the very beginning again with my meeting with Ashley Carmichael to Dottie Uttin to my first encounter with Maurice Beaumont to everything I'd pieced together about the ritualistic hazing and targeted rape culture at Camp Carmichael and Tomahawk. When I've finished, Hanratty sits with his chin pinched between two fingers, his expression grim.

"Why are you not a detective?" he asks.

"I prefer to work with the dead," I say.

He glances in my direction, and I try to find something in his look. I'm trying not to read too much into it, but the times I've seen Hanratty with Lisa the energy around him is quiet, like it is now. I wonder why.

He rocks back and taps his phone against his knee. "So you need me to question State Senator Starkley because he was there that night, and Elmer McQuiggan remembers him being soaking wet, and the other boys were picking on him."

I nod. "I know it doesn't sound like much, but I've found it's these little things that are critical to bringing an investigation to a close."

He looks to Logan and back to me.

"And Monica Davies fits into this how?"

"I think she was a victim of the hazing," I say.

"You don't think she killed Sadie Beaumont? She threatened you with a knife. Sadie Beaumont was murdered with a knife."

I straighten now. "She was?"

"Autopsy confirms she was stabbed. One deep slice to her chest right here." He indicates a spot on his chest where I'd seen the echo of blood on Sadie's ghost. "The stab wound had decayed enough that it couldn't be determined what kind of blade was used, but the cut was clean enough to suggest it wasn't serrated."

I sit with this, thinking, but after a few seconds, I reach the same conclusion.

"No," I say. "The feeling I got from Monica Davies was that she was scared. Not that she was a threat."

"So what or who was she afraid of? Afraid of getting caught?"

Hanratty has a point, but I ignore it.

"We need to talk to Starkley. He was there that night. Likely the only other person besides Monica Davies who knows what happened on the island that night."

Hanratty rubs the back of his neck with one hand. "We interviewed Ashley Carmichael. She said it was the usual Bonfire Night just like every other Bonfire Night the camp had held. The boys from Tomahawk came. There was singing around the campfire, some ghost stories, they roasted marshmallows and hot dogs. The boys went home, and the girls were in bed before curfew. Nothing happened."

I still, thinking of Elmer calling her a hostess. Hanratty's recollection of her interview matches with the image everyone has created of her then, a lonely girl struck by tragedy, trying to hold on to the parts left to her.

"Did Ashley say anything about Sadie Beaumont? Chief Wise said some of the girls on the camp testified that Sadie took a canoe out that night. That's why they searched the lake for her when Maurice reported her missing."

Hanratty shakes his head. "No, she didn't say anything about Sadie Beaumont. It's been forty years. Maybe she didn't remember."

I think of the woman I met that day, her exuberance for her mother's camp, the weight of her father's care, her actual bounce as she pranced about the kitchen.

"Maybe," I say. "A lot has happened to her. I wonder if Sadie's death is just one more."

Hanratty stands. "I'll see what I can do about Starkley, but I can't make any promises."

I stand as well and nod. "Thank you."

We've walked them to do the door when Hanratty says, "Just do me one favor in return."

I wait, expecting the usual admonishment to stay out of the investigation, but when he turns to face me, he's wearing the grin he had the first day we met him.

"Try not to end up as one of those dead people you're so fond of."

I sneak a peek at Lisa who is smiling softly at Hanratty.

"I'll try not to," I say.

Twenty-Four

True to form, I nearly immediately break my promise to Detective Hanratty.

I get to work early the next day. It's the first day of August, and I feel the press of the summer season winding to a close. Now the real rush begins. The last-minute tour groups before school starts again, the frantic scheduling of team-building outings and corporate events that were brainstormed when the beautiful fall season still felt so far away.

August is crunch time, and I need to stay focused. I can't let Sadie's murder investigation take me away like it has been. I was right to ask Hanratty for help. He is, after all, the law enforcement officer in charge of this investigation. I can trust him to find answers while I focus on my job.

I pull over across the street from the main gates and check for traffic before getting out of my SUV and heading to the gates. I'm sorting through my work keys, looking for the one for the gate, and the only thing that saves my life is the frantic honking of a truck horn.

I don't waste time looking up. I launch myself in the direction of the other side of the road. The next few seconds are a mess of ear-splitting sounds and pain. So much pain. There's the screech of tires, the incessant honking, gravel spitting, the crash of something heavy, and I'm sure I'm dead.

But I'm not.

The next I'm aware of what's happening I'm on the ground. In the ditch, more specifically, next to the gates to Lady Josephine Lodge. I threw myself out of the road, but I'd only made it to the gravel on the shoulder where I hit the ground, the small stones tearing through the skin on my right arm, which was completely bare thanks to my sleeveless shirt. From there, the momentum must have rolled me into the ditch. I'm wet along the side lying in the tall grass, and there's a distinct ringing in my ears that I realize is actually a dinging noise, like when you leave your car door open with the keys in the ignition.

"Della!"

I blink, the tall grass coming into focus as I lift my head. The voice I know, but it's so out of place for a moment I think the grass is calling my name.

"Della!" There's more crunching of gravel now, and the grass in front of me disappears, replaced by a solid chest and sturdy hands. "Della. Jesus. Can you hear me?"

I look up at Daryl Walden.

"Della," he says my name again. "Are you all right? Can you move? We need to get you out of this filthy water."

It takes a second for it to register he's right, and I make to stand but pain ricochets down my side. I make a noise I've never heard myself make and grab my bad leg, fear that it's broken again tearing through me.

"Okay, okay." Daryl's voice is steady, and I'm grateful he's calm in this situation. "Let's get your arm out of the water at least," he says, lifting my right arm above the grass. "Jesus," he breathes again.

I realize he's looking at my arm, horror etched in his features.

I risk a glance at my arm and look away when my vision starts to dim. It's worse than I had first thought, the skin nearly peeled off my elbow entirely.

"I don't want to seem ungrateful," I say through clenched teeth. "But what are you doing here?"

Daryl scoots through the grass on his knees now, and I see he's getting behind me. Relief shoots through my body as he comes against my back, holding me up out of the ditch water. I look down. He's fully seated in ditch water so he can hold me up. I'll think about that later.

"I saw the car back at the supermarket. No plates. No registration. Thought it was suspicious, so I followed it. I was already on the phone with Carmen when the driver went for you, so help is on the way. Just hang on."

"Daryl, help is already here," I say. "You're it, my friend."

I can only see the side of Daryl's face, but he shifts uncomfortably behind me.

"Oh," he says quietly.

Daryl spent a great deal of his life caught in the trap of untreated PTSD and alcoholism, and I know the role of hero is not one with which he is familiar. He had been engaged to Victoria Gustafson when she was murdered, and her death sent him into a pattern of disruptive behavior. In my investigation, I learned he was actually a man who cared deeply about things, especially about protecting the people he loved. It didn't surprise me at all he had a dash cam in his truck or that he would follow a suspicious driver.

"Did you see the driver?" I ask, changing the subject to put Daryl at ease but also to distract me from the pain radiating through my hip.

"It was a woman with long dark hair. I'm afraid that's all I saw."

My mind immediately connects the description with Monica Davies, and misgiving slips through me like ice. Had I been wrong about her? Was it really fear I had sensed, or was she truly trying to hurt me all along?

"But I got the whole thing on dash cam," he says. "I'll give it to Carmen and hopefully the police will be able to make something of it. I don't know who that lady was, but the minute she saw you she hit the gas and headed straight for you."

The pain has leveled out, and I'm able to take in the road in front of me. Daryl's truck is at eye level. The engine is still running, and I imagine he's left the driver's side door open in his haste to get me.

"You honked," I say. "You saved my life."

He shifts against me again, and I hear him curse softly under his breath.

He's saved from further accolades because the shrill siren of an ambulance overpowers the rumble of Daryl's truck engine.

I'm sick of paramedics. I'm sick of the stark expression on my best friend's face when she catapults herself into the ditch beside me, reaching for me even as paramedics with the help of Daryl try to lift me out. The pain in my hip is unbearable, my arm is on fire, and I've scared my best friend to death. Again.

"I'm sorry," I say. "This wasn't my fault. I was just going to work."

"I know, darling. I know," she says.

I'm on a stretcher now, but Carmen doesn't let go of my good hand, the one not burning with road rash.

"Logan?" I ask.

"Ryan and AJ are going to get him. I didn't want him to get another phone call like the one I gave him the other night."

I let my head fall back against the stretcher. She's right. I don't know how bad I look, but it must be bad for Carmen to have the same look on her face she had when she found out JFK Jr. had died.

My head only stays on the pillow for a second. The paramedics turn me as they pull me from the ditch, and I see the front gates of the lodge. The car had missed me, but it sideswiped the gate. One precious brick pillar lay in ruins, the heavy iron gate it was supporting nesting in the gravel drive where it fell.

"No!" I reach for it instinctively. The pain rips through my arm anew, but I keep crying, "No! No! No! That's nineteenth-century brick."

Carmen swats at my arms, pushes me back toward the pillow. "Will you cut it out? I'll get you Leonardo da Vinci bricks if it means you'll settle down!"

My good hand goes to my pocket, but my phone is in my SUV in my bag.

"Carmen, you need to call Steve Fitzpatrick," I say.

Carmen rears back, and suddenly she looks very much like her mom, and I shut up instantly.

"You did not just tell me to call someone you work with. Tell me you didn't do that while you're lying on a stretcher, going into an ambulance, where you will be taken to a hospital for more tests than a middle-schooler during state testing because you were nearly killed in a hit-and-run. Please—" She squeezes her eyes shut, squats and stomps her feet, and pinches her fingers together, her bright yellow nail polish flashing in the sun. "Please tell me you did not just do that."

"I didn't," I whisper.

She opens her eyes and straightens, lets her hands fall to her side. "I didn't think so. Now get in the damn ambulance."

I go, quietly, but mostly because I'm strapped to a stretcher, and my free will has been taken from me. I can't see Daryl anywhere. The front gates of the lodge are a mess of confusion. More law enforcement. They're the ones in Tyvek suits, and they swarm the collapsed brick pillar with small cases and plastic bags. Evidence bags.

Just before they lift me into the ambulance Detective Hanratty comes around the side of the ambulance door.

"Hey!" I shout it far too loudly, but the pain and adrenaline in my body are a heady biological cocktail.

He spins and peers into the ambulance. "Dr. James." His voice is hard.

I lift my good hand only to find it pinned to the stretcher as an IV goes into my arm. I smile at the paramedic as sweet, sweet drugs start to flow into my body.

"Technically, I'm still alive," I say. "Find Daryl Walden." I need to raise my voice over the confusion of the scene outside the ambulance. "He saw the driver that tried to hit me, and he has dash cam footage."

Carmen appears beside Detective Hanratty from around the opposite side of the ambulance.

"What are you doing." It is not a question. It's a scold.

I shut my mouth.

"That's what I thought," she says.

"Daryl Walden," I call after both of them as they retreat.

I know Daryl will find Carmen, and he will give her the dash cam footage, but just then the sweet elixir in my IV hits, and I collapse back against the pillow.

My eyes slide shut, and I'm about to let myself drift on a sea of painkillers when there's a clatter in the ambulance beside me.

"I'm her husband."

This is a phrase I'm hearing entirely too often, and my eyes spring open just before my husband kisses me.

"I'm so sorry," I say against his mouth. "I was just going to work."

He pulls away, and my breath catches at the stark lines of

his face. His eyes roam over me, cataloging, assessing, and I touch his face, bringing him back to me.

"I'm okay. I'm still on the alive list."

"Will you please stop flirting with the other side?" His words are playful, but his tone doesn't manage the same light-hearted note.

"I will really try," I say.

"Do I get to chase your ambulance?"

We both look at the open ambulance doors where my brother is standing, the dopiest, goofiest grin of pure glee on his face. Aunt Janine stands next to him with a slightly more appropriate, sober expression on her face.

"Possible concussion, multiple lacerations, and possible hip fracture on a previous femur fracture. We'll be going with lights and sirens, so you'd best better hurry," one of the para-medics calls to my brother.

Ryan gives a whoop of glee and starts running in presum-ably the direction of their car.

"Hey, frat boy!" Aunt Janine yells after him. "It's my car. I'll be doing the ambulance chasing."

The ambulance doors slam shut on their retreating forms.

———

"I knew someone was going to die, Greg."

"I'm not dead," I point out from my hospital bed.

"Well you could be," my mother shoots back.

"But I'm not, and don't you think bringing Father Patrick was a little much?" I gesture to the priest standing at the foot of my hospital bed.

He waves weakly in response, and how uncomfortable he's feeling is clear on his face.

My mother brushes this off. "We might have needed him to read you your last rites."

"We're not Catholic," Ryan says from where he's perched on the windowsill, popping jellybeans into his mouth.

"Isn't there a limit on the number of guests I can have in the room?"

Logan looks up from the bag my mother has brought me, my toothbrush in his hand. "It's six," he says and goes back into the bag.

I count. Damn.

I've been taken to the hospital in Plattsburgh, the extent of my possible injuries ruling out the clinic in Saranac. I've been X-rayed, scanned, poked, and prodded. No concussion, no broken elbow, no stitches, only three butterfly bandages and something likely spawned from Satan they used to clean the road rash, a job they pawned off on a poor intern, and no broken hip. Just a bruise the size and shape of Michigan minus the upper peninsula.

But because I'm the victim of a hit-and-run I'm being kept overnight for observation, a nice banal phrase used to charge the hell out of my insurance.

Aunt Janine appears with a takeout bag and a cardboard tray of drinks. Ryan reaches for one, and she beans him in the head with the takeout bag.

"That's for Logan and Moon Pie. They've been here all day. You went to the Bucking Bronco. I know you."

Ryan looks insulted.

"You've got barbecue sauce on your shirt," Aunt Janine says with a shake of her head.

Ryan covers the spot on his shirt with his hand. "No, I don't."

I reach for the bag, my stomach heaving in hunger. "Thank you, my dear auntie," I say in my most pleading voice.

She keeps the bag out of my reach. "No more risking your life for the dead."

I drop my hands. "Why does everyone keep asking me to do that?"

My phone dings where it sits on the table placed over my bed. I find a text from Carmen. It's a photo of Henry with her two girls. They've got him inside a bright pink sleeping bag, ribbons curled around his ears. His tongue hangs out of the side of his mouth, and one paw rests on Ella's head.

Your boy is happy.

I text back three heart emojis.

Daryl?

The three dots appear on the screen.

He's okay. Raymond's with him.

I text back another heart emoji and set my phone out of the way of dinner. Logan helps me unwrap a bacon cheeseburger and steak fries because my IV tube keeps getting caught on the bed rail. I finally give up and let him do it.

My mother hovers even if my father tries to convince her it's time to go home.

"We've delivered the bag. Let's let her rest. We'll see her tomorrow."

My mother shakes her head. "I knew this would happen."

"Nothing's happened," I say.

"Want to try out that new tiki bar in Saranac?" Aunt Janine asks Father Patrick.

He lights up for the first time since appearing in my hospital room.

"Sure," he says.

Aunt Janine waves at Ryan. "Come on, kid. You're the DD."

"Aww," Ryan moans but lopes after her. "See ya, snot rocket," he says to me.

"Thank you, dear little brother," I call after him.

His reply is a disgusted garble.

"Now listen, Delia Ann," my mother says as she

approaches the side of my bed. "I'm leaving for my retreat on Sunday, and I don't want you doing anything that will ruin this for me. I've waited years for this, and I'll—"

I hold up the hand that will not get stuck on the bed railing. "What retreat?"

Her lips part in that way that suggests she's talked to me about this before when I know she hasn't.

"My body painting retreat. You know. In Niagara-on-the-Lake? Del, we talked about it."

"I have absolutely no idea what you're talking about."

I can tell this is the wrong thing to say because my dad's eyes go wide and slide away from us, and he starts a conversation with Logan about golf. Neither of them golf.

My mother sets both of her hands on the bed rail. "Delia Ann, you know I've talked about going on this retreat, but I never had the vacation time. The retreat is four weeks long. It's with Gustav Renault, the master of the art form."

"What art form?"

"Body painting," she says, the exasperation clipping her words.

"Like tattoos?"

She rolls her eyes. "No, where you use your body as the brush."

An image pops into my head that is so deeply disturbing I know it will never leave my mind.

"What?" I say, even though I really don't want an explanation. It's really just a reaction.

Her face pinches with disappointment. "I've told you this. You spend the first week of the retreat getting comfortable with your naked body." Here she spreads her hands down her torso sensually, and my hunger vanishes. I eye the bacon cheeseburger despondently. "Only when you're comfortable with your true form can your artistry reveal itself."

I look to my father to find both he and Logan staring at the TV mounted in the corner, the sound turned low.

"Dad," I say. I'm not going to be alone in this conversation. "Do you know Mom is going to spend a week naked with some dude pretending to be an artist?"

Dad doesn't turn around, his voice robotic as he says, "I support her in whatever she wants to do."

I turn my attention back to her. "You cannot be doing this."

Her disappointment deepens. "I can, and I will. I am not going to allow any of you to ruin this for me. I knew that's what you were going to do."

"Ruin what?"

"My retirement," she says, her voice heavy with exasperation. "Del, I've waited so long for this."

"You've been going on for weeks about how somebody was going to die because you were going to retire."

"Yes," she nearly yells. "And ruin. It. For. Me." She enunciates each word carefully.

I try to sit up in my hospital bed. "Wait. This whole time you've been worried about someone ruining your retirement. Not about retirement itself?"

She blinks. "Why would I be worried about retirement?"

I think about her giant party, the list of classes she had started making at the beginning of the year that she wanted to take once she finished work, about how she was just learning to stand-up paddle board with Ryan.

"Retirement is a big change. It can be difficult to adapt," I say.

My mother scoffs. "Please, Delia Ann. Not all change is bad."

She gives me one more stern lecture about not ruining her life by dying and collects my father before heading out the door.

I only get to enjoy three bites of my now less appealing bacon cheeseburger before there's a knock at the door.

Detective Hanratty pokes his head in. "I don't mean to interrupt."

Logan waves him in and stands from where he'd taken the chair beside my bed. "Please. Any updates?"

Hanratty steps inside the room, followed closely by Perez. I set down my burger. If they've come in pairs, it means business.

"We've reviewed the dash cam video from Mr. Walden's truck. There's no clear shot of the driver's face, but it is clear it's a woman with long, dark hair. She's wearing large sunglasses, though that obstruct most of her face."

"Dr. James, were you able to observe the driver before the incident?" Perez asks, rather more stoically than his usual demeanor.

I shake my head. "I didn't know anything was happening until I heard Daryl honk."

Hanratty and Perez exchange a glance.

"It would appear from the dash cam footage the driver of the vehicle knew your movements. Mr. Walden picked up her location at the supermarket located off the county highway in Bellegrave. From there, she proceeded to a community center."

Perez checks his phone, but I offer the name.

"The Gale Center," I say. "The Gale Center is at the turnoff where the county highway splits, and the lake road goes north where the lodge is."

Perez nods. "Mr. Walden followed the suspect to that location where she parked for a short time. Your vehicle is seen passing the Gale Center, and the suspect starts moving again."

"She was waiting for me." A chill grips me, but as soon as the fear starts to take hold, a warmth spreads inside of me. It's small and swift, but it banishes the cold.

Before I can think about it, Logan sits down on the side of my bed and takes my hand.

"So what does this mean?" he asks.

Perez nods to Hanratty.

Hanratty says, "We've dispersed the description of the vehicle to all law enforcement in the area and indicated the likely damage it would have sustained after the collision with the brick pillar. We have Bellegrave deputies canvasing the village with an image of the driver we were able to pull from the video, but it's likely no one is going to recognize her. The image isn't very good frankly."

"May I see it?"

Hanratty pulls his phone from his pocket, taps the screen, and holds it out to me. He's right. The image is grainy, and at best, I can make out the long, dark hair and sunglasses.

I shake my head. "That could be anyone."

Hanratty nods, grimly. "In a professional capacity, I will tell you we're doing everything we can to locate the suspect."

"And the unprofessional capacity?" Logan asks.

Hanratty puts his phone away. "I think you'd better figure out pretty quickly who is trying to kill you."

"That is a long list, my friend," I mutter. "Would the driver of the vehicle have been hurt?" I ask then.

Hanratty nods. "Most likely."

"We've notified area hospitals, clinics, urgent cares. That sort of thing," Perez says.

I think about the destroyed brick pillar. "She must have hit the brick pillar pretty hard," I say. "Her injuries would be visible, right?"

"Are you suggesting we go around and check people for bruises?" Hanratty asks.

I think about the map of Michigan on my hip.

"Maybe," I offer.

Hanratty steps forward and puts both hands on the rail at the foot of my bed.

"Look," he says. "You know something, or someone thinks you know something. Something damning enough that they're trying to stop you before you can tell the authorities."

His words are too painfully close to the feeling Sadie pressed on me that night on the island.

"I've told you everything I know," I say.

He shakes his head slowly. "There's something we're not putting together. Something big."

I swallow. "Sometimes people think ghosts give me the name of their killer, but it doesn't really work like that."

Hanratty stills. "What do you mean?"

"A spirit will choose the thing that's important to them. The piece that connected the puzzle for them or the thing they were thinking about when they died. It takes so much for them to manifest I think there's an element of panic, and they get out whatever it is they can." I picture Sadie, her arm raised, the bee charm dangling from the bracelet at her wrist. "Sadie was trying to protect those girls on the island. I know that much now, but who was she trying to protect them from?"

"From whoever is trying to kill you," Hanratty says.

He's right, and the enormity of what I've been investigating comes together. In my mind, I'd been researching the past, something I was trained in, something I was comfortable with. It only occurs to me now that the killer is still out there and alive.

"What should I do?"

Hanratty straightens. "I would tell you to let us do our jobs, but you've been doing them better than us." He glances at Logan and back to me. "Do you two have any vacation time you can take? Lay low for a while?"

I shake my head. "Summer is my busy season. I can't leave the lodge. We already had to cancel this morning's sessions while the debris from the brick pillar was cleaned up. We can't lose any more time."

"Someone is trying to kill you," Hanratty says like I've just tried to convince him the world is flat. He looks at Logan again. "You can't talk sense into her, can you?"

"Nope," Logan says plainly. "She will do what she wants to do, and I can only hope she'll let me help her."

For some reason, my husband's words sting, and I can't help but think once more about how I retreated into my own pain when our daughter died, leaving him alone with his.

"I'll lay low," I say.

I don't know who I've surprised more. Hanratty, Logan, or myself. Perez is the only one who seems unperturbed.

"I still need to go to work, but I can make sure I'm not the one opening, and I'm not the last person to leave at night. I'll make sure someone is with me at all times. I'll just go from home to work and back. No errands. No outings. I'll curtail any of my activities for the time being. Will that help?"

I can feel Logan's stare on the side of my face, but I can't look at him or I'll give in to the tears I can sense brewing. I only squeeze his hand as he's still holding mine.

"You would do that?" Hanratty asks.

"Yes," I say. "Of course, I will. I'd carry a gun for protection, but mine was confiscated after I shot someone with it. Carmen says I might get it back after the trial."

Hanratty turns to Perez, and I think they might exchange words, but something on the television behind Hanratty catches my attention.

I point. "Turn it up," I hiss.

Logan grabs the remote to turn up the volume on the TV while Hanratty and Perez turn to see what I'm pointing at.

Monica Davies's face fills the screen of the television, a title card running along the bottom of the shot.

The sound of a reporter fills the small hospital room.

"A break in the 1999 hit-and-run that left shipping mogul Donald Carmichael critically injured has led to the arrest of Monica Davies," the reporter says. "Fifty-eight-year-old Davies has no fixed address but was reportedly a camper at Carmichael's Camp Carmichael in Bellegrave before its sudden closure in 1984. While Davies has previously been arrested on drugs charges, police are still trying to determine a motive in the hit-and-run that nearly killed Carmichael."

The image on the screen is the mugshot I'd found when searching Monica Davies's name, and I wonder why there isn't a more current photo. The reporter goes on to say Davies is being held at a jail in Plattsburgh until her arraignment.

I don't look away from the TV, but I can feel three pairs of eyes on me as I say, "I need to talk to her."

TWENTY-FIVE

anratty makes the arrangements for me to visit
Monica Davies at the Clinton County jail the
following day. I go directly from the hospital to the
jail, an experience I never thought I would have.

Carmen arrives at my hospital room a little after nine, just
after the doctor has cleared me to go but before the nurses
have finished my discharge paperwork. She's usually discreet
when it comes to her firearm, but today she has it holstered
directly on the belt of her fuchsia cropped pants, her badge
clipped next to it.

"Ah, my date has arrived," I say.

Logan is putting my shoes on because I can't bend that far
down, and he looks up to glance at Carmen.

"So this is who you're leaving me for," he says melodra-
matically.

"Only for today," I say and attempt to stand.

I can't. Logan catches me by the elbows.

"I'm afraid not for today either," he says as he sets me back
on the bed. "I'm going with you."

"You have to work." It sounds like an excuse I'm making for him to go back home, but really, I'm feeling guilty.

No sooner had I promised to lie low than I arranged to meet my possible murderer in jail.

"Bridget's canceling my meetings," he says, referring to his secretary as he gathers the bag of things my mom brought the night before.

The hair on the back of his head is sticking straight up, probably because he slept wedged in the plastic-covered chair beside my bed. The guilt blooms.

"What about Henry?"

I want to tell him he should go home, have a hot shower, eat real food, and fall asleep on the couch with our dog, but it's not something I know how to say to him. Those kinds of words are another victim of the space I've let grow between us.

"Henry's with AJ and Ryan," Carmen says. "They said something about taking him dock diving."

Logan swings the tote bag on his arm and reaches for me with the other one. "Come on," he says. "I'm taking you to jail." He wiggles his eyebrows. "This will be fun."

He's making fun, but I can see the strain in his eyes. I still him with my hand on the one he has on my arm.

"Logan, I promise this is it. I meant what I said about staying out of it. Letting Hanratty and Perez investigate. I just —" I lick my lips, suddenly nervous. I need him to believe me, and I've never felt that before. "I think if I talk to Monica, somewhere where she can't hurt me, we might be able to find out who is behind this, and it will all be over." I watch his face, study the strain in his eyes. "I need this to be over," I say.

He studies me the way I study him, and I watch the hardness leave his eyes.

"Okay," he says.

Hanratty and Perez meet us at the jail. Hanratty has had to

arrange for this visit, and I thank him for the strings I know he's had to pull. He brushes off my thanks.

"If you can make some progress in this case, then that's thanks enough," he says.

I'm stripped of anything that could be considered a weapon, including my *History Done Dangerously* hoodie I got at an archivist conference a few years ago.

I'm taken into a small room that disappointingly looks nothing like any of the visiting rooms I've seen on any crime drama ever. It's sterile and plain, but it's clean and well lit. Hanratty said Monica was offered a public defender for this meeting, but she declined.

I take a seat at the table with the laminate top and connected plastic disc seats and wait. When the guard brings Monica into the room, I'm momentarily confused. She looks nothing like the outdated mugshot, sure, but more she doesn't look like the woman who accosted me that night at the boathouse. It's like she's aged ten years. It lies on her face like a bad tattoo, digging into every line and crevice. Worse, her eyes are flat and lifeless.

She's no longer afraid, I realize. She's simply resigned.

"Hi," I say when she takes the seat across from me. "Thank you for agreeing to speak to me."

In the dim light of dusk, I'd been unable to appreciate how old this woman is. Closer to sixty than fifty, she's worn down at the edges and tired. So unlike Ashley Carmichael with her bouncing ponytail.

Monica doesn't say anything. I glance at the guard who remains at the door and shift in my seat.

"I know what happened on the island."

This at least brings Monica's attention to me instead of the laminate top of the table.

"I know the girls at Camp Carmichael were forced to

endure some kind of hazing, which likely included being raped or at least assaulted by boys from Tomahawk."

I wait, thinking my words might bring a reaction, but the one I get is not the one I hoped for. Monica looks away, out the bank of windows to the side of the room, disinterested.

"Were you a victim of the hazing?" I ask.

Monica snorts, her mouth lifting in a terrible grin, but she doesn't say anything for several seconds.

"No one knows what happened on that island," she says, her voice gravelly today, worn out as much as the rest of her. But then her eyes lock on me, and her voice is suddenly hard. "We made sure of it."

Her tone is unlike the night she threatened me with the knife. It doesn't tremble or waver. The roller coaster of emotion is absent. Her words still register a note of alarm.

"Made sure of what? What are you hiding?"

She snorts again, her mouth twisting as she looks away. "You think you're going to figure this out, Nancy Drew?" she sneers. She moves her head slowly left and right in a mockingly slow shake of her head. "You won't. That's the whole point. Always has been. What happens on that island stays there. It always stayed there."

I lay my hands on the table. "Then help me figure it out. Tell me what happened that night."

My voice comes out sharper than I mean it to, and it draws her stare back to me. She still doesn't speak though.

"What does Jonathan Starkley have to do with this? How was he involved with Sadie Beaumont's murder?"

Something flashes across her eyes at Starkley's name, but she remains unmoving, perched on the seat opposite me.

"Was Starkley part of the hazing?"

She snorts. "Jonathan wouldn't kill the snake that bit him."

"So then what *did* he do?" I ask.

Her eyes are still on my face. "He did the same as the rest of us."

I'm getting nowhere.

"What happened to Debbie Fraser?"

Again there's no reaction for a long time, and when she does speak, her words are slow.

"Debbie died." She says this so softly I almost can't hear her over the buzz of the overhead lights. "She couldn't take it. She couldn't live with what happened. With what we did."

"What who did? Are you talking about Starkley now?"

Monica's eyes drift to the windows again, but her expression has softened, almost reflective now.

"I took Debbie to Vermont when she found out she was pregnant." Monica doesn't look away from the window as she speaks. "Abortion was easier there. I borrowed my mom's Mercedes." She snorts again, the laugh humorless. "What a fancy car for such a terrible thing. Debbie was sick after. I got her home, but she didn't stop bleeding. Her mom found her. Figured out what we'd done." Monica's laugh is harder now. "Ah, the pain they inflicted on us. Her mother and mine." She shakes her head slowly again. "But they didn't know. They didn't know the worst thing we'd done."

"Did you kill Sadie Beaumont?" I ask the question that lurks at the edge of our conversation.

She turns her gaze back to me, and her eyes have turned sad.

"No," she says. "I didn't kill Sadie Beaumont."

I believe her. It's in the forlorn expression on her tired face. The one thing she's been truthful about since we sat down at this table.

"Then why did you try to kill me yesterday with your car?" It's a gamble, but it's one I must take.

She straightens. I watch her head lift and tilt in question, her hands come to rest on the table like mine, but hers are laced with scars.

"Someone tried to kill you? With a car?"

I think she's playing, but I can play along too.

"You know they did. They tried to run me over. Tell me. Is that what you do? Hit-and-runs?"

Her gaze drops slightly but instead of ignoring me, I think she's thinking, gathering her thoughts as though they're scattered about the table.

"Of course." Her smile is sick, knowing. "I wondered why. After all this time."

"Wondered what?"

But I know she's not going to answer, and she doesn't.

I change course again.

"I heard after Sadie died Jonathan Starkley and Ashley Carmichael started dating."

Her eyes flash up. "He didn't love her."

Curious.

"I didn't say that."

She picks at the table now, the first sign of agitation I've seen since she walked in.

"He didn't love her," she says again. "His mom wanted him to marry Ashley."

"But they didn't marry," I say.

Monica scratches at the table, the sound soft and swishing against the harsh buzz of the lights.

"I know," she says, contemplative. "I always wondered if his mom found out what he'd done."

She says the words to the tabletop, and I think for a moment she's forgotten I'm there.

I want to reach out and take her hand, remind her that I'm human and vulnerable just like her, but the guard is watching us.

"Monica." I speak her name softly.

Her eyes lift from the table to me.

"Tell me what happened that night," I say. "I can help."

Her expression doesn't change when she says, "Nobody will believe an addict."

She gets up then and walks back to the guard, and our interview is over.

TWENTY-SIX

After a short debrief with Hanratty and Perez afterward, I head home to do nothing for three blissful days.

I try not to think about Sadie Beaumont, Jonathan Starkley, or Monica Davies. I try not to think about my poor brick pillar and the funds that we'll need to raise to restore it. Peevishly, I hope Allie will be the one to tell Arnold Fairchild what's happened, so I can avoid being on the receiving end of whatever diatribe might ensue.

I binge the BBC adaptation of Agatha Christie's *And Then There Were None*, but I still can't stop thinking about Monica's conflicting words. We take Henry out on the boat, and I float on the inner tube along our beachfront, careful to keep my bandaged arm out of the water, but still I find my gaze locked on the island out in the middle of the lake, my mind working the pieces of the puzzle together.

Monica said Jonathan Starkley wouldn't hurt the snake that bit him, but then she'd gone on to say she thought Starkley and Ashley hadn't married because his family had found out what he'd done.

Had they discovered he'd killed Sadie Beaumont?

Was he the voice I'd heard that day on the phone with Ashley Carmichael?

When Logan takes Henry for a run, I sneak on to my forbidden laptop to try to piece together where Starkley might have been the day I called Ashley. Photos from the publicity tour he'd been on for the last several weeks were all over social media, and I found one from July fifteenth of him in Tupper Lake, eating ice cream with a group of kids at a STEM summer camp.

Tupper Lake isn't that far from Bellegrave. He could have been there.

But then why?

Had he heard they'd found Sadie's body and gone to warn Ashley not to talk? But then that would suggest Ashley knew something about Sadie's death.

I think about Elmer's and Chief Wise's impressions of Ashley as well as my own and just can't put together that bubbly person weighed down by responsibility and tragedy having anything to do with Sadie Beaumont's death.

When I get to the lodge Monday morning, there's still one question that refuses to leave my mind.

How could someone conceal a murder on an island filled with campers and staff?

Miriam Carmichael was dead. Donald Carmichael wasn't there. Were the staff and counselors complicit? Was there someone on staff who arranged all of it, and their crimes would never be uncovered because the records were likely gone? How powerful was Donald Carmichael that he could wield such control from Kingston?

Solving Victoria Gustafson's murder seemed so easy now with a clear path to the killer. I'd survived two attempts on my life and am no closer to finding who killed Sadie Beaumont, nor who I'm meant to save.

Steve Fitzpatrick meets me in the parking lot, his ubiquitous Buffalo Bills coffee cup in one hand.

I raise an eyebrow as I walk up to him. "What's happened now?"

He shakes his head, his smiling growing. "Nothing. Just walking you to your office."

I stop so quickly in the parking lot, my sandals shuffle gravel. I stare at Steve and a movement out of the corner of my eye catches my attention. Frances is waiting for me on the lodge's porch. Her hands are folded in front of her, a long letter opener glinting in her grasp.

"Are you both serious?"

Frances raises her chin. "Logan called."

I figured he would. I allow my army to walk me into my office. Allie and Lisa are waiting. Allie has the Cake & Cookie box in hand, Lisa the tray of coffees.

I let out an exaggerated sigh as I set down my bag by my desk.

"This is going to suck, isn't it?" I ask.

Allie gives me a one-sided hug, avoiding the arm that's still covered in bandages.

"Yeah, but at least we're the ones who get to torture you."

There's a knock at my office door, and I'm not in the least surprised to see Detective Hanratty.

"Hey," he says with a small wave of one hand. "You doing okay?"

"You're checking on me too now?"

I don't miss the glance he slides Lisa's way. Part of me is envious. The ease of a new relationship. No baggage. No years of shared trauma. But as I look between them, I know they carry their own personal trauma into the relationship, whatever it may turn out to be, and that I don't envy.

"Afraid so," Hanratty says, his smile kind. "I plan to meet

State Senator Starkley's team at the square when they arrive in the village this morning."

"You're going to ambush him," I say.

Hanratty straightens from the door, his smile turning knowing. "Ambush is a strong word. I would say surprise is more appropriate."

The detective leaves, and I'm left with my small army of historical society staff and volunteers. It feels good to settle into work I'm familiar with that contains an incredibly low risk of murder, namely *my* murder.

When I drove into the office that morning, I saw the preparations in town for the state senator's visit. It had made my stomach turn, and I drove through as quickly as possible.

The morning is busy with the usual Monday tasks of cleaning up whatever fires were extinguished over the weekend. Thankfully none included calling the fire department to free a kid stuck in a safety barrier.

By noon I'm starving and sick to death of everyone following me around.

As if sensing my mood, Carmen appears with a greasy paper bag I know can only be from Shelly's.

"Logan thought of everything, didn't he?"

Carmen smiles flirtatiously. "Whatever do you mean?"

The Reuben and fries are not enough to distract me. The vanilla milkshake Carmen brought with them helps though, and by the afternoon, I'm somewhat mollified.

I compulsively check my phone every few minutes. Starkley was due to arrive in the square around eleven. Surely Hanratty would have spoken to him by now. When I check my phone for the billionth time, I remind myself I'm not a police officer, and Hanratty does not need to update me on the investigation.

I've been staring at a draft of a newsletter for so long my

eyes have started to water when there's a frantic scuffle in the hall and Diana Milton appears in my doorway.

"Starkley is here."

For a second, her words don't register. I'd nearly fallen asleep trying to read the newsletter, and with my mind relentlessly on Sadie Beaumont and the state senator, I think I'm dreaming.

"What do you mean he's here?"

Allie appears next to Diana. "Starkley and his team just pulled onto the grounds. Steve radioed from the creamery where he's fixing the ground on that outside outlet. He saw their cars pull in and wanted to warn us."

Allie doesn't know the double meaning of her words. While everyone is aware someone has now tried twice to take my life, they don't know of Starkley's connection to the murder of Sadie Beaumont.

I look between them. "This isn't a planned stop."

Allie shakes her head. "No. We have no idea why he's here."

I check my phone again, but there's still nothing from Hanratty.

"Okay, this is fine," I say, although I don't really feel that way. "It's fine. Let's welcome the state senator."

The crunch of gravel in the parking lot is like gunfire through the open windows, and I turn to see a trio of black SUVs pull into spaces near the entrance to the lodge.

My body tenses instinctively, and I take a deep breath. I don't know if the state senator is really a murderer. He just most likely is one.

We meet Starkley and his team on the front porch.

"State Senator Starkley, what a surprise," I say, forcing a civil tone.

It's apparent Jonathan Starkley is a fan of sunscreen. His face is remarkably unlined, and his teeth have seen plenty of whitener. He wears his brown hair cut short in a style more suited to an elementary school kid in the nineties with the khakis and blue button-down shirt to match. I wonder if his tie is clip-on.

I don't offer him my hand, but then it doesn't seem he expects it.

"Thank you for having us. I'm sorry to just show up here, but someone in town thought we should stop by." His smile is just the right amount of enthusiastic, and I realize he's had years to perfect it.

"Oh, lovely," I say. "I'm Dr. Della James, the executive director here. Please allow me to introduce my staff."

I make it as far as Allie before my phone beeps. Allie must see my hand go to it in my pocket because she picks up the introductions. I slip my phone from my pocket and check the screen.

Hanratty.

Starkley stonewalled us. Insisted on a lawyer. We're trying to arrange it now.

Insisted on a lawyer.

I look up from my phone, dazed. I should have known Starkley would push back. I was naive to think Hanratty would get anywhere with him.

Starkley and his entourage have now moved into the lodge and into the conference space where Diana is showing him the 360 cameras we offer for virtual meetings, how the historical space has been adapted to suit modern needs. There are so many people surrounding the state senator, and as I'm already unbalanced from Hanratty's text, it's as though the room is closing in around me.

There are a handful of aides marked by the phones glued to their hands, their sensible shoes, and the caffeine-crazed look in their eyes. One aide is taking photos with a real camera while another holds her phone vertically, following the state senator as he listens to Diana explain the twig and branch decor that is a distinctive mark of Adirondack camp design. The aide filming shifts, and I can see her phone screen now. It's populated with floating emojis.

She's live on some social media outlet.

I turn my attention back to Starkley. Detective Hanratty must answer to the law. I only answer to the dead. I step through the crowd of people until I'm in front of Starkley.

"Jonathan Starkely," I say. "You were at Camp Carmichael the night Sadie Beaumont was murdered."

He's good. I know I've startled him, but the political gloss is so thick it hides all his secrets from his face. I don't let it deter me.

"I confirmed you were there with the man who ran the launch that night that took you and the rest of the boys from Tomahawk over to the island. He said when he brought you back you were soaking wet, and the rest of the boys were being particularly cruel to you." I pause but only long enough to let this sink in. "What happened that night? Who murdered Sadie Beaumont?"

My persistence is rewarded when the political gloss cracks just the tiniest bit. I don't think it's going to work, and then finally there it is. His expression changes for just a moment, and anyone else in the room might have missed it. But I'm watching him too closely, and for just a second I see it.

His face hardens, his eyes grow cold, and for just a moment, he looks like a man who could kill someone.

I've made a mistake. The instinct to step back is strong, but I won't back down. It doesn't matter. Starkley turns and whispers something to the aide next to him. Without so much as another glance at me, he walks away, turning deeper into the lodge.

I go to follow when a hand clamps down on my arm.

"Dr. James, you're coming with me."

I turn, the voice unfamiliar, and see a Bellegrave police deputy I don't recognize standing next to me, his hand holding my arm.

"What?" I'm so confused it's the only word I manage.

In the crush I must not have seen the police deputies, but there's actually two of them, and one of them is turning me. The cold snap of handcuffs on my wrists jolts me awake.

"Wait. What are you doing?"

The deputy straightens. "You're under arrest for threatening a public official."

I snort. "I didn't threaten anyone."

He ignores this. "Come along, Dr. James, or I'll add resisting arrest."

"I'm not—" I shut my mouth, turn as far to the side as I can. "Frances, call Logan."

"I'm already on the phone to him," she shouts back over the sudden buzz in the crowd.

I go peacefully with the deputy as he reads me my rights. It isn't until I'm locked in the back of the cruiser that the panic sets in.

It isn't because I'm being arrested.

It's because I've just realized *where* they're taking me.

TWENTY-SEVEN

"I can't be here," I say, my voice trembling with panic I try to lock down.

The deputy who arrested me laughs. His name tag says Brodsky on it. I'm going to remember that.

"Then you shouldn't have threatened a public official," he says.

I sit on a metal chair by a metal desk in the basement police station beneath the Bellegrave Opera House. My hands are still cuffed behind my back, and though I'm trying to calm down, my breath is coming in shallow gasps. My lungs sting as air turns cold around me.

"No, you really need to listen to me. I can't be in here. It's dangerous for me."

I look around frantically, but the open office space is eerily empty. There's a pair of officers at a desk in the corner I don't recognize, and Delilah who usually sits at the front desk isn't there. Is everyone out in the village for Starkley's visit?

Deputy Brodsky laughs again. "Is that right? Well, think about that the next time you want to break the law."

The temperature drops more, and instead of breathing air it feels like I'm sucking ice water into my lungs.

The deputy is going through paperwork on his desk, blissfully ignoring me. When the frost spreads across the arms of the metal chair in which I sit, I kick the metal desk beside me violently.

"Jesus," the deputy mutters and jumps in his chair.

"Listen to me." My voice is unyielding. "You need to call Detective Carmen Neil. She can explain. You need to get me out of here."

The frost spreads up the arm of the chair. It oozes closer and closer. I lean back in the chair as far as possible, but it's coming up the legs now.

I shoot to my feet, stumble backward into the desk behind me.

"That's it," the deputy says, snagging a ring of keys from his desk as he stands. "Maybe some time in the cell will calm you down."

"No." The word comes out involuntarily. "No, you can't lock me in there. You can't—"

Mist clouds my vision, and I stop speaking, the darkness stealing my words.

The deputy has hold of my arm again, my bandaged arm. The pain is nothing compared to the cold. He drags me toward the holding cells at the far end of the basement and tosses me inside the farthest one. I trip. My shoulder crashes into the concrete block of the wall at the back of the cell, and when the pain shoots down my arm, I'm only grateful it wasn't the one that's still bandaged from the road rash.

"No!" I'm screaming now. "You can't leave me in here."

At some point he removed the handcuffs. I launch myself toward the cell door, but the clang of the key in the lock cuts off my next words.

"Just calm down, lady," he says. "We'll probably get you arraigned by Wednesday."

I watch him walk away. I don't realize I'm gripping the cell bars until the frost closes over my hands. I jerk them away, the skin tearing. I flex my fingers as I stare at the blueness invading the tips. I shake them, willing life back into them.

The mist from the open space at the end of the hall has reached me by the time I can feel my fingers again. At first it's just a fog, hazy and indistinct. It lingers in the hallway just beyond the cell bars. It watches me without eyes.

"No," I say, the word quiet and subdued.

The mist gathers, darkens, and it's several beats of my heart before I can see it's forming a shape.

"No." This is louder now, fear driving the word from me. "No." This is screamed as fear turns to terror, and the shape solidifies.

It has arms now, and they're reaching for me.

"No!" I scream again, but I know no one is coming.

No one is going to save me.

The black void comes together in the snap of a second. The arms stretch into a torso, into a head hidden in a black hood of smoke. There are no legs. It drifts toward me, arms held out in front, black fingers reaching for me.

Della.

My name is like the hiss of a snake in my head, but the thunder of my beating heart doesn't drown it out.

It's going to kill me.

This.

This thing.

This evil spirit is going to kill me.

No.

The word is only in my head, but it's stronger, surer than any of the *nos* I've spoken so far.

No.

I feel the word. Feel it course through me, running through my veins.

No.

The blackness is almost to me. I can see the decayed nails of its fingers like the dried wings of dead flies.

No.

It crooks a single finger in front of my face.

I close my eyes against the evil and speak a name, a name I never got to use.

"Audrey."

The warmth comes first. It bubbles softly in my very center, bubbling and convulsing, growing until it rushes through me. I force my eyes open, force myself to watch what happens. The light shoots from me in a sparking arc, showering the cell with drops of fire. The black void recoils, its anger a shriek in my head.

"Audrey." I speak her name more loudly, call on the warmth inside of me, summon it, beckon it.

Let it free.

I keep my eyes open until the light grows too bright. Only when I can't look anymore do I let the warmth take me.

————

When I open my eyes again, I'm surprised to see Hanratty's face hovering over mine.

I jerk and smash my head into what feels like concrete.

It is concrete I realize when the wrought iron railing of the police station stairs come into focus.

"Crap, Della, are you okay?" Hanratty says, picking my head up from the sidewalk.

I blink against the afternoon sun. Hanratty is above me. Perez is kneeling at my feet.

"Did you guys carry me out of there?" My voice is gravelly, but the words are mostly discernible.

"Yeah," Perez says. "We heard you screaming from out here." He thrusts a thumb over his shoulder. "Detective Neil said we had to get in there."

I let my head fall back into Hanratty's hands and close my eyes. When I open them again, I see Hanratty studying the building beside us, his neck tense.

"Something bad is in there," he says.

It's not a question. I know now that it's not.

"There is," I say. "Very bad."

He looks down at me, something passing over his eyes.

I don't get to question it though because I suddenly become aware of a squawking noise.

"What is that?" I ask.

Perez's expression is nearly childlike. "It's Detective Neil reaming out that snot-nosed deputy."

Hanratty shakes his head. "Kid deserves it. Can't have somebody with that holier than thou mentality on a police force."

I sit up enough to see Carmen at the top of the stairs. She is indeed reaming out Deputy Brodsky. The poor man. I have no sympathy. Not even when Carmen morphs from her second-grade-teacher stare to her third-grade one. Mrs. Michaels. Any infraction in her class resulted in immediate suspension of bathroom privileges for the day. Bathroom. Privileges. The woman was a witch.

"I confronted Starkley," I admit then, letting my head collapse back against Hanratty.

"I heard." His tone indicates his displeasure.

"How far have I set back the investigation?"

I can see in his eyes I've done irreparable damage to his investigation, but he doesn't say so.

He only says, "Let's not worry about it right now."

Later, much later, after Logan once more collects me from outside the police station, when we're sitting together on the hill that slopes away from our little cottage and down to the lake below, as we watch Henry try to catch the bubbles he's making in the water, while I tell my husband about the echo our daughter has left inside of me, only then do I let myself think about what I saw in the jail cell.

Logan doesn't ask me any questions. He's heard what happened from Carmen, Hanratty, Perez, and a very apologetic Chief Tom. He doesn't say anything. He just sits beside me on the hill and holds my hand while I stare at the abandoned camp on the island in front of our cottage and wonder who killed Sadie Beaumont.

I don't go to work the next day and neither does Logan. We don't do much besides sit on the couch and watch old James Bond movies. Henry is happy to nap the day away, taking turns snuggling with each of us. For a single day, I let myself not think about the investigation, about how I might have prevented Hanratty from ever bringing Starkley to justice.

Because I know now it must have been Starkley who killed Sadie. He was the only one who could have. The pieces fit together. He was soaking wet that night because he was forced to jump in the lake and wash off Sadie's blood. That must be it. It's the reason Ashley Carmichael didn't marry him. He was a murderer.

It didn't matter what I thought. I'd jeopardized the whole case by confronting him like that.

But I try not to think about it for one day. Just one. I'll deal with the dead tomorrow.

For now, I kiss my husband good night for the first time in a very long time.

TWENTY-EIGHT

I go back to work on Wednesday.

The board meeting is two weeks away, and the first thing I do is update my resume. I'm nearly certain the board is going to fire me, not only for getting the nineteenth-century brick pillar demolished but also for accusing a state senator of murder in Lady Josephine Lodge while it all streamed live on social media.

I haven't heard from Hanratty, and Chief Tom has already gotten Starkley to drop any charges. Starkley likely didn't want the bad publicity if he truly was going to announce his run for governor soon.

I focus on the upcoming board meeting and the end of the busy summer season. With the help of the entire staff, we draw up a list of things that need to be completed in the lodge before the meeting to make Lady Josephine look her best for the board. It was more than we could tackle in a couple of weeks, and it was agreed we'd assemble our usual volunteers to sort out the tasks.

By Friday, David Knoll has taken over control of the list, doling out responsibilities like a mom with the candy bowl on

Halloween. He's commandeered the use of the small table in my office where I usually meet with staff. It's late in the afternoon, and I know we'd all rather be at Domingo's for happy hour despite the incessant rain, but he's diligently drawing up physical checklists for the volunteers he's organized for maintenance duty over the weekend.

I can feel him watching me where I sit, sorting through the donor lists Diana has given me to review for the board report.

"What?" I finally say when I can't take it any longer.

David shuffles his to-do lists, punching holes in them to make binders for each volunteer.

"I just don't get it," he says. "If I had any of those Camp Carmichael people pegged for a murderer, it wouldn't be State Senator Starkley. The man drives a hybrid and not a good one."

I look at him. "Who said State Senator Starkley is a murderer?"

He waves this away. "Everyone is talking about it now that your little video has gone viral."

I frown. "It's not my video."

He snorts. "You've achieved what every tweenager dreams about. Social media stardom."

He says this as if we're discussing my Broadway debut.

"It doesn't matter," I say. "There's no evidence to prove who murdered Sadie Beaumont. It was too long ago, and I've messed up the only solid lead."

David stops his shuffling for a moment, but his attention remains on me.

Finally he shakes his head, "You know I'm not sure why anyone still talks about Ashley Carmichael."

I sit back in my desk chair. "What do you mean?"

David shrugs. "It's just she was washed up before she even started, you know?"

"Washed up?" I wonder if somewhere in my many adventures of late I've hit my head because David is not making sense.

He shakes his head. "I forget how young you are sometimes."

"We're nearly the same age," I remind him.

He stands and comes over to my desk, leans on the edge. "Yeah, but you never ventured out beyond the confines of Bellegrave much before you left for college."

This is true. I tell him to go on.

"Ashley Carmichael opened a restaurant down in Kingston, right? Place got panned by food critics almost immediately. It was in danger of closing within the first month."

Vaguely I recall a publicity photo of Ashley in chef's whites.

"So her restaurant wasn't successful? I thought the food business is difficult. Low margins and what not."

"Yeah, but it helps when Daddy can step in and give a little money to keep the business afloat."

"Donald Carmichael bankrolled his daughter's restaurant?"

"Sure did. At least for a while." He shakes his head, his eyes going to the rain streaking the windows behind my desk. "If you ask me, Daddy's accident was awfully convenient. She got to close shop without losing face. In fact, people praised her for giving up her dream to take care of her father." David snorts. "Please. That place was going under as it was."

There's a small tug deep inside my brain.

I open my mouth to ask a question, but a more relevant one comes out instead. "How do you know all this?"

David's smile is full of pride. "My dad was one of the critics who panned her. I remember him talking to my mom about it. He couldn't believe with all that wealth Ashley Carmichael had turned out to be nothing."

Nothing.

Nothing.

Nobody.

The tug again, deep in the recesses of my mind.

I'm stopped from going further at a small knock on my door. Allie sweeps in with a tablet in her hands.

"I got those marketing photos from the Starkley team's photographer," she says as she props the tablet on my desk and begins swiping through photos.

Even though I had accused the state senator of murder and been arrested, the visit had been mostly a triumph. Starkley had seemed to enjoy the tour of the lodge and had made an impassioned speech about historical preservation on the lodge's front porch. It had been Allie's idea to use some of the Starkley team's photos from the visit to show the board it hadn't been a complete debacle.

The photos are what I expected. State Senator Starkley looking like a campaigning politician with the rolled-up sleeves and intense expression while Diana likely explains how the hallways were once open walkways to incorporate nature.

David goes back to his checklists, but I'm not done with him.

"Why do you bring this up now?" I ask as Allie continues to swipe on the screen of the tablet.

"Because Ashley Carmichael was here when Starkley stopped by for that unplanned visit," he says.

The tug in my mind is replaced by a bulldozer that attempts to knock me clean out of my chair.

"Ashley Carmichael was here?" My gaze swings frantically between Allie and David.

Allie nods. "Yeah, she showed up near the end of the tour. She really wanted to talk to the state senator, I guess."

I stare at Allie. "Why do you say it like that?"

Allie stops swiping. "Because she asked to speak to him

alone for a minute." Allie shrugs. "I thought it was weird, but the state senator seemed fine with it. They went into the library for a few minutes. That was all."

"Do you know what they talked about?"

Allie's eyebrows knit together. "No, but Ashley Carmichael looked weird. That I remember."

"Looked weird how?" My heart has begun a staccato in my chest, and vaguely I'm aware I'm gripping the arms of my chair too tightly.

"She was wearing way too much makeup, and she kept her sunglasses on indoors." She makes circles out of her fingers and holds them dramatically to her eyes. "They were these big honking things like Jackie O might have worn."

"Did the photographer take a picture of her that day?"

Allie looks at me like I've just asked her if Santa Claus is real.

"Probably," she says and goes back to swiping on the tablet.

There are several more shots of the crowd in the conference room, a few of Starkley on the porch, and then at the very end a series of candids as the visit broke up.

"There." The word comes out far more loudly than I mean it to, but the staccato has turned into a stampede.

Allie swipes back one.

The photo was taken in the hallway that leads from the conference space to the library. Starkley and Ashley are walking away, but they've turned toward each other for a moment as Ashley says something. The photo captures her profile. The weather had been gorgeous that day, and the windows along the hall illuminate Ashley's face like a spotlight.

Allie's right. Ashley is wearing far too much makeup, and just beyond the rim of her oversized sunglasses, a green tint seeps across her cheek, the kind of sickly color that appears when bruises leak through makeup. But I don't need to see the bruises. The sunglasses are enough.

They're the same ones the driver who tried to kill me was wearing.

Footsteps wet with rain squish their way down the hall then, and Lisa appears in my office, tendrils of damp hair stuck to her cheeks.

Her expression is stricken when she says, "You know that woman that threatened you down by the boathouse? I swear I just saw her walking up Byre Road."

I pick up the tablet. "Allie, I need you to send this photo to Detective Hanratty. Lisa will have his number."

Carefully I pull on my raincoat over my still bandaged arm. I stop in front of Lisa.

"Are you sure it was Monica Davies?"

Lisa nods. "I was going to stop and see if she needed help. It's pouring out there, and she was really struggling to get up that hill, but then my headlights caught her face when she looked up." Her voice goes dry, and she swallows. "Her mugshot was on the news for days. It was definitely her."

I touch her arms, so she knows how serious I am. "I need you to call Daniel." It's weird saying his first name like that. "Tell him to meet me at the Carmichael residence as quickly as possible."

I don't wait for her reply. I run for my SUV, wishing once again I had my gun.

TWENTY-NINE

I find the door open when I get there.

I'm soaked by the time I make it under the overhang of the side door, the rain finding ways through my rain-coat until I can feel the icy drops on my skin.

I push open the door the rest of the way, take a step inside, and call, "Hello?"

There's no answer.

My footsteps are muted against the hunter green carpet. The hallway is dark today, no lingering scent of delicious food. Just the sound of the rain on the roof, the cold rivulets like fingernails scraping at the windows.

I head for the kitchen, but I stop abruptly when the scene in one of the rooms off the hallway catches my attention. It's the room with the twig and branch furniture I saw on my first visit. Unlike last time though, it's not empty.

Ashley Carmichael stands next to Jonathan Starkley in front of a dormant fireplace while Monica Davies stands in front of them. Monica Davies is holding a gun.

"Della, please." Ashley's voice wobbles with dread. "Please help us. This woman is crazy. She's an addict, and she wants drugs. She's trying to rob me. She needs cash to feed her habit."

I look between Monica and Ashley.

"Is that the story you're going with?" I say.

Ashley's mask of terror fades until her expression turns to stone.

I jerk my thumb at Monica. "Besides, I'm on her side."

I turn and leave abruptly so Ashley's protests are mumbles fading in the distance. When I get to the kitchen, I rip the shadowbox with the roll of knives off the wall. I don't bother opening it there. I wait until I'm back in the room with Ashley, Jonathan, and Monica.

I pick out the twig and branch table I think is worth the most before I take the shadowbox in both hands, lift it high in the air, and bring it down, smashing it into the corner of the table. The glass shatters, and Ashley screams, jumping into Jonathan who shoves her away.

I pluck the leather roll from the center of the shadowbox and toss the remains to the side. Using the same table that I've now rendered worthless through my act of vandalism, I unroll the knives. The lethal metal of kitchen knives flash in the orange light of the lamps lit at the edges of the room, but the slot in the dead center of the roll is empty.

I straighten and look at Ashley Carmichael.

"You got sent home from Paris because you didn't have the right knife." I point at the missing knife. "You didn't have the right knife because you used it to kill Sadie Beaumont." I swing my finger toward Jonathan Starkley. "You were soaking wet that night because you took the knife out in the canoe along with one of Sadie's sneakers. You ditched the knife and the shoe in the lake and swamped the canoe, so it looked like Sadie had drowned. You swam back to shore and came back on the launch like nothing had happened, but Elmer McQuiggan noticed you were wet, the same reason the other boys were picking on you that night." I turn to Monica now, but I drop my accusatory finger. "Ashley made you help her get Sadie's body into the oil drum. You and Debbie Fraser. That was the price she forced you to pay as her friends." I shake my head sorrowfully. "Debbie killed herself rather than live with that."

Monica's angry face unwinds, her eyes growing wide, her lips parting on unspoken words. I take a step toward her.

"You were wrong, you know," I say. "I would have believed you."

Her eyes scan my face, and I know she's looking for the truth there, but she doesn't get the chance to find it.

Ashley takes a step forward. "You little—"

Monica swings the gun around, pointing it directly at Ashley, wrapping both hands around the grip.

"Stop." She fires the word at Ashley. "I told you to stop." Monica shakes the gun now.

I slide carefully back at the same time I try to see if the safety is still engaged on the gun, but the light is too dim to make out what kind of gun it is or where the safety is.

"You don't get to do this anymore." Monica's voice is rough with emotion. She shakes the gun again. "You don't get to play with people's lives. Sadie tried to stop you, and you killed her."

Ashley seems annoyed more than anything. "Listen. The cops are going to get here, and I'm going to tell them you're an addict tripping on whatever bad drugs you just got on the street, and you're here because you tried to kill my father and when you weren't successful you came back for round two."

She sounds like she's seen one too many after-school specials.

I hold up a finger. "Yeah, actually I know it was you who tried to run your father over."

All three people turn to me.

I touch my arm. "You tried to kill me the same way." I tilt my head. "That's all you've got, isn't it? You either stab them or run them over." I shrug. "Not very original. But then I heard your restaurant wasn't either."

The fire flames in her eyes, and she takes a step toward me.

"Stop," Monica breathes, raising the gun higher.

Ashley freezes.

"Rather convenient that dear old dad needed you right when your restaurant was going to go under," I repeat David's words. I tap my finger to my chin. "Let me guess. He stopped bankrolling you when he realized you were a wash-up, so you tried to kill him. You told me yourself he got his affairs in order after your brother died. I bet one of those affairs was some hefty life insurance you would get if he died. But you couldn't even get that right, could you? Dear old Daddy lived, and now look at you. Condemned to a fate worse than death."

Ashley's lips press so tightly together they nearly disappear.

"You don't know anything," she seethes.

"I do," I say. "Because Sadie told me herself."

Ashley hesitates and then laughs. "Yeah, sure. That story about how you see the dead. Right."

"Tell me," I say. "Do you still have your bracelet with the bee charm on it or did Sadie not give you one?"

For the first time, Ashley looks genuinely afraid.

"How do you know about those?" Monica's question is soft, childlike, and I hurt for the young woman who never got a chance.

"Sadie showed me her own. The one she was wearing when you shoved her body into an oil drum."

Ashley starts toward me, and this time she ignores Monica's attempts to get her to freeze.

"That bitch got what she deserved," Ashley spits, her eyes alight with an unholy fire. "She was trying to change things. She was trying to stop the way things were done at the camp. She wanted to—" Her voice breaks, but she recovers herself quickly. "She wanted to change my mama's camp. She had no right."

"Tell me. Did your mother start the culture of rape at the camp or was that you?"

Ashley's eyebrows shoot up in defense. "It was not rape. Those girls had to learn to submit. They were going to be the wives of doctors and lawyers, governors and even presidents."

"Calling it something else doesn't change the fact that it was rape."

Ashley screams then like a child throwing a temper tantrum. "People like you wouldn't know. You don't understand what my mama was doing there. How she sacrificed for those girls."

"People like me?" I ask, even though I know what she means. "You mean smart, accomplished, kind, and fair?"

She takes another step toward me. "Poor," she spits. "Poor, stupid people like you. You don't have what it takes. Those girls can thank me for what I did. I prepared them to be the wives those men needed."

"I guess you should have taken a little of your own medicine then. It seems nobody wanted you for their son's wife."

Her scream is guttural now, and she comes at me with both fists raised.

Surprisingly, Jonathan Starkley grabs her with both arms around her waist and hauls her back toward the fireplace.

"Stop!" he shouts. Really I didn't know his voice could achieve that volume. "Just stop. You've done enough."

"Did your parents discover your role in Sadie Beaumont's murder? Is that why they stopped you from marrying Ashley Carmichael?" I ask when Jonathan's attention turns back to me.

He can't maintain eye contact, and he looks away. "*I*

stopped it from happening. I couldn't marry her." He says this with disgust, but I don't miss how his eyes travel unerringly to Monica.

He didn't love her.

No, he didn't love Ashley Carmichael, but he had loved someone else.

I cross my arms. "So you killed Sadie Beaumont because she was trying to stop you from allowing those girls to be bullied and raped, and you got your friends to help you cover it up." I shake my head. "Monica was right. You *are* a nobody."

The rage that illuminates Ashley's face then is other-worldly, and she launches herself before Jonathan can catch her this time.

Two things happen at the same time.

Ashley Carmichael for all her painted toenails and bouncy ponytail is still in her late fifties. Even with my bad leg and multiple bruises from her attempt to kill me, I'm still faster. I jump out of the reach of her fists at the same time her feet hit the broken shards of glass on the floor. Her feet shoot out from under her, and she falls hard. She screams, her hand cupping her opposite elbow.

"Oh god, it's broken," she moans, rolling on the floor.

"Stop," Jonathan says, coming to crouch uselessly beside Ashley. "You're on broken glass. You'll hurt yourself."

I see now what Monica had meant about Jonathan not hurting the snake that bit him.

I'm not looking at either of them though. I'm looking at Monica. The gun in her hand has steadied, and it's pointed directly at Ashley, writhing on the floor.

"Don't do this," I say.

Ashley goes quiet. Jonathan looks up.

"Don't do this, Monica," I say again. "She's not worth it. I know the truth now. This isn't a burden you must carry alone."

Monica's eyes float up to my face, and I see the unshed tears in them.

She shakes her head slowly. "No," she whispers. "You don't know the burden I carry."

"You're right. I don't," I say.

"She gave me the drugs," Monica whispers. "When the pain wouldn't go away. She gave me pills first. Then powder. Then—" Her voice breaks on a cry, her gaze never leaving Ashley. "She made me an addict. She trapped me."

Ashley's face doesn't change. If anything it hardens.

I reach for Monica. "Killing Ashley won't help it."

Monica's head tilts ever so much. "You're right," she repeats what I've just said. "But this will."

For the rest of my life, I'll think about that moment. About whether or not I could have gotten to her in time, but every time I go over it I know it would have been impossible. She was too far away.

So when she raises the gun to her own temple, all I can do is scream.

"Monica, no!"

But it's too late. She's already pulled the trigger.

I watch her go down. Her body hits the floor with an unholy thud, but Monica is still standing there.

At least, Monica's spirit still stands there.

I hold out both hands reassuringly. "It's okay. You're okay," I say as softly and calmly as I can to her, but her face morphs, contorts with fear.

It's not the Monica who just held the gun to her head that I see. It's young Monica from the photo, her hair braided along her forehead.

There's no static. There's no sound at all. Just me and the dead.

"You're going to be okay," I say again.

Confusion seeps quickly from her face, and she moves, her hand slipping into her pocket. When she pulls it back out, she shows me what she holds.

A leather bracelet with a single, carved bee charm.

I glance down at her dead body. "You want me to get it?"

Her eyes flick away from mine. She's looking at something behind me.

Before I can turn, she says, "Sadie?"

The single word echoes in my head long after Monica's spirit vanishes in a halo of warm light.

Suddenly in the vacuum of silence, I hear the sirens. They're close, and I know I must have missed their approach in the chaos.

I don't hesitate. I walk over to Monica's body and lift her hip, slide my hand into her pocket. My fingers find the leather strap, and I tug the bracelet free. I stare at it for only a moment before I shove it deep into my raincoat pocket.

There's crying behind me, but it's not Ashley. Ashley is still whining about her elbow. Jonathan is crying. He's crying great, big messy sobs.

"No," he says over and over. "No."

Finally he picks himself up to all fours from where he'd been crouching on the floor to help Ashley. He crawls across the hardwood to Monica's body. He lifts her head, cradles her face.

"No, no no," he says over and over again.

My feet crunch broken glass as I head for the hallway just as the sound of cars in the driveway outside reach us through the open door.

"So did she pass over or what?" Ashley sneers from the floor, her hand still clutching her elbow.

Hanratty is in the doorway then along with Perez, guns

drawn. They announce their presence but don't move into the room.

I crouch and meet Ashley's gaze. "I thought you said I couldn't see dead people."

Her mouth twists into a sneer, but her eyes skitter to Monica's body. "Who were you talking to just now?"

"Monica," I say.

Ashley's eyes dart back and forth. "So did she go? You know. To the other side?"

It's my turn to sneer. "I guess you'll just have to find out."

The terror spreads slowly across her face, her lips opening and closing without sound.

I stand and walk to the door.

"Wait!" she shouts after me. "Wait. No. You need to tell me. Is she still here? Is she still in this room?"

I look over my shoulder. "You'll just have to live with not knowing."

I walk out of the house, the rain muffling the anguished cry of Ashley's terrified screams.

———

It's stopped raining by the time Hanratty finds me.

I sit on the stoop, my butt both wet and cold. He sits next to me.

I wait for a scolding, but one doesn't come. Instead, he pulls out his phone, taps the screen, turns it sideways, and holds it out in front of me.

At first I don't know what I'm seeing. It's a video of some kind, and judging by the low quality, it's some kind of security footage. After a second, I realize it's me, standing in the jail cell of the Bellegrave Police Department, and I'm screaming my head off. I'm screaming until I'm not. I hear my daughter's name instead. I watch several frames, but the black mass doesn't appear in the video. Something else does.

The lights above me flicker right before the entire frame fills with a bright light. When the glow fades, the lights above me are out. Security lights have blinked on, and they give just enough light to see me prone on the floor.

Hanratty shuts off the screen.

We sit for several more seconds as a scene I'm growing far too familiar with unfolds around me. The evidence team going in and out of the house. Jonathan Starkley is in the back of a cruiser. He's still crying. Ashley's already been carted off in an ambulance, but I refused my own ambulance ride. One a month is enough. I glance at the house, wondering if Donald Carmichael is in there somewhere and if he's been told what his daughter has done.

Finally Hanratty speaks. "My mother was murdered. I think her ghost is with me. I'm afraid she's stuck here because of me."

"She's not here," I say.

He turns his head to me, relief making his eyes go wide.

"She left her imprint on you though." I tap the phone he's still holding between his hands. "Like my daughter left an imprint on me." I consider this. "I think your mom is protecting you somehow, but she's not here. She's passed on."

He looks away, and there's a wet noise when he swallows and wipes a hand across his face.

It's several more seconds before he says, "Are you going to help me find who killed her?"

"Maybe," I say.

THIRTY

I wave to Logan and Henry where they stand on the dock as I ease my boat around and point the bow toward the island.

Logan had wanted to go with me, but I assured him it would be safer if I went alone. He'd asked me to wait for Aunt Janine, but she's in Plattsburgh playing paintball with Ryan, and I didn't want to interrupt their bro time.

I make a wide arc around the island, heading for the opposite end where Maurice Beaumont said the caretaker's cabin had been. I'd gone to see him in Raquette Lake to bring him Monica Davies's bracelet. He cried when I gave it to him, proof that his daughter had never changed. She'd stayed true to the moral compass he'd helped instill in her to the very end.

Grandma Beaumont looked up from her wrestling long enough to offer me a lemon-lime soda and some Philly cheesesteak.

Ashley Carmichael was formally arrested for the murder of Sadie Beaumont after State Senator Jonathan Starkley reached a plea deal with the district attorney. Starkley confessed to his own role in Sadie Beaumont's murder, how he had taken the shoe and the knife out in the canoe that night, dumping the knife and planting the shoe and the canoe to look like Sadie had simply drowned. He confirmed my suspicions that Debbie Fraser and Monica Davies were forced to hide Sadie's body in the barrel.

Jonathan Starkley paid for Monica Davies to be buried. He, Detectives Hanratty and Perez, and I were the only people who attended her funeral.

The evidence team found a late model sedan without plates in the garage of the Carmichael residence. It had sustained damage to its right front fender consistent with a collision with a brick pillar. A wig of long, dark hair had been discarded in the passenger seat containing hair fibers the evidence lab would later confirm belonged to Ashley Carmichael. The car had been towed away for evidence collection. Red dust found on the front, passenger side bumper would later be matched to the bricks recovered at the scene where Ashley Carmichael tried to kill me.

My little stunt that had gone viral took an unexpected turn once Starkley confessed to his role in the murder. Someone started an online fundraiser for the badass history nerd who had stood up to the corrupt politician. Not my words, but I wasn't angry about being called a badass. The online fundraiser had raised enough to repair the brick pillar, but that, in turn, caught the attention of one of those cable reality television shows about weird history. They are coming to film a series at the lodge next spring. Their filming fee was enough to run the living history museum at the lodge for the next two fiscal years.

For the first time in its existence, we were forced to turn people away at the gates of the lodge when we met capacity daily. The staff and I are making plans to manage the numbers we will likely see over Labor Day weekend. Matt plans on roasting three more pigs.

Maurice is right. This side of the island isn't as thickly overgrown. The slope down the beach where I tie my boat is less death-defying, more hard dirt slope than brush. I make it to the top faster than I would expect.

I don't have much time. Lisa and Daniel—still weird to use his first name, but I'm trying—are coming over for charcuterie and board games as I attempt to make connections with people who are still alive.

The laughter comes as I expect it to before I even make out the faded lines of the caretaker's cabin through the trees. This time instead of looking away I look toward it.

I find the eyes glowing between branches, the giggles skipping from a fallen, rotting log to an impenetrable wall of overgrown thorns, to the top of the forest canopy.

I hold my stare steady on them, and from deep inside of me, comes a warm wave of strength.

"Ashley Carmichael has been arrested," I say into the trees. "They know what happened to you on this island."

The giggles cease so abruptly they leave behind a hum of silence. Not even an insect beats its wings.

I move on. The caretaker's cabin is in much the same shape as the rest of the buildings on the island. There's a tree growing directly out of the front porch of the small cabin, and its branches sprout from beneath its eaves. I find the tall oak just behind the cabin like Maurice said I would, its rope swing surprisingly still intact. The rope is black with mildew, and moss grows thick on the swing's seat, but it's still there. I make my way to the base of the tree and kneel in the dirt, extracting the small, stone plaque from the pocket of my jacket.

I press it into the dirt beneath the tree, digging some out to make sure it's level. When I'm finished, I brush it clean to read the two lines of text.

Here lies Atticus Beaumont,
the goodest good boy.

I kneel there for several minutes, listening to the sound of the wind in the trees, the buzz of insects, the occasional chirp of a bird, and nothing else.

I make my way back to my boat. The sun is setting by the time I untie and shove off. The engine starts with a throaty roar, and I give it speed, letting the boat plane above the water until I feel that rush like flying.

The lake unfolds before me, its surface glassy with possibilities, an untold future beckoning me from the opposite shore. If I let the boat go, it will carry me there, away from everything that's ever hurt me and toward something new.

But I don't let it.

Instead I change direction and head toward home.

Acknowledgments

I have always wanted to conceal a dead body in a fuel drum.

For working out the science behind doing so, I owe an immense amount of gratitude to Dr. Kathleen M. Sandman. Thank you for talking microbes, decomposition in diesel, aerobic and anaerobic, and oxidation states. Your assistance was invaluable to this murder.

This story was a difficult one to write. I knew going into it that it would be, but the seismic effect of systemic rape in a subculture was one I've wanted to address, especially in terms of lost time as a result of serious trauma. I took several breaks while writing *The Lost Summers*, and I leaned heavily on my creative community. Special thanks to Kate Homan and Lee Hall. You have kept me sane.

Thanks as always to my dogs. It was in the writing of this that I truly put the power of chicken to the test. You are, as ever, the goodest good boy and girl.

About the Author

Jessica Ann is the author of over 25 novels of historical fiction and fantasy.

A magna cum laude graduate of the University at Albany, Jessica has degrees in history and English with Honors in creative writing.

Jessica lives in New Hampshire where, if she's not at her writing desk, she's probably letting the dog out. Again.

For more, visit her website at authorjessicaann.com.